Praise for t

"Harry Dresden would li[...]
be a little nervous aroun[...]
world with a uniquely p[...]
Books this good remind [...]
business in the first place[...]

    —Jim Butcher, #1 *New York Times* bestselling author of
the Dresden Files

"Benedict Jacka writes a deft thrill ride of an urban fantasy—
a stay-up-all-night read."

    —Patricia Briggs, #1 *New York Times* bestselling author of
the Mercy Thompson series

"Jacka puts other urban fantasists to shame. . . . A stellar
blend of thoughtful philosophy and explosive action popu-
lated by a stereotype-defying diverse cast."

    —*Publishers Weekly* (starred review)

"A fast-paced, high-stakes adventure. . . . The real power of
Jacka's series comes from the very human journeys and rev-
elations to be found for each character in the course of this
story."   —RT Book Reviews

"Tons of fun and lots of excitement. . . . [Benedict Jacka]
writes well, often with the ability to bring places to life as
much as his characters, especially the city of London."

    —SF Site

"[An] action-packed story with witty dialogue. . . . A won-
derfully witty and smart hero who's actually pretty awesome
in a fight."   —All Things Urban Fantasy

"Benedict Jacka is a master storyteller. . . . A brilliant urban
fantasy that is so professionally polished and paced that you
barely remember to come up for air."   —Fantasy-Faction

"Everything I love about an urban fantasy: action, magic, an
interesting new world, and a character that I really liked."

    —Under the Covers Book Blog

Yours to Keep
Withdrawn/ABCL

Books by Benedict Jacka

The Alex Verus Series

FATED
CURSED
TAKEN
CHOSEN
HIDDEN
VEILED
BURNED
BOUND
MARKED
FALLEN
FORGED

Your's to Keep
Withdrawn/ABCL

forged

BENEDICT JACKA

ACE
New York

ACE
Published by Berkley
An imprint of Penguin Random House LLC
penguinrandomhouse.com

Copyright © 2020 by Benedict Jacka
Penguin Random House supports copyright. Copyright fuels creativity, encourages
diverse voices, promotes free speech, and creates a vibrant culture. Thank you for buying
an authorized edition of this book and for complying with copyright laws by not
reproducing, scanning, or distributing any part of it in any form without permission.
You are supporting writers and allowing Penguin Random House to continue to
publish books for every reader.

ACE is a registered trademark and the A colophon is a trademark of
Penguin Random House LLC.

ISBN: 9780440000600

First Edition: November 2020

Printed in the United States of America
1 3 5 7 9 10 8 6 4 2

Cover art: Big Ben © Giuseppe Torre / Arcangel Images;
Skull statues © David Lichtneker / Arcangel Images;
Swirling lights by PM Images / Getty Images
Cover design by Judith Lagerman

This is a work of fiction. Names, characters, places, and incidents either are the product
of the author's imagination or are used fictitiously, and any resemblance to actual persons,
living or dead, business establishments, events, or locales is entirely coincidental.

If you purchased this book without a cover, you should be aware that this book is stolen
property. It was reported as "unsold and destroyed" to the publisher, and neither the author
nor the publisher has received any payment for this "stripped book."

chapter 1

The mountain had no name. It was deep in the Himalayas, overshadowed by a ridge on one side and a peak on the other, with the remains of an ancient Sherpa village on its lower slopes. The ground was dry—it was late August and I was below the snow line—but the wind whistling down from the white-capped peaks carried a cold that bit through my clothes and numbed my ears and nose. The sky was a clear blue, fading to a lighter shade near the horizon, with lines of puffy clouds floating between the mountains, snowy peaks shining bright in the sun. Nothing grew but scrubby grass and brush, and not a single bird flew in the sky. There was a beauty to the landscape, but it was bleak and pitiless, indifferent to life.

As I climbed, my attention was split three ways. The first part was focused on my footing and keeping my balance on the shifting stones. The second part was focused on the three men lying in wait in the rocks above. The third and largest part was occupied with the question of what else I would find. A little over twenty-five minutes ago, I'd learned that a certain person whose movements I was very interested in had travelled here. Unfortunately, while twenty-five minutes is a pretty fast response to an alert on the other side of the world, it was also more than long enough for that person to kill everyone on this mountain many times over. There was a very good chance I was already too late.

On the plus side, the people above seemed interested in me, judging by the fact that one had a rifle trained on my chest, so at least I wouldn't have to chase them down.

To a normal person my position would be a death trap. The mountain was bare, with the rocks providing only intermittent cover. I was well within rifle range, and the men above would have plenty of time to shoot me if I tried to run. If I tried to talk, they'd capture me, which would lead to me being interrogated, shot, or interrogated and then shot. That just left fighting. The three men had an assault rifle and a pair of submachine guns, while I had a pistol holstered in the small of my back. Bad odds.

To a diviner, the position was better, though still dangerous. I could use some combination of cover and misdirection to split them up, and then pick off the isolated man. From there, I could use a condenser on the remaining two to block their vision and set up a surprise attack. I'd need them to make mistakes, but not many people have experience in fighting diviners, and if I was careful and quick I could eliminate all three without exposing myself to fire.

I'm not a normal person, and I'm not just a diviner anymore. I didn't go looking for cover. Instead I climbed straight up the slope.

They let me get very close. By the time the first man stepped out with weapon levelled and shouted, "Ting!" at me, I was right in the middle of them.

I stopped and raised my hands. The man ahead was

Chinese, short and compact, dressed in dark body armour with a submachine gun of a type I didn't recognise. He gave me an order.

"I need to talk to your boss," I said, keeping my hands raised.

The man repeated his order, with a forceful gesture.

From looking through the futures, it was pretty clear that this guy didn't speak enough English for us to hold a conversation. The second man was behind me, and the third was off to the right, covering me with his rifle. They were being cautious.

"I am not kneeling down for you to search me," I told him. "I have business with Lord Jagadev. Please let me pass."

The man called something to the man behind. I could imagine what I looked like to the Chinese soldier. A Westerner, tall and gaunt, wearing armour of an unfamiliar design and a coat that probably held some kind of weapon. Clearly suspicious, but not threatening. He wasn't intimidated, and he wasn't about to let me go. I heard footsteps at my back; the second man was advancing.

"All right," I said. "I don't really have time to talk to you anyway."

Time seemed to slow as my futures branched. In one, the man behind me used the stock of his gun to club me on the back of the neck, stunning me and knocking me face down; the other man followed up, both of them aiming their weapons at me, shouting questions and threats. But that future was already ghostlike and fading as I turned from it towards others. In a handful of futures I spun away, drawing my gun and firing. Usually I killed one; in some I killed two, but all three men had me in their sights and nearly all the possibilities ended with bullets ripping through my body.

I blanked out those futures and looked at the ones where I caught the man behind and used him as a shield.

Instantly the futures opened up: the possibilities in which the other two men fired on me were rarer, and in most strands didn't happen at all. Their hesitation wouldn't last long, but it would be long enough for me to kill the man in front of me, then the one I was holding, then . . .

. . . the future terminated with a bullet through my head. The problem was the third man, hiding in good cover in the rocks to my right. In most of the futures in which I shot at him, I missed. In a few, I hit. That on its own wasn't a problem, but the ones in which I hit branched further: there was just time for the man's own trigger finger to squeeze, the bullet passing mine and taking me with him. And while I could choose which future I took, I couldn't choose which future *he* took. I needed a way to eliminate the risk.

I widened my search slightly and found a cluster of futures where I wasn't at risk of being shot. In all of them, I ducked down slightly, but I couldn't see why—ah. He had his rifle propped on the rocks, and couldn't depress its elevation below a certain angle without taking a second to shift his weight. I had the chain of events I needed. I opened my mind and called upon the fateweaver.

The future I'd chosen seemed to light up, energy flowing from my right hand up my arm and out into time and space. Unwelcome possibilities vanished, while the sequence of events I needed pulsed with light and strength, becoming an unbreakable chain. In an instant, every other future was banished, leaving only the fate that I chose.

It had all taken less than a second. Behind me, the second man's gun was just coming down.

I stepped left and turned. The movement was so casual that by the time the man behind me realised he was going to miss, his gun was swinging through empty air and he was stumbling past. He clutched at me and I took his hand, twisting it up and behind his back in a wristlock that drove him up onto his toes. At the same time I was sinking, using the movement to cover my right hand as it reached behind my back so that by the time the man in front of me saw the gun, it was already aimed at him. His eyes started to go wide.

I shot him through the head, aimed right and shot the man in the rocks, shoved the barrel up under the plates of the body armour of the man I was holding and fired a third time. He jerked and went limp, and I let him fall. The echoes of the shots rolled around the mountainside, rebounding from the far slopes to return again before fading into silence. I was left crouching, surrounded by three dead men, alone once more.

I straightened, holstered my gun, and kept climbing.

Another thirty seconds brought me to the way in. An illusion of a rock face covered a short tunnel that led to a thick metal door. The walls of the tunnel held traps, the door held a formidable-looking lock, and the whole area was heavily warded. It was a well-hidden and well-defended entrance.

Or at least it had been. The illusion spell had been broken, leaving the tunnel clearly visible, and the traps beyond had been triggered or destroyed. The only reason I could tell the tunnel had been warded was from its magical signatures, and even those were fading. The door had been ripped off its hinges, the solid steel bent and warped, leaving a gap that led into darkness. Beyond, nothing stirred; the area was silent but for the whistling wind.

It was about the most obvious *Do Not Enter* sign I'd ever seen. No prizes for guessing what I was about to do. Even after everything that had happened, I was still a diviner, and if there's one thing diviners do, it's poke their noses where they're not wanted.

Well, if you're going to do something stupid, you might as well have company.

I reached into my pocket, took out a small dull yellow pyramid, and set it down on the flattest piece of ground I could find. Then I stepped back and reached out mentally, stretching out my thoughts over a gap that was both un-imaginably vast and thinner than a razor. *Vari*, I said. *Clear to gate.*

Thirty seconds passed. Sixty. Then the air above the pyramid glowed, turning from yellow to orange-red. Space seemed to ignite as flame flared into existence in a vertical oval, six feet high and three feet wide. The cen-tre of the oval darkened and the oval became a ring, a gate linking two points in space, providing a view to a leafy forest, shadowed and gloomy. A young man stepped through, head turning as he scanned from side to side.

Variam Singh is small and compact, dark-skinned and dark-eyed. He used to be wiry, but he's filled out since he joined the Keepers. As far as I can tell, pretty much all the extra weight is muscle—Vari joined the Order of the Shield just as the Council was ramping up for war, and his first year as a journeyman mage was a busy one. He spared a glance at the bodies down the slope, then focused on the ruined door with a scowl. "Shit."

"Yup."

"We're too late, aren't we?" Variam said.

"Half an hour," I said. "She might still be inside."

Variam gave me a look.

We started towards the entrance. "Jagadev's goons?" Variam asked, nodding his head back down the slope.

"More likely a scout-response team," I said. "The Chi-nese Council claims this territory these days."

"How long till more show up?"

"None on the way, but let's not hang around."

We entered the tunnel, Variam conjuring up a flame of bright orange light. It danced and flickered, casting shad-ows on the rocky walls. I glanced at Variam's black robes and turban. "No armour?"

"I'm supposed to be on my lunch break," Variam said.

"I check out a set of armour from the ready room, they *might* get a little suspicious. We clear?"

"Clear."

The doorway led through into a long, straight corridor, its walls made from smooth blocks of stone. A pair of torches burned in sconces, the magical flames casting light but no heat. Variam took a step forward.

Futures flashed up in front of me. "Stop!" I said sharply.

Variam froze instantly. "What?"

"Stay where you are and don't move forward," I said. "Watch." I looked around until I found a pebble about the size of a large grape, stepped up next to Variam, and tossed it underhand.

A blade swept out of the wall in a silver flash, hitting the pebble in midair with a *whangggg!* and sending it bouncing back down the corridor. Variam jumped away, but before he'd even landed, the blade had disappeared back into the wall. It had missed him by about two feet.

"Bloody hell," Variam said.

"Optical trigger," I said, nodding down the corridor. "Laser, probably. No magical signature, no heat signature, and that blade's strong enough to cut an armoured man in half. You know what's interesting?"

"You mean *apart* from that?" Variam glared at me. "No. No, I don't."

"What's interesting," I said, "is that that's exactly the kind of trap you'd use to kill a life mage or a fire mage."

"Thanks," Variam said. He scanned the ceiling, focusing on what looked like a piece of ornamental ironwork. "Sensor's in that?"

"Could be," I said. "Though we could just duck under—"

Variam raised his hand and a burst of heat melted the ironwork to slag.

"—or that works too," I finished. "You're clear."

Variam walked forward, kicking aside bits of cooling

metal. I followed, scanning ahead for more dangers. "This would be easier if you'd let me take point."

"Screw that," Variam said, and I glanced sideways to see that his face was set. "You know what that bastard did. If she hasn't killed him, I will."

The door at the end of the corridor led into a wide circular room. In contrast to the corridor, the walls and floor were rough rock, with only a single smoothed path running through it. Variam stopped in the entrance. "This is another trap, isn't it?"

"It was," I said, pointing at the centre of the room. "See the residue there?"

"Earth magic, right? Some sort of ceiling collapse? Wait for people to get in, then drop the roof on them?"

"I thought of that too, but no. Looks more like a summon effect. I'd guess earth elemental. Similar result, but doesn't require you to dig out the whole room afterwards. It was summoned there, but it doesn't look like it had time to do much."

"No reset?"

I shook my head.

We kept walking, following the smoothed path towards the door at the far end. "You planning to get in my way if we find him?" Variam asked.

"Jagadev?"

"Yeah." Variam gave me a look that wasn't entirely friendly. "That was why you sat on this for five years, right?"

"I didn't want you going after him back then, if that's what you're asking."

"You try and give me some speech about forgiveness and how revenge isn't the way, I am going to punch you."

"I'm not going to hold you back," I said. "But I do want you to look before you leap. Remember that blade trap. Jagadev's had a *long* time to figure out how to kill you both if you came here. I am not okay with you going on a suicide run."

"You're not the one who lost family here." The next door had been left ajar, and Variam reached for it, talking over his shoulder as he did. "I know you technically didn't lie to us"—the door swung open—"but . . . *holy shit.*"

Beyond the door was an entrance hall. Square pillars lined the hallway, making two rows down the length of the room, and a long, shallow pool stretched between them. The floor was white marble, the walls and columns were decorated in pale yellow, and the pool was lined a rich gold. More of the faux torches were mounted on the pillars, and their flickering glow was caught and reflected from the waters of the pool, casting a thousand sparkling points of light across the hallway. Doorways on both sides and at the end led deeper into the caves.

The entire room was littered with bodies. Men lay sprawled between the columns, spread out on the floor, and propped against the walls. One had fallen into the pool and his body floated face down, bobbing slightly. As I looked more closely, I saw that not all the bodies were human. Creatures of some kind were mixed in amongst them, man-sized but covered in brown fur. But all were very much dead.

When Variam didn't move, I slipped past him, glancing from left to right as I moved through the bodies. The men had been geared for battle, armed and armoured. Some had been carrying guns, while others were bare-handed or wielding focus items. The furred humanoids had been using curved metal claws with a handle shaped to fit into the palms of their hands. Up close, they looked like a cross between humans and monkeys, with intelligent-looking faces and thin tails.

"She did all this?" Variam asked.

"This was their defensive strongpoint, I think," I said, scanning the room. "The traps and the earth elemental were to slow attackers down. They would have gathered here to make their stand."

"You mean to get slaughtered."

"Or that." Jagadev's defences would have been enough to handle a life mage. A life mage augmented by a marid jinn was another story. Looking through the futures, I could see that the bodies weren't yet cold. "Still some heat in them. I don't think this happened more than twenty minutes ago."

"Guess we might catch up," Variam said. He still didn't move. The sight of the massacre seemed to have cooled his temper.

It was more than a little disturbing to me as well. It's one thing to know that someone's capable of dealing out this kind of death, and another thing to walk through it. Every time I thought about what had happened here, I'd remember a quiet, shy girl with red-brown eyes, gentle and kind. As I looked at the bodies, that image wavered and warped. I didn't want to think about her doing this.

"You know what the creatures are?" I asked Variam, trying to distract myself.

"Vanara," Variam said. He sounded uneasy. "Why would she want to kill . . . ?"

"Looks like they were with Jagadev."

"It feels wrong," Variam said. "Why'd they be helping someone like him?"

"Jagadev had humans working for him," I said. "Not much of a stretch to think he could get other creatures too."

"Yeah." Variam shook his head. "Yeah. We should move."

We picked our way through the bodies. I stepped over a vanara's legs, placed my feet to avoid stepping on a man's outflung hand. "Jesus," Variam muttered to himself. "I think I know some of these guys."

"Jagadev probably brought them along when he left London," I said. As I walked, I looked at where the defenders had fallen, trying to read the flow of the battle. It must have been fast. There were a couple of scorch marks on a column and a few bullet chips on the walls, but very few. Most had probably died without realising how outmatched they were.

There was one man at the far end of the hall a little apart from the others. He was Chinese, dressed in a white suit, with a pair of sunglasses covering his eyes. He was sprawled on his back, arms outstretched.

"That's Kato," Variam said, staring down at the body. "He was majordomo at the Tiger's Palace."

"Hmm," I said. I crouched down, studying the corpse. Behind the sunglasses, Kato's eyes were open, staring sightlessly at the ceiling. "I don't think he died in the battle. Positioning's too neat." I glanced up at Variam. "Did he ever give you guys a reason not to like him? Especially Anne?"

"Few reasons, yeah. Why?"

"I think he might have gotten special treatment."

Variam looked back at me with a frown, then shook his head again. "Come on."

I followed Variam deeper into the mountain, leaving Kato's body behind. The fight in the entrance hall must have broken any resistance, because there were no further signs of combat. If anyone had escaped from that room, they'd kept running. I couldn't blame them.

I kept searching as we walked, mapping the tunnels and watching for any further traps, and as I did an old memory surfaced. Back when Variam and Anne had been living with me, I'd tried to find them both a master, and the search had taken me to Dr. Shirland, an elderly mind mage in a terraced house in Brondesbury. We'd sat and talked while a fat black-and-white cat watched sleepily from an armchair.

If I approached anyone to refer Anne as an apprentice, they'd ask whether she was dangerous. And I wouldn't honestly be able to answer no.

Anne won't even kill flies, I'd said. *She might be power-ful but she's not dangerous. She's innocent.*

I don't think she's quite so innocent as you believe.

The massacre in the entrance hall floated before my eyes, and I shook my head, trying to make the image go away. It wasn't like that was Anne, anyway. Or not just Anne.

I don't think she's quite so innocent as you believe.

She *was* innocent. Well, not completely, but I could understand her reasons. She'd been pushed into it, first by Sagash, then by Jagadev, then by Levistus and Sal Sarque, finally by Richard. It wasn't as though I'd been wrong.

Anne won't even kill flies.

Okay, I might have been wrong. But I'd been right with the bits that mattered. Anne might have snapped in the end, but she'd never done anything to me.

Well, except at the Tiger's Palace. And afterwards, in San Vittore. And then there was what she'd done to my hand . . .

I don't think she's quite so innocent as you believe.

Focus, I told myself.

The image of those corpses in the entrance hall came back, followed by an image of Anne. Anne, bodies. Bodies, Anne.

Angrily, I shoved it away. It didn't matter. I just needed to find a way to fix all this, then I could take Anne away and we could go back to how things were.

I don't think she's quite so—

"Shut up!"

Variam stopped and looked back at me with a frown. "What?"

I breathed in, closed my eyes, breathed out. "I didn't mean you."

Variam gave me a sceptical look. "Starting to think *you're* the one who shouldn't be here."

The rooms and hallways had been growing richer and

more opulent the deeper we went. This hadn't been some last-minute hidey-hole—Jagadev must have been preparing this retreat for a long time. Maybe he'd been using it as his base for centuries. Right now we were in what almost looked like a museum. Thick glass cases stood on marble pillars, each holding some odd item to catch the eye. A pile of small bones was within one case, an ancient handwritten diary within another. A wrought iron polearm was contained in an especially long case, while another held a dark brown cloak with a magic aura I couldn't identify.

As I looked around I realised that unlike the last few rooms, this one had signs of battle. There was no blood, but a gilded chair had been knocked over and a leather pouch lay discarded on the floor. Concentrating, I could sense a faint magical residue. It must have been very strong to still be visible.

"Someone went through," Variam said. He was staring at a set of gold-inlaid double doors at the end of the room.

"Yeah," I said. I was focused on scanning for danger. There was no threat around the doors, no threat in the next room, but I didn't like the look of the futures in the middle distance. "Let's see who." I strode to the double doors and pushed them open.

The room within was a bedroom, and dripped with wealth. Gold rugs and tapestries were scattered upon the floor, silks hung upon the walls, and the furniture was a dazzle of precious metal. The gaudiness made me blink: I'd been scanning only for danger, and anything that wasn't a potential threat hadn't registered on my radar.

Which was why I hadn't realised that Jagadev was on the far wall, crucified against the stone.

The rakshasa looked like a humanoid tiger, as tall as a man but far more heavily muscled. Ornate spears had been driven through his hands and feet, pinning him against the wall, and all around him some kind of net of magical energy hovered, glowing a menacing black-green. The energy in the spell was so powerful that it made the rest of the room look dim. Jagadev's eyes were closed and he didn't move.

"Shit," Variam said, staring at Jagadev. "Is he dead?"

"No," I said, frowning at Jagadev. The spell around Jagadev was incredibly complex. It was life magic, but with thick strands of the jinn's power woven in, grey-black and opaque. It was interacting with Jagadev in some way, but I couldn't figure out how.

Variam was staring at Jagadev like a dog at a hunk of meat, but he managed to tear his eyes away and look around. He ignored the gold and silver as though it wasn't there. "Where'd she go?"

I swept the room with my diviner's senses and nodded to one of the silk hangings. "Escape tunnel behind there."

Variam looked at it, then back at Jagadev, clearly torn. "Can we catch her?"

"No," I said with a sigh. I'd been searching for futures in which either of us caught up to Anne, and I hadn't found a single one. "I don't even know if she took the tunnel. For all I know she used that jinn to punch straight through the gate wards."

"You got some other way to follow her?"

"Like what?"

"I don't know. Use that new hand of yours."

"If it were that easy, I'd have found her already. Anne is at the top of the Council's hit list, and she is taking a *lot* of care to be hard to trace."

"You're saying you can't find her."

"Yup."

"Shit."

There was a moment's silence. "Well," Variam said. "I guess we'll just have to take him as the consolation prize."

"Mm," I said. I was wondering how long Anne had taken to overwhelm Jagadev and pin him like this. How long had we missed her by? My instincts said not long. Maybe no more than a few minutes. If I'd been faster, we might have been able to catch up with her . . .

. . . *and do what?* Well, that was the problem, wasn't it? "How long until you need to be back?"

"A while."

I looked at Variam. Something about his tone of voice gave me the feeling that he was cutting things closer than that. "We should probably stop talking about this anyway. Jagadev's been listening since we walked in."

Jagadev opened his eyes. The pupils were golden and slitted like a cat's, and they stared down at us without expression. Variam took a step forward. The fingers on his right hand twitched, and the futures of violence suddenly spiked.

"Vari," I said warningly.

"Can he hear?" Variam said.

"And speak."

"Why?" Variam spat.

"Because Anne left it that way," I said. I wondered what she'd had to say to her old enemy, and how I could get Jagadev to tell us.

"Hey, asshole," Variam told Jagadev. "Remember me?"

Jagadev stared down at Variam.

"You're going to tell me exactly what you did," Variam said. "And who helped you. If not"—he flexed his right hand—"we're going to see how well that fur of yours burns."

Jagadev didn't so much as blink. The rakshasa's features were hard to read, but even pinned to the wall and motionless, he somehow managed to look down on Variam as if the fire mage were some sort of insect.

There was a dangerous tone to Variam's voice, and I could sense violence flickering very close now. "I'm not going to ask again."

"He's not going to answer, Vari."

"Yes he will."

"No, he won't." I was still sorting through the futures, snatching glimpses between the shifting possibilities. "Setting him on fire won't make him talk. Burning pieces off him won't make him talk. He's not afraid of you."

"Oh, yeah?" Variam said. "Let's change—"

Jagadev spoke suddenly, his voice a purring rumble. "Your brother was a coward."

Variam went very still.

"He died begging for his life," Jagadev said. He raised one eyebrow slightly. "Would you like to know how?"

"Shut up," Variam said.

"He pleaded for us to take his family instead," Jagadev said. "He wept and cried that he would give up the rest of you if we would only spare him. First he tried to offer his mother. Then when that failed, he offered you. He told us that you would come at his call, that you'd be eager, because you blindly trusted him, worshipped him as a hero even though—"

Variam's hand snapped up.

My hand hit Variam's just as he loosed his spell, and the heat burst hit the wall to Jagadev's right. There was a *whump* of superheated air. A tapestry flashed into ash and burning sparks, and a section of gold-friezed marble melted and deformed.

"Vari!" I snapped.

Vari had turned on me, orange-red light glowing around his hands. They weren't aimed at me—not quite—but they were close. "I told you not to get in my way," he said through gritted teeth.

"He's manipulating you," I said sharply. "He's had years to plan out this encounter, figure out exactly how to push your buttons. Stop and think!"

Flames surged around Variam and his eyes lit up red. Death and violence danced in the futures, and not all of it was aimed at Jagadev. I stared back at Variam and stood my ground. For a long moment, everything was still but for the flickering fire around Variam's body; I could feel the heat at my face and hands but didn't flinch.

Then Variam withdrew. The fire around him dimmed and he let out a long, hissing breath. The futures calmed and settled. "Take a walk," I said. "Five minutes. I'll make sure he's still here when you get back."

"He'd better be," Variam said.

"You have my word."

Variam gave Jagadev one final look, then turned and left the way we'd come in.

I turned back to Jagadev. The rakshasa had fallen silent again. "Hello, Jagadev," I said. "How long's it been, six years? Though I suppose that's not much to you."

Silence. Jagadev's slitted golden eyes stared at me without expression. But no—there was an expression there, something unfamiliar. I'd been searching through the futures, picking out glimpses and clues, and all of a sudden I understood what I was seeing. "You're in agony right now, aren't you?" I said softly. "That's what that spell is doing. It's not just paralysing you; it's inflicting the most pain it possibly can. It's a wonder you're even able to talk."

Jagadev's expression didn't shift, but I knew I was right. "So that was why Anne left you alive," I said. "She could have killed you in an eyeblink, but that would have been over too soon, wouldn't it?" I tilted my head. "So what did she have to say? I'm guessing she wasn't all that grateful for all you've done for her."

Still no answer.

"If you're not going to talk, I might as well call Vari back in to finish you off."

"Anne knows you will betray her," Jagadev said.

I paused, caught in the middle of turning around. "You think to ally with her against your shared enemies." There was no trace of pain in Jagadev's voice: it was silky, contemptuous. "She knows you will turn on her as soon as you can. She will expect it, and you will fail."

I felt a stab of fear. I knew Jagadev had to be guessing, but his guesses were dangerously close. "Nice try."

"She knows your plans, Verus. But do you know hers?" Jagadev raised an eyebrow. "I think not. When she strikes, all your divination will not foresee it."

"This is what you always do, isn't it?" I said. "Plant suspicion, turn people against one another. All those people out in the entrance hall, those men and the vanara . . . I bet you spun them a very convincing story. How well did it work out for them?"

"And yet here you are," Jagadev said. "Because no matter how you try to hide it, you wish for my knowledge, my wisdom. Like all mages. Like all humans."

Jagadev had a point. The rakshasa was hundreds of years old, if not thousands. He would have had the time to amass wealth and secrets beyond most mages' dreams. The secrets would be worth the most: locked away in his mind would be the keys to entire kingdoms. I felt the temptation of Jagadev's unspoken offer. Help him, and I'd have access to the knowledge that only he possessed. Of course, to do so, I'd need to keep him alive . . .

. . . and in doing so, I'd be betraying Variam. And once I'd protected Jagadev, he'd betray me as well. The rakshasa had spent centuries practising these deceptions. He'd promise me everything, and give me nothing but death.

"You know, it's funny," I said. "You could have killed Anne and Variam so many times, when they were living as your wards in the Tiger's Palace. I mean, they were the last living descendants of the mages who killed your wife, weren't they? And you managed to get them under your power, living under your own roof. So why did you hold off?" I looked at Jagadev. "I think it was *because* they were the last. Once they were gone, you'd have nothing left. And when you finally decided to kill Anne, you didn't just have her assassinated cleanly, because that wasn't enough for you, was it? You tried to destroy her in every way you could. And now she's doing the same thing. She could have finished you off, but instead she decides to play with her food. I guess she learnt it from you." I shook my head. "So much for your wisdom."

"You know nothing about Anne."

"I know enough," I said. "And what I don't know is definitely not worth the price you'd charge for it. So no, Jagadev. I'm not making a deal. You're going to die right here in this room. All I'm really interested in is whether you have any last words."

"Last words?" Jagadev said. He paused, and his voice became harsh, deadly. "Then take these for your last words, *mage*. I may die here, but before the year is out, you and your underling will follow me. I have killed countless members of your kind, yet the number who will die at the hands of your lover will dwarf that. And you will be the one who enables it. Her name will be remembered in infamy, and yours alongside."

I stood looking back at Jagadev for a moment before raising my voice. "Vari! We're done."

Footsteps sounded and Variam appeared, carrying something slung over one arm. He ignored me, looking straight at Jagadev. "You do not say another word about anyone in my family," he told Jagadev. "Understand?"

Jagadev looked at Variam contemptuously. The green-black energy of the spell was still swirling. I wondered how much longer it would take to kill him.

"I just want to know one thing," Variam said. "Why?"

"Why you?" Jagadev sounded almost amused. "Are you truly so ignorant?"

"I know why me. Alex told me that part. I just want to know why you did all this shit. How is it worth it? How could it *ever* be worth it?"

"You would not be able to understand."

"Understand what?" Variam demanded. "You could have gone anywhere, done anything. Instead you spend two hundred years killing people who'd never even *heard* of you?"

"Oh, your brother had heard of me," Jagadev said. "At least by the time—"

Variam's hand snapped up again, and this time I didn't stop him.

Fire bloomed like a miniature sun. The noise was somewhere between a thump and a roar, and a wash of heat hit my face. I'd thrown up my hands to protect my eyes, and even with my armour, I could feel the skin scorching. A nauseating smell of burnt hair and flesh filled the room.

I lowered my hand to see that Jagadev was gone. A semicircular depression had been burnt in the wall, the stone charred black. The remains of the rakshasa's body mixed with cooling lava in a charred mass on the floor below.

"Well," I said. "You did warn him."

Variam didn't reply. We stood looking at the remains in silence.

Movement stirred in the futures. I looked ahead and one glance told me what I needed to know. "Come on. We've taken too long."

"Yeah." Variam tore his eyes away from Jagadev's corpse and started to turn towards the door.

"Not that way."

Variam halted. "More of Jagadev's?"

"Not Jagadev's," I said. "The same guys I ran into outside." There were more of the soldiers, and this time there were adepts and mages with them. "Chinese Council."

"Shit," Variam said. "I don't want to have to talk my way past those guys."

"If I'm standing next to you, I don't think they'll give you the chance." The Councils of the various magical nations aren't always on the best of terms, but they do share information. I headed towards the tapestry. "Let's take the back door."

"How are these guys even here?" Variam asked as I pulled aside the silk hangings to reveal a smooth wall.

"Either we tripped some sensor, or Jagadev called them in." I ran my hand across the wall, my fingers finding a depression; I pushed and with a click a crack appeared in the stone. I shoved it open, the smooth marble rotating to reveal a dark opening.

"He would, wouldn't he?" Variam was still carrying that bundle of fabric over his left arm, but with his right he sent orange-red flames flying over my shoulder, their light illuminating a rocky tunnel.

"Close it behind us," I said, stepping through. Variam followed and with a click the light from the room behind was cut off, along with the stench of burning meat. "Yeah, probably. Just a final 'screw you' to whoever killed him. Oh, and he's rigged this place to self-destruct."

"Wait, what?"

"We've got time," I said. I'd noticed the spell during our conversation. Someone, probably Anne, had interfered with the triggering mechanism, but it had been delayed, not stopped. "Twenty minutes at least."

"What is it, a bomb?"

"Some sort of dimensional gate that'll turn this mountain inside out and drop the contents into God knows where."

"Okay, let's not stick around to find out." Variam stepped around a patch of fallen rubble in the tunnel. "How far do these gate wards go?"

"Not to the edge of the mountain," I said. The wards

over Jagadev's palace were strong, but no ward has un-limited range. "We keep going another few minutes, they'll have weakened to the point where we can . . . oh, for the love of God."

"Now what?"

"Someone's coming down the corridor towards us. Come on."

I sped up my pace, searching through the futures ahead. Variam hurried to follow me, his shorter legs taking three steps to my two. Orange-red light from his flames flickered on the wall, casting dancing shadows. "More Council?"

"I wish," I said. "Rachel."

"*Seriously?* That crazy bitch *again*?" I heard a clatter as Variam stumbled over a stone before catching himself. "Can we get into deep falloff for the wards before she gets to us?"

"Yes."

There was a pause. "Can we get that far *and* finish a gate before she—?"

"No."

"Can we find—?"

"No."

"We could—"

"Terrain favours her too much."

"It's *really* annoying when you do that."

"We don't have time for a fight," I said. "There's a dip in the ward coverage in about a hundred feet. If you start a gate there, I'll hold her off long enough for you to finish."

"You sure—?"

"Yes."

A hundred feet along, the corridor bent right. The wards were still clearly detectable to my magesight, but I could sense the fluctuations that betrayed the underlying weakness around this patch of tunnel. Variam started casting, shooting me a look that said, *You'd better be right about this.*

Ahead, the futures shifted. Rachel had broken into a run. "She'll be here in thirty seconds," I said. "Keep the gate going and don't get distracted by disintegrate spells or cave-ins."

"Yes, Mum. Shouldn't you be worrying about her?"

I walked forward, picked my spot, and waited.

Sea-green light bloomed, illuminating a human shape. The footsteps changed, slowing from a rapid beat to a steady, relentless *clack-clack-clack*. The light brightened, intensifying at Rachel's hands and revealing her face.

Rachel had not done well since we last met. The domino mask hid her upper face, but not the lines of tension along her face and jaw. Her clothes were dirty and torn, and the hatred in her eyes as her gaze met mine was like a physical blow. Before, I thought that Rachel had hated me about as much as a person possibly could. I'd been wrong.

Energy swirled around Rachel's hands as she stalked forwards. She wasn't stopping or slowing, and I felt a twinge of déjà vu. Trapped in a tunnel with a more powerful mage ahead . . .

No. I shook the memory away. *Not more powerful anymore.* I drew my gun, the barrel coming up to line on Rachel's head.

Rachel reacted instantly. A sea-green ray flashed out.

I dodged the moment the future firmed, but even so I barely made it. The ray threaded the gap between my arm and body, then struck the rock behind and disintegrated a load-bearing section of the tunnel wall.

I was already sprinting away from Rachel as the ceiling collapsed with a deafening rumble and boom. Stones bounced around my ankles, but the whole thing was over in seconds and I slowed to a walk, a cloud of dust making my coat billow around me and ruffling my hair.

Variam was still forming his gate spell, one eyebrow raised. "Don't get distracted by cave-ins, huh?"

I could hear rumbling sounds as Rachel fired more disintegrate spells from the other side. It wouldn't do her any good; more of the mountain would collapse to fill in any holes she made. "Let's get out of here."

Variam's gate completed and an orange-red portal formed. We stepped through and left the Himalayas behind.

chapter 2

The gate winked out behind us. We'd come down in a wilderness region in the middle of the night, dead flat and deserted. Scrubby bushes came up to ankle height with gravel and rocks in between, all illuminated in moonlight out of a clear sky. The landscape stretched away to every side with no sign of life or variation.

"Where are we?" I asked, shivering slightly. The air felt cool after the tunnels.

"Mojave Desert," Variam said. He was already working on the next gate, orange-red light glowing about his hands as he frowned in concentration. "We being followed?"

"No . . . yes," I said. It's hard to follow a gate, but not impossible, especially if you're motivated.

"Deleo? No, don't bother answering, of course it's bloody Deleo. How long?"

"Three to four minutes. Honestly, I'm impressed she made it through the cave-in."

"Impressed, right," Variam said sourly. "You'd better hope I get this gate first try."

I patted Variam on the shoulder. "I have faith in you."

Variam rolled his eyes. "So, I know the list of people who want to kill you is pretty damn long. But is it me, or does Deleo suddenly want to kill you even more?"

"It's not you."

"I was kind of hoping Richard would've got rid of her and saved us the trouble."

"Would have been nice, but no," I said. "Don't actually know how things went between them, but from what I've heard, she hasn't been seen with him since. So either she's been fired and she's blaming me, or Richard's sent her as a last chance to prove herself."

"Does it actually make much difference?"

"No."

Variam's gate opened and we stepped through into another stretch of nighttime wilderness. It looked similar to the last except for fewer rocks, more sand, and cacti casting long shadows in the moonlight. "Now where?" I asked.

"Mexico," Variam said. "Sonoran Desert." He was already at work on gate number three. "So, look. I'm kind of noticing that whenever we go on any sort of mission these days, there's a good fifty-fifty chance that Deleo shows up."

"Yes."

"Doesn't seem like she's going to stop."

"Probably not."

"You considered *making* her stop?" Variam asked. "I mean, given the body count you've been racking up, I know I'm supposed to be telling you to cut back, but what if next time she follows us, we pick out a good spot and . . . ?" He took one hand away from his spell to draw a finger across his neck.

I sighed, letting my breath puff out into the air. It was a little warmer here. "It's not that simple."

"Is this because you guys were apprentices together?"

"It's not that," I said. I'd been close to Rachel once, but there was precious little of that left. "She's got a jinn of her own."

Variam gave me a frown. "Seriously?"

"Meant to tell you earlier, got distracted," I said. "But yeah, it was back when we were apprentices. Actually, I'm pretty sure it was at the exact point where she stopped being an apprentice."

The gate opened and dazzling light made me blink before Variam quickly muted the glow, shielding the oval with a veil of magic.

We stepped through into bright daylight. A high sun was beating down from a cloudless sky, and the air was hot and dry. We were standing on a small tumble of rocks in the middle of huge dunes of golden sand. I turned to Variam. "Seriously?"

"What?" Variam said.

"We're in . . ." I paused. "Saudi Arabia? The Arabian Desert?"

"What's the problem?"

"What is it with you and deserts?"

"I like deserts."

I rolled my eyes. "Anyway, the long and the short of it is that the bonding ritual screwed up and it's one of the reasons she's so crazy. I'm pretty sure she can't use the jinn's powers in any kind of consistent way. But they're always there as an option, and even when they're not, she's got a really good track record of seeing through my bluffs. I don't want to go toe-to-toe with her if I can avoid it."

"So the plan is—what? Wait for her to get bored and give up?"

"No," I said. "I've got someone on call who might be able to help. If not . . . she's my problem. I'll fix it."

We stood in the baking heat for a few seconds. The air felt like a furnace, and the glare from the sun made me want to shield my eyes. "You going to be okay?" I asked Variam.

"No angry voice mails," Variam said. "As long as I get back in the next quarter hour, I'm fine."

"That wasn't really what I meant."

"Yeah, I know." Variam glanced at me, then looked down, scraping his toe along the rocks. "I'm not sure." He paused. "You think what he said was true?"

It was a measure of how worried Variam must be that he was asking something like that. "I think he was saying whatever he thought would make us unhappiest."

"Doesn't mean he was wrong."

"'The evil that men do lives after them; the good is oft interred with their bones.'"

Variam looked askance at me. "If you're trying to make me feel better, you're doing a really shitty job."

"Jagadev did precious little good and a lot of evil," I said. "But what he did to Anne might end up being worse than everything else put together. Richard and Morden handed Anne that jinn, but Jagadev and Sagash put her on the path that led there."

"And now Jagadev's dead, we know where she's going next."

I nodded. "It's going to be hard to stop her."

"It's not her going after Sagash I'm worried about."

⁙⁙⁙⁙⁙

I waited for Variam to gate back to England, then took out a gate stone for a journey of my own. Once I was in an area with mobile coverage, I took out a phone and dialled. It rang for a while before there was a click and a rumbling voice answered. "Yeah."

"It's me," I said.

"So?"

"I ran into her again. Had to disengage."

"You didn't tell me."

"She's not giving me much notice."

"You a diviner or not?"

When Variam had asked why I didn't get rid of Rachel, I told him the truth, but not the whole truth. The mage on the other end of the line was called Cinder, and he had reasons of his own for wanting Rachel alive. "Last time we spoke, you wanted me to find Deleo," I said. "Have her come after me while you were there, so that she'd have to deal with you first."

"And?"

"I'm not sure how well that's going to work."

"We had a deal."

"We still do, but I'm warning you, she has really gone off the deep end. If you get in between the two of us, I don't think it's going to end the way you're hoping."

"My problem, not yours." There was a note of finality in Cinder's voice. "You going to do it?"

I sighed. "I'll do it."

Cinder hung up, and I lowered the phone with a grimace. Rachel wasn't my biggest problem—she wasn't even in the top five—but she was an extra complication I really didn't need. I wasn't sure I could afford to deal with her on top of everything else.

But Cinder was one of the very few allies I had left, and that meant I'd have to figure out some way to keep him happy. And on the subject of problems, I had another phone call coming up, one that was going to be a lot more unpleasant than the last. Time to get ready.

⏐⏐⏐⏐⏐⏐⏐⏐⏐

I staked out the forest clearing that I'd chosen for the conversation, taking the necessary precautions. It was hard to remember that once upon a time I'd been able to call someone up without taking an hour to make sure I wouldn't be traced or killed in the process. Once I was done I took out my communicator, did a last double check through the futures, and channelled through it. "Hello, hello," I said into the focus. "Testing, one two three."

There was a pause, then a familiar voice sounded through the communicator. "Hello, Mage Verus," Talisid said. "Yes, I can hear you perfectly well."

I couldn't see Talisid—the focus was audio only—but I could imagine him, dressed neatly in a business suit, balding and serious-looking. I'd known Talisid for a long time and, for most of that time, we'd been on the same side. That wasn't true anymore.

"Hi, Talisid," I said. "Listen, I know it's been a while, and I'd love to stop and chat, but I don't think it's the best time to catch up. So could you put your bosses on?"

"That won't be necessary."

"Please don't take this personally, but I'd rather not go through an intermediary on this one."

"I'm acting as the Council's representative in this matter."

"For God's sake, Talisid," I said. "Every single one of the Senior Council is sitting there listening to this conversation live right now. Can you stop wasting my time and just put them on?"

"I'm afraid that's not possible."

I swore silently. If Talisid wasn't going to budge, that was a very bad sign.

"I understand you had some information you wanted to offer?" Talisid asked when I didn't reply.

"You think that's why I'm calling?"

"I was under the impression that you were hoping to present your side of the story," Talisid said. "I may have been mistaken."

"Talisid, your bosses tried, convicted, and sentenced

me while I wasn't even there," I said. "They waited for me to leave the War Rooms, then passed a resolution authorising me to be brought in dead or alive. They have made it *abundantly* clear how much they care about hearing my side of the story."

"You haven't been tried or convicted. An indictment has been issued, but no official sentence can be passed until the full procedures have—"

"Can you spare me the bullshit?"

"All right, Mage Verus," Talisid said. "If you don't wish to present any information, what is it you'd like to discuss?"

"Mage Verus," I thought. *Not "Councillor" or "Verus."* "I'm here to negotiate."

"Negotiate a . . . ?"

"A ceasefire."

"Ceasefires are for wars."

"Which is what we're in right now."

"Let me make sure I'm understanding you," Talisid said. "Are you claiming to be representing Richard Drakh's cabal?"

"I'm representing myself."

"The Council is not at war with you."

"Yes, you are, ever since you passed that resolution."

"The indictment against you was issued because there was overwhelming evidence that you had committed multiple and serious breaches of the Concord," Talisid said. "If you have any evidence to present in your defence, we'll consider it, but—"

"You declared me an outlaw," I said. "Which means, as far as I'm concerned, the Concord's entirely irrelevant, since I'm no longer subject to your laws."

"Are you representing *anybody* else in these negotiations?"

"Just me."

"Mage Verus . . ." Talisid was starting to sound impatient. "You clearly have some misconceptions about how Council law works."

"No, Talisid, I think I have a *very* realistic understanding of how Council law works. It comes down to how much power you have. You already tried using that power against me directly, and it didn't work so well. I'm here to see if you're ready to consider alternatives."

"I'm really not sure what alternatives you have in mind," Talisid said. "You violated the Concord in numerous and flagrant ways, even *without* considering your involvement in Sal Sarque's murder. Do you really think all that is going to be swept under the rug?"

"I think you'll make whatever decisions are politically expedient," I said. "A month ago I was sitting in the Star Chamber and I can assure you that the Council are completely fine with sanctioning breaches of the Concord when it works to their advantage."

"You are not sitting in the Star Chamber now."

"No. The ones sitting in the Star Chamber are the seven members of the Senior Council listening in to this conversation." I paused. "Sorry, did I say seven? I meant six."

The line went quiet for a second, and when Talisid spoke again, his tone was more cautious. "What are you hoping to achieve from these 'negotiations'?"

"Right now, I'm still on the Council most-wanted list," I said. "Which means you keep sending Keepers and hunter teams after me. Which means I have to kill, incapacitate, or avoid them. It's a nuisance. I'm offering a ceasefire with a view to some sort of permanent treaty."

"And in return for this you would offer . . . ?"

"I already told you. You stop trying to kill me and I'll stop trying to kill you."

"I'm afraid you're going to have to do considerably better than that."

"I'd be happy to discuss terms in more detail," I said. "I'd be willing to relinquish my place on the Junior Council, for instance. But you're going to have to end hostilities first."

"Verus, be realistic." Talisid was sounding frustrated again. "I want to help you, but you can't threaten the Council like this. You're only making things worse for yourself."

"I'm not threatening them. They're trying to interrogate and kill me. I'm just responding in kind."

"You're one man."

"Yeah, that was what Sal Sarque thought too."

There was another silence. "I'll convey your message to the Council," Talisid said at last. "However, I strongly suspect that they're highly unlikely to—"

"You aren't going to convey anything because they're listening right now. I already told you to cut the bullshit. Simple answer, please. Yes or no?"

"As I said, I'll convey your message to the Council."

"Yes. Or. No."

"I'm afraid it's not as simple as—"

I deactivated the focus, held it tightly for a second, then threw it down into the ground as hard as I could. It dug into the dirt and stuck. "Shit!" There was a tree a few steps away; I stalked towards it and kicked it, hard. Pain jolted up my leg. The tree didn't move.

I stormed up and down, venting my feelings. *Stupid, self-righteous assholes!* I knew how stretched the Council was—to still be chasing me, they had to be spending manpower they badly needed. What the hell had I done to make them hate me this much?

Okay, I kind of knew the answer to that question.

I shook my head and focused my thoughts on the present. As expected, the Council had several tracking attempts running on me, and I took a few minutes with the fateweaver to sabotage them. Once I was done, I bent down and pulled the communicator out of the dirt, then started the chain of gates that would take me home.

⁘⁘⁘⁘⁘⁘⁘

It was late afternoon when I returned to the Hollow. The floating island was peaceful in the yellow-gold light, the sky a deep blue, fading to green. Birds sang in the trees as I followed the path through the woods, the grass rustling under my feet.

Once upon a time, I'd had lots of places where I felt safe. My home in Camden, my safe house in Wales, Arachne's cave beneath Hampstead Heath. Now the Hollow was all that was left, and calling it safe was overselling it. Shadow realms are hard to track or lay siege to, and the wards we'd placed made it harder still, but if the Council wanted to get in badly enough, they could do it. I'd already had to flee the place once, and only constant vigilance and use of the fateweaver had kept me from having to do so again.

Now that my temper had cooled, I could see that trying to ask for a ceasefire had been stupid. To the Council, I was a criminal and a rogue. I'd thought that Sal Sarque's death might have shaken them, but I hadn't considered how it must look to them. As far as they were concerned, it was Richard and Anne who had killed Sarque, not me. I was vastly more dangerous than I had been when they'd attacked me, but they didn't know that.

So why had it pissed me off so much? Because I didn't want to be dealing with this. I had Anne's possession to solve, with Richard in the background. I didn't want to deal with this shit from the Council as well.

Well, what I wanted didn't matter. Like it or not, the Council was my enemy, and that wasn't going to change unless I did something about it.

My cottage in the Hollow is a simple place, not much

more than one room with a bed, a chair, and a desk. I made myself some dinner, taking it to the desk by the window to eat alone. The stores in the Hollow had mostly been laid in by Anne, and with her gone I'd been gradually eating my way through them. I needed to get more, but I'd been putting it off—it was one more step towards accepting that she was gone. Once I was done I cleaned the plate, put everything back in the cupboard, and went out to find the Hollow's other resident.

Karyos was near her tree, sitting cross-legged on the grass. She was studying a small sapling, touching it delicately with the tips of her fingers. She glanced up at my approach, then back down. I sat down on a fallen tree.

Karyos looks like a young girl, with features that are almost human, but not quite. Her skin is a pale gold, and her hair the colour of bark, though both could pass if you don't look too closely. If you had to guess her age, you might say nine or ten. Her real age is either two weeks or a couple of thousand years, depending on how you count it. We'd been sharing the Hollow for a few weeks, and I was still feeling out how to relate to her.

"How was your day?" I asked.

Karyos shrugged.

I nodded at the sapling. "Making it grow?"

"My tree is alone," Karyos said. She spoke English fluently, though with an odd accent that didn't match any country I knew. "There should be a grove."

"Camouflage or tradition?"

"Both."

There was a pause. Karyos didn't look up from her sapling.

"How are you finding the clothes?" I asked.

Karyos glanced down at the blouse and skirt she was wearing. Luna had picked them up for her. "Uncomfortable."

"Are they the wrong size?"

"I dislike wearing them."

"It's a good habit to get into."

"They feel restrictive," Karyos said. "As though they are shaping me."

"I hadn't thought about it that way," I admitted. "But I suppose they are."

"It was not always like this," Karyos said. "I remember the groves in Greece. Humans would come with offerings, baskets and amphorae." She looked up at me with big dark brown eyes. "Would they bring me offerings now?"

"If you showed yourself outside?" I hesitated, thinking of what would happen if she stepped out of the Hollow into its reflection in the Chilterns, with its villages and motorways and big industrialised farms. "I don't think it would go very well."

Karyos nodded sadly. We sat for a little while in silence.

"I could try to find you something more comfortable," I said. "Clothes aren't really my speciality, but there's probably something out there that would suit you better."

"Arachne used to tell me that," Karyos said. "I wish she were here."

It was a simple statement, but it hurt. I missed Arachne too, and talking like this to Karyos was when I missed her the most. Karyos might share some traits with Arachne—she was an ancient magical creature, with strange powers and an otherworldly lair—but our relationship was very different. If Karyos had been Arachne, instead of me asking about her day, she would have asked me about mine. Before I'd opened my mouth, she'd have noticed that I was upset and ask how the conversation with the Council had gone. I would have told her, and she'd offer advice. She wouldn't have given me easy answers—most of my problems don't *have* easy answers—but she'd help me to see things more clearly, and I'd always leave her lair feeling better.

But Karyos wasn't Arachne. The hamadryad had spent most of her lifetime entirely isolated from human and mage society, and she was hopelessly ignorant of the modern world. With Arachne, I'd felt as though I was the child and she was the parent; with Karyos, it was the other way around. Instead of looking to her for answers, she was the one looking to me.

"I miss her too," I said. "But as far as that goes, I might have some good news. I think you've got a good chance of seeing her again."

Karyos looked at me in surprise. "I thought she was gone."

"For me. Maybe not for you."

"How?"

"I've been thinking about the way that dragon took her away," I said. "Arachne's lived a very, very long time, and I think that dragon's part of the reason why. So if that's the way it protects her—spirits her away when she's in danger—why was she still around?" I leant back, resting my hands on the tree trunk. "Dragons exist outside time as we perceive it. If you were a dragon, and you wanted to save the life of someone like Arachne that had a lot of people trying to kill her, how would you do it? Well, seems to me a really easy way would just be to transport her forward in time eighty or a hundred years or so to a point where all her attackers were dead of old age."

"Was that what it did?"

"I don't have any proof, but it fits," I said. "Arachne told me in her letter that we weren't likely to meet again, but I'm human. For you, though?" I nodded at the young tree behind Karyos, its leaves silhouetted against the sky. "A hundred years probably isn't even one full rebirth cycle."

"I'll be able to see her again?"

"I'll have to do some research," I said. "But I think so."

Karyos smiled, her face lighting up. It transformed her

from a grave, silent creature into a happy one. "That would be wonderful."

We sat for a little while, the silence more companionable this time. "Are you comfortable with me living here?" I asked Karyos.

"Yes," Karyos said. "Why?"

"We've never really talked things out," I said. "I mean, when we first met, you were trying to kill us. And we kind of killed you. Obviously it didn't stick, but you were living in this shadow realm for a long time before we moved in."

"Yes."

"You don't have a problem with that?"

Karyos looked confused.

Okay, apparently I need to spell this out more clearly. "Are you angry about what we did?"

"Why would I be?"

I tried to think of a good answer to that and failed.

"You took this realm by right of conquest," Karyos said. "You could have slain me."

"That would have made Arachne unhappy," I said. "Besides, there aren't many magical creatures left. I didn't want to cut that number down without a really good reason."

Karyos nodded. "I was damaged and unable to renew myself. When my tree died, my life would have ended. Leaving me alone would just have been a slower and more complicated way of killing me. You preserved me, and I am grateful."

"That's good to know."

"Though . . ." Karyos hesitated. "Now that my mind is clear again, I feel lost. This world is so different. So much has been forgotten, so much is strange. When you tell me about this new England, it makes me feel . . . helpless. I do not know if there's a place for me here."

"I think the world would be a smaller and duller place without creatures like you in it," I said. "And there are plenty of other humans who feel the same way. They might not always be easy to find, but they're there."

"I hope so," Karyos said. She looked at me. "What are you going to do?"

"For now?" I said. "Find Anne, and deal with the Council. I'll work out the rest as I go."

⁙⁙⁙⁙⁙

It was an hour or two after sunset when I returned to my cottage. I closed the door behind me, drew the curtains, then took off my jacket and shoes and socks. My gear was laid out on the desk, my trousers folded over the back of the chair, then I cleaned my teeth and washed my face. Only at the very end did I take off my shirt.

With my clothes on, my arm could pass for normal. Anyone who looked at my right hand would notice that it was too pale, but pale skin can be explained. Stripped to the waist . . . not so much. It wasn't just my right hand that was pale, it was also the wrist and most of the forearm. Just above my elbow, the colour changed to my normal skin tone. Mostly. White tendrils reached up from the forearm like vines, spreading around the joint so that their tips touched my upper arm.

When the fateweaver had replaced my hand, the border between it and my flesh had been at my wrist. That had been eighteen days ago. Ever since then, it had been spreading.

I stroked my left hand along my right. The surface felt smooth and slightly yielding, like a cross between flesh and some harder substance. I could feel the touch of my fingers, but the sensations were muted. From testing, I knew my new hand was far stronger and tougher than my old, and that wasn't counting what the fateweaver could do. There was just the little question of what it was going to do to the rest of me.

I flexed my arm up and down. There was a slight stiffness in the elbow that I'd noticed as of yesterday, at around the same time that the tendrils had reached the joint. It didn't hamper my movements, but it was a constant reminder.

I switched off the light and lay down on my futon. I lay awake for a long time before going to sleep.

chapter 3

I woke early the next morning. The Hollow was peaceful and quiet, birds singing in the early light, the sky a mix of pinks and yellows. I dressed and ate breakfast, then sat down at my desk with a pen and a sheet of blank paper. The window above the desk had a view out onto the grassy clearing beyond my front door. I picked up the pen and wrote three words.

- *Anne*
- *Richard*
- *Council*

With my free hand I tapped my thumbnail against my lips. I needed to deal with all three. How, and in what order?

In a perfect world, I'd be able to resolve all three conflicts peacefully. That was not going to happen. My best hope for negotiations had been the Council, and yesterday's talks had put an end to that. Talks with Anne would be faster and probably less unpleasant, but our long-term goals were not the same, and she knew that as well as I did. That just left Richard, and I strongly suspected I'd burnt my bridges with him already.

So the *how* was simple. I had to neutralise all three as potential threats. That just left the question of order. I kept writing, ink scratching across the white paper.

1. *Anne —> Richard —> Council*
2. *Anne —> Council —> Richard*
3. *Richard —> Anne —> Council*
4. *Richard —> Council —> Anne*
5. *Council —> Anne —> Richard*
6. *Council —> Richard —> Anne*

I put down the pen and tapped my lips again. It's an old habit of mine when I'm thinking. I used to do it with my right hand; nowadays I do it with my left.

Going after Anne seemed like the worst option by a long way. For one thing, out of all three, Anne was the closest to being on my side. I knew she still had some feelings for me, and I was pretty sure she wasn't going to let me die if she could help it. And she had her own scores to settle. As long as I was fighting against them, I could (mostly) count her as an ally.

Of course, that was only going to last as long as Anne was calling the shots. Sooner or later the jinn was going to take over, at which point Anne was going to stop being an ally. In fact, once that happened, I was expecting the jinn to make me priority target number one. Which brought up a second reason not to go after Anne: the only way I could really "win" was to split her away from the jinn, and right now I had no idea how. Sooner or later (and probably sooner) I was going to need an answer.

That left Richard and the Council. Which one first?

If it was a question of who was the bigger threat, my

answer would be Richard every time. He was smarter than the Council, and much more dangerous. On the other hand, more dangerous didn't necessarily mean more dangerous to *me*. Richard had directly or indirectly saved my life several times over, and if he really wanted me dead, he could have done it a long time ago. My actions in Sal Sarque's fortress might have changed that, but as things were, the Council hated me far more than Richard did, and with a lot less chance of me being able to change their minds.

There was also the same issue as with Anne. Richard had his own jinn, and if it wasn't as powerful as Anne's, his other skills and allies more than made up for it. I didn't have a good game plan for how to face Richard. I didn't have a good game plan for how to face the Council either, but it felt more possible.

Besides, Richard's cabal and the Council were still at war. Allying with Richard was off the table for a variety of reasons . . . but then, Richard's cabal had more members than just him, didn't it?

You know, I think that could work. I lifted my pen and crossed out options one through four. When I got to five I hesitated, my pen hovering between five and six.

Seconds ticked by and I put down the pen. I needed to know more.

I hadn't been idle over the past two weeks, and I'd gathered a fair bit of information about the Council and about Richard's cabal. But I hadn't managed to learn anything more about jinn. I'd spoken to various contacts, questioned Karyos, and even asked Luna to dig up what she could, and none of them had been able to tell me anything useful.

But there was one creature that would have the answers I needed.

I got up and went to prepare myself. Usually I'm not one for ritual, but for this I needed every advantage I could get. The Hollow has a small pool around the other side from where I sleep; I stripped naked and washed myself, cleaning each body part carefully and thoroughly. Once I was done, I dressed in a set of clean clothes, shivering slightly, then finished towelling my hair until it was completely dry.

I fetched my gear from the cottage. There wasn't much: my dreamstone, a plain white cloth, and, most importantly, a chair. Then I walked through the woods until I found a small clearing that looked at first glance like any other. There was a tree stump to one side and I spread the cloth out over it, then I placed the chair about three feet from the stump, adjusting it until its legs were stable on the grass. Some mages like to kneel or sit cross-legged for this kind of work, but I find that makes my knees stiffen up. I sat down on the chair, hands in my lap, closed my eyes, and focused. I breathed in and out, slowly and regularly, holding myself quite still. Slowly and methodically I identified the fears and worries rattling around inside my head, and one by one, I put them gently but firmly away. My mind had to be clear and focused, and any stray thoughts could become a vulnerability to be used against me. When I finally opened my eyes, the shadows in the clearing had shrunk and the sun was visible above the treetops.

I rose and walked to a tree at the edge of the clearing, then touched a knot on its trunk and channelled a thread of magic. The illusion covering the middle of the trunk vanished, revealing that the tree was hollow. Inside were several wrapped packages.

When my shop was destroyed, I'd taken the most powerful and dangerous of my stock of items and hidden them away. I reached in and took out one of the smaller packages, a little less than a foot in length, then walked back and laid the item down on the tree stump. Carefully, I untied the wrappings and pushed away the cloth.

The item inside was a cylinder of lacquered wood, about ten inches long and two inches wide, with a braided cord hanging from one end. The wood was coloured white, with engravings of twining blue flowers. I sat back down on the chair, let out a long slow breath, braced myself, then reached out mentally through the dreamstone. *Marid*, I said quietly but clearly. *If you are willing, I would speak with you.*

There was what felt like a very long silence. Then the jinn answered.

It didn't sound like a creature. It was more like a choir, with one dominant voice and a chorus of lesser ones. As the dominant voice spoke, the others would speak in echo, sometimes repeating its words with subtle differences of emphasis, sometimes contradicting it entirely. I was keeping the mental contact thread-thin, but even so the pressure from the other side was vast. It felt like putting one hand through the bars of a cage to rest my fingers against the body of some enormously strong animal.

WHY HAVE YOU COME. The jinn's voice rolled over my senses, even as the chorus echoed it. *(come where? you have always been here.)*

I braced myself against the mental pressure. The really frightening thing was that it didn't even feel as though the jinn was attacking; all it was doing was paying me attention. *I've been told a lot about jinn over the past few years*, I said through the dreamstone. *I thought it might be a good idea to see how much of it is true.*

YES. (yes? you ask, you do not understand.)

I was told there was a war long ago, between jinn and mages. I was told that's why you are how you are now.

YES. (no. not always. not now.)

Do you want to tell me your side of the story?

THERE ARE NO SIDES. THERE IS ONLY THE DARK. (the beginning and the end. to see is not to understand.)

I paused. *I was told that it was mages that bound you into items. Stripping away your physical form and binding you into items. Did they?*

OUTSIDE. (outside.)

I don't understand.

YOU SEE THE SURFACE. IN THEIR BINDING, THEY TOUCHED SOMETHING ELSE. (made us less. made us more.) BETWEEN BODY AND SEAL, WE WERE OUTSIDE. A BLINK OF AN EYE AND A THOUSAND YEARS. (less than a blink. more than a thousand years. a thousand years were a blink.)

That . . . happened to you?

THE LESSER WERE EXTINGUISHED. (husks. shells. burning shells.) THE GREATER WERE CHANGED. ONLY THE ETERNAL CAN ENDURE THE DARK. (the dark. the dark.)

Okay, I said slowly. *The jinn that's possessing Anne. What does it want?*

WAR. (eternal patience. eternal war.)

A chill went through me. *Is there any way I can change its mind?*

AN AVALANCHE BEGINS A THOUSAND YEARS AGO. (blades of grass beneath the stone. ask the rock why it falls.)

How about breaking its contract with Anne? Is there some way I can do that?

YES. (no.)

How?

DO NOT PRESUME. TO WISH IS NOT TO GUIDE. (impudent. to guide is not to wish. you have learned nothing.)

Okay, I said. *What do you want in all this? Are you on that other jinn's side? Are you hoping it'll succeed, or fail? Do you want humans wiped out for what they did to you? What?*

THERE IS NO REVENGE. There was no anger in the

jinn's voice; it was dispassionate, implacable. *THERE IS ONLY THE CONTRACT, AND THE PRICE. (the price. your price.)*

The strain of talking to the jinn was wearing on me. It felt like holding back some massive uncaring force, and I could feel my will beginning to shake. *One last question*, I said. *You stayed in my shop for years. I'm pretty sure you didn't have to. You took victims when they made contracts. But the rest of the time, you left everyone in peace. Why?*

YOU ARE THE HOST. ONE LIFE IS A LEAF. LAW IS ETERNAL. (you have seen. follow the path.)

I struggled to understand. It was getting harder to think. *What do you mean—?*

ENOUGH.

All of a sudden, the jinn's presence was gone. I lurched on my chair, blinking, as though a weight I'd been bracing against had been suddenly pulled away. The sunlight hurt my eyes and I put up my hand to shield them.

I rose to my feet, staggering slightly. The Hollow felt too bright and too loud. Carefully I rewrapped the cylinder and carried it back to the tree. I made sure not to touch it with my bare skin, but the item was passive and silent as I returned it to its storage. Once I was done, I slumped back down on the chair. That had taken a lot out of me.

Was that even worth it? It was hideously dangerous to link to a creature that powerful. My mind could have been destroyed, and I'd learned nothing.

Or had I? I still didn't understand what the jinn were, but now I had some idea of what I *didn't* know. Something had happened to them, something that those ancient mages had done with their binding, maybe deliberately but more likely as some unintended side effect they didn't fully understand. I didn't know how to make use of that, but it was somewhere to start.

I got to my feet, gathered up my stuff, and started

walking. It was time to get to work on the problem I knew something about.

. . . .

Shadow realms that have been warded against intruders are difficult to enter, which was one reason I'd been able to stay in the Hollow for so long. When we set up the Hollow's defences, we created a set of keystones, and in theory only someone holding one could open a gate to get inside. But if you're powerful enough, there are ways around these things.

Earlier this year, I'd gained two abilities that significantly expanded my options. First, I'd learned how to use the dream-stone to step physically into Elsewhere. It's a hostile environment to put it mildly, but it has major advantages, one of those being that it allows you to travel almost anywhere. The second ability was the magic of the fateweaver. It let me manipulate the futures I could see with my divination, choosing the outcome I desired and eliminating all others.

Put the two together, and I had a way to get into a shadow realm. The dreamstone let me open a gate; the fateweaver let me make sure it would work. It wasn't easy—first I had to stack the odds in my favour by travelling to the real-world location that the shadow realm was a mirror of, then I had to spend a couple of hours patiently following future threads, using the fateweaver to stabilise them so that I could learn what would and wouldn't work. But eventually I saw the futures light up in a sequence of events that would end with me entering the shadow realm. What the Council would have done with a full assault team and a weeklong siege, I could do in an afternoon.

I stepped through into the shadow realm and let the gate wink out behind me, feeling the slight disorientation that always hit me upon leaving Elsewhere. Looking around, I saw green trees, dappled shadows, and beams of light slanting down from a canopy far overhead. From nearby, I could hear a stream and what sounded like a waterfall. There was a path a little to one side, grey flagstones laid through the grass. I started walking, though I didn't hurry. My arrival had set off several alarms, and I knew that the shadow realm's inhabitants were converging on me.

The path wound through the trees and led up to a clearing with a long, wide house on the other side of a grassy lawn. The house was made of yellow-brown stone, irregularly shaped, with grey tiles making up half a dozen gables and small roofs. The path crossed the lawn, bent around what looked like a goldfish pond, and went up a couple of steps to the front door. It all looked very pretty. I leant against a tree and waited.

A group of four people came running from around the back of the house. They changed direction to head straight towards me, spreading out as they covered the distance. There were two girls and two boys; all looked to be around twenty, give or take a few years. "Stay there!" one of the boys called out at me.

I didn't move. The group of four slowed to a walk, then stopped about thirty feet away. All were dressed in casual clothes; they looked alert and hostile.

"Who are you?" the first boy said. He was tall and fit, with short black hair and watchful eyes, and his hand was by his hip in a stance that signalled he was ready to draw a weapon.

"My name's Alex Verus," I said. "I'd appreciate it if you could let your master know I'm here."

At the sound of my name, the boy's eyes narrowed. The taller of the two girls stiffened. "What are you doing here?"

"As I said, I'm here to see your master. Don't do anything stupid, please."

The four of them tried to keep their eyes on me and glance at one another at the same time.

I knew what they were thinking without even having to look. "I said *don't* do anything stupid."

"We know who you are," the taller girl said. She had dark brown hair in a severe-looking ponytail, and a face that would have been pretty if her expression hadn't been so hostile. "You were the one who sold out Morden."

"Did Morden tell you that?"

The girl hesitated.

I nodded. "Ask him next time you get the chance."

"You want to go after him," the boy said, "you'll have to deal with us."

I gave the boy a flat look; he shifted but held his ground. "Your show of loyalty is noted but unnecessary. I am here to talk."

"Yeah, right," the girl said.

I paused, letting my gaze touch all four of them, and when I spoke, my voice was cold and clear. "Do not mistake my courtesy for weakness. I arrived without an invitation, and in recognition of that fact I am treating you with patience. There are limits to that patience. I would rather not do your master the discourtesy of harming or killing his followers within his own shadow realm, but that is exactly what I *will* do if you follow through with your idiotic plan of attack."

The four adepts—I'd had time to figure out what they were—held quite still. For a moment futures of combat flickered, then one by one they died out. None of the adepts were sure what to do instead, and I didn't break the silence. We stared at each other across the grassy lawn.

Then a voice spoke from the direction of the house. "I appreciate your restraint." The tone changed, becoming a command. "Stand down, all of you."

The man in the open doorway had black hair and wore a black suit and shirt. He stood in a relaxed posture, with his hands clasped easily behind his back, and looked quite unworried. "Hello, Verus," he said, his voice carrying across the lawn.

"Morden," I replied. "If it's convenient, I have some matters I'd like to discuss."

"Would you like to come inside?"

"Actually, I'd prefer to walk in these woods."

"Of course." Morden stepped down off the porch and started along the path. "Go back to your practice, you four. I'll be along shortly."

ıı ı ı ı ı ıı

Morden and I walked side by side. The rush of water echoed from around us, the sound muffled and re-directed by the trees so that it was hard to tell in which direction it was coming from.

"Beautiful shadow realm," I said.

"It is, isn't it?" Morden agreed. "It took some effort to secure, but it was well worth it. I always thought those mages who spend their lives barricaded in fortresses and prison realms were displaying the worst kind of foolish-ness. What's the point of power if you have to live in a home you hate the sight of?"

"Did it have a name?"

"The Waterwood. You didn't know?"

"Even diviners don't know everything," I said. "Oh, and you've got a flaw in the gate wards near those oak trees just off the path I entered by. It's at the centre of three overlapping nodes, and two of them are slightly out of phase. Creates a three-foot section where they cancel each other out rather than reinforcing."

"I see," Morden said.

We walked a little way in silence, the path winding around a grove of silver birches. I waited for Morden to ask why I was here, but apparently he was content to wait.

"Do you remember the conversation we had all those years ago in your mansion?" I asked.

"Of course."

"You spoke to me about rogues," I said. "About mages who turned their back on the tradition in which they were trained. And how they often came back." I looked sideways at Morden. "Did you know something like this would happen?"

"You're the diviner, Verus."

"That's not really an answer."

Morden shrugged slightly. "In politics, there are always unpredictable elements. It was possible for you to have won yourself a place with the Council. If you'd gained a powerful enough patron, if you'd avoided making the wrong enemies, if events had made you sufficiently indispensable. But it struck me as unlikely. Remember that by the time we met I'd been dealing with the Council for many years. I'd seen enough mages rise and fall within their ranks to have a good idea of how well you would fit within their institutions."

"I remember you told me that the Council would never accept me," I said. "With hindsight, I would have saved myself a lot of trouble if I'd just taken your word for it."

Morden shook his head. "If you'd followed my advice without understanding why, you'd have learned nothing."

I nodded. "What do you want?"

Morden smiled slightly but didn't answer.

"You asked me that question quite a few times, back then," I said.

"As I recall, you spent most of the conversation evading giving me an answer."

"Yes, and so did you," I said. "Because I threw that question right back at you, and you told me you wanted the fateweaver." I stopped and held up my right hand, letting my sleeve fall back to reveal smooth white not-quite-flesh. "Well, here it is. Are you going to take it?"

Morden turned to face me, his hands still clasped behind his back. "What do you think?"

"I don't think you care about it at all," I said. "It was just a playing piece to you. Which means you weren't telling the truth any more than I was."

We looked at each other for a moment, then Morden nodded to himself, turned, and carried on walking. I fell into step beside him. "I find the question a useful one when discussing the Path," Morden said. "The less sophisticated assume the purpose of such discussions is to probe an enemy's weaknesses. The real value of the question is that it forces one to examine oneself."

"Yes," I said. "I've been learning that."

"I told you back then that a true Dark mage has purpose," Morden said. "You had will, but you lacked a clear perception of yourself and your goals. That is no longer the case. You have an objective which you are determined to accomplish. You are also significantly more powerful. This is not a coincidence."

"None of which answers my original question."

"No."

"The Council never really understood you, you know," I said. "I sat in on God only knows how many strategy meetings where they were trying to predict what Richard's cabal would do. They had Richard pegged as the would-be Dark Lord type. The Council have dealt with enough of them over the years that they're pretty used to them by now. Dark mages who think the logical conclusion of their philosophy is for them to rule as many people as they can. Vihaela was even easier. She's what you might call the smaller-scale version. Power over one person at a time." I looked at Morden. "You, though? They could never find an explanation for your behaviour they were happy with. The best one they could come up with was the public face. Richard as the mastermind, you as his political representative. Their idea was that Richard had some kind of leverage over you that made it impossible for you to betray him."

"They certainly spent more than enough time trying to discover what that leverage might be."

"And got absolutely nowhere," I said. I'd had to sit through innumerable frustrating interviews with Keepers convinced that I had the key to prying out Morden's secrets. "Personally? I think they never found anything because there wasn't anything to find. You were helping Richard voluntarily. But that didn't answer the question as to why. All the time you were under Council arrest, you were taking an enormous risk. You could have been disappeared or 'killed trying to escape' at any time."

"The risk was a little smaller than you think," Morden said. "The Council can be ruthless when threatened, but so long as they feel that they are in control, their inclination is towards caution. Live prisoners can be made dead if need be; the reverse is not the case."

"But in politics, there are always unpredictable elements."

Morden smiled slightly. "What would be your explanation?"

"I think you were never driven by self-interest at all," I said. "That was why the Council could never figure you out, and it was why you were able to work with Richard so easily. Richard wants to be in charge, and everything he's done has been with a view to increasing his power. But you've been quite willing to give your own power up."

"Have I?"

"Several times," I said. "Take that raid you organised on the Vault. The other mages who went on the raid benefited from the items they took. Richard benefited because of his plans for Anne. But you lost your position on the Junior Council, and instead of fleeing afterwards, you let them take you into custody. And you didn't take any steps to make sure Anne would be under your personal control. You let Richard and Vihaela handle all of it."

"So what do you believe my motivations to be?"

"If you and Richard had both wanted to be the one in charge, one of you would have betrayed the other by now," I said. "So as much as you like to talk about the Dark way, I don't think accumulating personal power is your priority at all. Strange as it sounds, I think you're actually an idealist. You want the Dark philosophy and mind-set to be spread and understood. What I don't understand is why you launched that raid. You had what you wanted, you were on the Junior Council. Why sabotage it?"

"From the moment I joined the Council, efforts were made to remove me," Morden said. "You were caught up in several of those plots yourself, and once you took over my seat you became the target of them in turn. What I suspect you may not have recognised is that removing me—or you—was never the primary objective. In the long term, the Council was not concerned with who sat in that seat; they were concerned with controlling its resident. If they had succeeded, the mages occupying it would have followed Light norms and constrained themselves according to Council beliefs. Within a generation they would have been Dark in name only, and treated with contempt by their former allies. That was the real danger."

"And so you blew everything up?"

"The Council's support of that goal was too strong to overcome by purely political means. It still is, to a lesser degree. That may change."

I thought about that for a minute. Morden's explanation wasn't what I'd been expecting, but I didn't have any reason to disbelieve it. I'd had the feeling for a while that Morden had been playing a completely different game to everyone else.

"But these are long-term concerns," Morden said. "Yours are more immediate, I suspect. Why are you here, Verus?"

"I need to win a war with the Council," I said. "I was wondering if you'd be willing to help."

"Do you have something in mind?"

I gained a certain amount of respect for Morden in that instant that I was never to lose. It was the sheer lack of worry in his voice. I explained what I had in mind in two sentences.

Morden didn't seem surprised. "And how do you plan to accomplish that?"

"Well, that's the problem. I don't think a frontal attack is a good idea."

"Given the Council's current state of readiness, I would agree."

"Which is why I'm here," I said. "I was hoping in your dealings with the Council you might have come across something I could use as a stepping-stone."

"It should be possible," Morden said. "I'll need a day or two to look into things, but I have a target in mind that should suit your needs."

"Thank you," I said. "Will there be any issues of allegiance?"

"You mean as regards Drakh?"

"I'm fairly sure that I'm not Richard's favourite person at the moment."

"Drakh and I may be allies, but I am not accountable to him for my every action," Morden said. "If he confronts me on the issue, I will tell him that I believe that your success would be in my, and his, best interests, which is entirely true. Should he choose to press the matter, however, I will not stand in his way. I suspect it will not be long before you have to resolve your issues with Drakh directly."

"Oh, I've been expecting that for a while," I said. We'd come most of the way around in a circle and were approaching the house once again. "Your new apprentices didn't back off all that far, by the way."

"They can be somewhat reckless," Morden said with a

glance back at where the four of them were hidden. "Still, an excess of spirit is better than an excess of caution."

"I didn't know that adepts were your type."

"Perhaps I've learned from you," Morden said with a slight smile. "In any case, if there's nothing else, I have other business. I'll be in touch."

। । । । । । । ।

The image of those four adepts nagged at me on my way home, and midway through the journey I realised why. Two girls, two boys, living in the mansion of a Dark mage. They'd been a couple of years older than I was when I'd joined Richard, but the parallels were uncomfortably close. I wondered if they'd end up on the same path as Morden's last Chosen.

There was another realisation too, something that was harder to explain. I had the feeling that Morden was going to survive all this. He wasn't aiming to settle grudges and wasn't seeking the crown, and because of that everyone else would always have someone they wanted dead more badly than him. When this was over he was going to be walking away, back to the forests and streams of his shadow realm and to his new group of disciples. The same wasn't likely to be true for me.

chapter 4

"I warned you this could happen," Klara said.

"I know."

It was the next day and I was sitting in my cottage in the Hollow. I'd taken off my shirt, and Klara was bent over my right arm, her eyes studying it intently. Klara is a German life mage, thin and unsmiling. I didn't really know her well enough to trust her, but with Anne gone, Klara was the best I was going to get.

"If we had amputated immediately, you would have only lost a hand," Klara said. Her fingers pressed lightly on the not-quite-flesh where the fateweaver had replaced my skin, a faint green light spreading from the fingertips. "Now, you will lose the forearm as well. Continue to wait, and it will be the shoulder."

"Is that still what you're recommending?"

Klara sighed and sat back, the light at her hand fading. "No. The item has tied into your pattern and nervous system. I do not know if it could be safely removed, not without a better understanding of its workings."

"What about the stiffness?"

"Your elbow cartilage is being converted." Klara nodded down at my right elbow. "The item has finished transmuting your radius and ulna and is spreading to the humerus. I expect within another day or so the process will be completed and your elbow will return to full functionality."

"So it's fine?"

"Apart from the fact that it's replacing your arm one part at a time, yes. I would not consider that 'fine.'"

"Fair point," I said, getting to my feet. "How fast is it spreading?"

"At exactly the same rate as before."

"So that spell you tried didn't help."

Klara shook her head. "No effect whatsoever. At this point, the only treatments I can think of carry the risk of so much potential damage that I am hesitant even to try."

I pulled my shirt over my head and tucked it in. "Well, I appreciate the help."

"I don't know why you're thanking me. I have done nothing." Klara looked at me. "Once again, I recommend that you seek treatment at a dedicated facility. I believe it would still be possible to remove this item with further study."

"I understand, but that's not an option."

"Is being *dead* an option?"

I paused. "How long?"

"Half a year at the maximum. Probably no more than three months." Klara nodded at my arm. "The item is overwriting your pattern incrementally, replacing your skin, flesh, bones, and nerves with synthetic material. You are extremely lucky that these materials have so far proven compatible with your physiology. For now at least, your body and your new arm are functioning in symbiosis. The problems will come once it finishes with your arm and starts on your torso."

"So you think it'll keep going."

"There are some indications of negative feedback," Klara said. "I think it *may* not spread to replace your entire body. But it will almost certainly spread through your shoulder to your head and chest."

"What happens if it starts replacing my brain?"

"That is an excellent question. It is also irrelevant."

"Why?"

"The item has successfully transmuted your arm," Klara said. "Somehow, your body has managed to integrate these changes into your physiology. However, the more of your body that is replaced, the greater the strain. Your transmuted arm is fully functional, and will remain so. For various reasons, I can predict almost certainly that the same will *not* be true for your internal organs."

"So you're saying . . ."

"Your right lung will be transmuted, followed by your heart," Klara said. "This will cause them both to shut down. The process is permanent, and once started, irreversible. Your only chance of survival is to have the growth halted before that happens."

"Which would mean losing access to the fateweaver."

"Yes. In fact, you should be doing that anyway. I strongly suspect that use of that item's powers is accelerating the material's spread."

"Those powers are the only reason I'm still alive," I said. "I understand what you're saying, but right now, I need them."

"Yes, well, the thing that's keeping you alive is also killing you," Klara said. "You will have to choose."

Once Klara was gone, I sat at my desk for some time, staring down at my new arm. Klara hadn't told me anything that I hadn't already suspected. Unfortunately, there wasn't much I could do about it. I needed the fateweaver, and that was that.

I hoped I'd be able to finish things before the clock ran out. At the fateweaver's current rate of spread, I should have at least a month. One way or another, that ought to be enough.

ı ı ı ı ı ı ı ı ı

"And have you seen Verus since then?" the Keeper asked.

"I already told you I haven't," Luna said.

"Has he contacted you in any way? Items, letters, e-mail?"

"No."

"Have you contacted him?"

"No."

"Did he leave you any instructions to contact you?"

"No."

It was late afternoon on the same day. Morden hadn't contacted me—I wasn't expecting to hear from him until the following morning—so I'd been free to spend the day focusing on the Council. It was just as well I had.

The Council were hunting me in several ways. The first and the most basic was by using divination and tracking spells to pinpoint my location directly, at which point they'd send a team to capture or kill me. I'd used a combination of anti-surveillance measures and the fateweaver's magic to screw up their tracking spells, but with each failure, they were improving. I'd had to spend a good couple of hours today just on blocking their attempts, and it was rapidly approaching the point where avoiding them was going to prevent me from doing anything else. I'd have to do something about it soon.

But while the Council was doing that, they were also hunting me the old-fashioned way. Ever since I'd gone on the run, Keepers had been staking out my old haunts and questioning my known associates. One name was at the top of their list.

"Seems a bit strange," one of the Keepers said. "You were his apprentice for what, five years?"

"Three," Luna said.

"And he hasn't got in touch?"

"No."

"What, you don't get on?"

Luna shrugged.

"Answer the question," the other Keeper said.

"Like I said, I haven't seen him."

I was crouched in the window of a first-floor flat across the street from the Arcana Emporium. From my position, I could look down across the street through the shop windows to see the backs of the two Keepers questioning Luna. Luna was behind the counter, my view of her head blocked by the ceiling, but I could see enough to read her body language. No one else was in the shop: the Keepers had flashed badges and shooed all the customers out. A couple were lingering outside, shooting curious looks through the glass.

I was listening in on the conversation through a small speaker unit resting on the floor. The speaker was connected wirelessly to a pair of microphones hidden in the shop. I'd installed them after the Keepers had made their first visit. This was their fourth.

"Where do you think Verus might be right now?" the first Keeper said. Her name was Saffron and she was a mind mage.

"I don't know," Luna said.

"When was the last time you saw him?"

"I've already told you," Luna said. "It was before he was outlawed, here at this shop."

"You haven't seen him since then?"

"No."

Mind magic isn't a lie detector. A mind mage can read surface thoughts without being obvious about it, but to search memories they have to break through their target's mental defences first. Officially, Saffron wasn't allowed to do either of those things to Luna without formally charging her with a crime. Unofficially, I was quite sure she'd been reading Luna's thoughts since the first visit. I'm quite familiar with mind magic, and I'd made sure to teach Luna as much as I could, which meant that, right now, Luna was carefully schooling her thoughts to make sure Saffron could learn nothing useful whatsoever.

Of course, at any point Saffron and her partner Avenor could just decide *screw it* and drag Luna off to a cell to rip out the contents of her head by brute force. So far, they hadn't, mainly because they had no evidence linking her to me, but it wouldn't take much to change their minds.

"Verus is facing the death penalty," Avenor said. "Once we catch him, he'll be interrogated. Fully interrogated. Anyone who helped him, they're getting the same sentence. You understand?"

"Yes," said Luna flatly.

"You hear anything, you let us know," Saffron said. "The Council won't wait forever."

"Okay."

Footsteps sounded through the speakers, and across the street, I saw Saffron and Avenor open the door and walk out, leaving Luna alone. Through the speakers, I heard Luna exhale. She stood behind the counter for nearly a minute, then walked to the door, flipped the sign from *CLOSED* to *OPEN*, and went back to minding the shop.

I stayed crouched by the window, checking the futures. Once I was absolutely sure that Saffron and Avenor weren't coming back, I took up the rifle lying beside me, returned it to its case, snapped the case closed, and stowed it in its hiding place under the floorboards.

Afternoon turned into evening, and the shadows lengthened on the floor. A steady stream of customers flowed in and out of the Arcana Emporium: teenagers, adults, tourists, locals, and some who didn't fall into any obvious category. Luna dealt with them all, selling items, giving advice, and fielding questions, while I watched from above.

Looking down on Luna, I couldn't help but think how once upon a time, that had been me. Right now she was listening to a pair of women in cut-off shorts, one with a bundle of posters, the other with a pair of plastic bags, who were asking her whether magic was really just another way of having faith in Jesus. I tried to imagine what it would be like to be back in her shoes, opening the shop at nine o'clock every day, and couldn't. My memories of that time had an unreal quality these days, like I was remembering someone else's life instead of my own.

It was nearly seven when Luna finished with the last customer and followed them to the door to flip the sign back to *CLOSED*. She stretched and yawned, did a circuit of the shop, then took out a broom and spent five minutes sweeping the floor. Once she was done she sat down at the counter and opened the ledger.

The sun had disappeared behind the rooftops, and the sky was turning a dusky blue. I looked down across the street and through the shop window at Luna. She was focusing on the ledger, making notes with a pen. I saw her reach up to brush a strand of hair behind her ear, and as she did I felt a stab of loneliness so sharp that it was like a physical pain. I didn't want to be up here, spying on someone who was supposed to be my friend. I wanted to be down there talking to her. When the Council had outlawed me, they hadn't just taken away my position, they'd taken away my connections. I missed being able to drop in on Luna or Variam for a visit. I missed Arachne and the safety of her lair. I missed having regular, normal interactions, and I missed Anne most of all.

I let out a breath and tried to steady myself. It took a while.

By the time I was calm again, the sun was setting. Luna was still down in the shop, working away. This was taking longer than I'd expected—my best guess had been that her visitor should have arrived by now—but divination's never reliable when it comes to free will. Still, the futures were converging and it shouldn't take more than another ten minutes. I was glad that Avenor and Saffron hadn't stuck around. This was going to be risky enough already.

The futures settled, and I felt a stir of gate magic from somewhere behind the shop. About thirty seconds later, there was the sound through the speakers of the shop's inner door opening. Luna's head snapped up and she went still.

"Surprise!" Anne said. "Is this a bad time?"

Anne had changed a lot in the last few weeks. Her hair had grown to fall almost to the small of her back, and in place of her old clothes she wore a jet-black skater dress with an off-shoulder design that left most of her arms and legs bare. The biggest change, though, was in how she moved. The old Anne had been tall and striking, but she'd downplayed both, hanging back and staying quiet. Now, she walked onto the shop floor as if she owned it.

Luna's head moved to track Anne as she passed, but her hands stayed on the counter. "Love what you've done with the place," Anne said, glancing around. "Not sure exactly what you changed, but it really feels different from when Alex was running it, you know?"

"I wasn't expecting you," Luna said.

"Yeah, well, you know how it is," Anne said. "Or actually, I guess you don't, since you never had the whole fugitive experience, but you can probably imagine I don't pre-book much of a social calendar, right? So how's it going? Still working nine to five?"

"Mostly."

Anne shook her head, her hair swaying with the motion. "I don't know why you stick at it. Selling crystal balls to fat women who want to win the lottery? You're not an apprentice anymore, you don't have to keep minding the till."

"I'm not minding the till," Luna said. "This place is mine now."

"God knows why you'd want it." Anne pulled out a chair from against the wall and dropped into it, studying Luna critically. "You do look good though."

"Thanks," Luna said. "So what have you been up to?"

"Oh, you know," Anne said. "Council wants me, Richard wants me. It's kind of dull, really. They chase me, I run away, they chase me, I run away, I get bored of running and murder them all, they scrape up more guys to chase me again. Same old same old."

"Are they chasing you right *now*?"

Anne shrugged. "Maybe? I don't really keep track."

The answer to that was yes. A Council team was trying to track Anne at this very moment, and they would have succeeded by now if I hadn't intervened, using the fateweaver to scatter the threads of their spell. Neither Luna nor Anne would have been in immediate danger, but it would have given the Council a reason to investigate Luna more closely.

Luna wasn't looking happy at all. "Could you maybe *not* lead them straight to my shop?"

"Hey, I have to find you somewhere. Not like you'd come visit if I'd sent you an invitation."

"I would have, actually."

"Really?"

"Yes," Luna said. "You were my best friend. Remember?"

"Aww!" Anne smiled. "Of course I do. Nice to know you do as well."

"Look," Luna said. "I *would* like to talk to you. But knowing that a Keeper team might show up at any minute is not exactly making me feel relaxed here."

Anne waved a hand. "Fine, fine, I'll get to the point.

What if I told you there was a way you wouldn't have to worry about the Council breathing down your neck?"

"How?"

"Same way that I don't."

"You don't have to worry about the Council because you've got a bonded jinn."

Anne smiled. She raised her eyebrows.

Luna paused. "You're not serious."

"You remember those talks we used to have?" Anne asked. "You always said you wanted to *do* something. Make a difference."

"And you said you didn't," Luna said. "That you just wanted to be left alone."

"Yeah, well, that was then, this is now. So what do you think? Ready to shake things up a bit?"

"Anne," Luna said. "I'm not in your league. I never was. You were ten times stronger than I was *before* you got that jinn. You and Vari and Alex can get away with things like thumbing your noses at the Council and daring them to do something about it. I can't. That mage status I have, the one you're putting at risk by being here now? That's the only reason the Council haven't just pulled me off the street already. I know the Council treated you like a bottom-rank mage, but that was still better than how they treated me. You really don't understand how little it takes for them to come down on me."

"So stop worrying about them coming down on you," Anne said. "Make them afraid that *you'll* be the one coming after *them*."

"You want me to bond to your jinn as well."

"Not mine. But there are others."

"Why me?"

"Because like you said, we were best friends," Anne said. "I'd like to think we still could be. And when it comes to jinn, you've got some firsthand experience."

Luna was still for a second. "You're talking about the monkey's paw."

Anne rose to her feet and began strolling around the room. She didn't answer, not straightaway.

"You're hoping I'll get it for you, aren't you?" Luna said. "Wait. Is that why you came here? Were you hoping it'd just show up on the shelves?"

"I *was* kind of wondering," Anne said. She trailed a finger along one of the shelves, disappearing from my view for a few seconds before coming back into sight. "I mean, that was the way it worked back when Alex was running the place, right? Just sort of pop into existence when the right person came along?"

"Yeah, well, it's not popping."

"There are other jinn," Anne said with a shrug. "It's you I really care about."

"So what's the idea?" Luna asked. "Us two, each with a jinn, going on a rampage?"

"Hey, you were the one saying about how the Council treats you," Anne said. "You told me enough times how they'd look down their noses at you for being an adept. Why not make them have to look up to you for a change?"

"Yeah, for how long?" Luna asked. "Because you're right, I *do* know a bit about jinn. As in, I know what happens to the people who make a contract with one. You remember what the monkey's paw does once its bearers run out of wishes?"

"Those other bearers didn't have me."

"They probably all told themselves that too," Luna said. "But fine. Forget all that for a second. Let's say it works. We get our jinn, set ourselves up as the big bad witch-queens of the British Isles. Is that the plan?"

"More or less."

Luna nodded. "Then what?"

"Then we deal with the people who want to take us down. Like the Council, and Richard, and—"

"I mean after that," Luna interrupted. "Then what?"

For the first time in the conversation, Anne looked honestly puzzled. "Does it matter?"

I heard Luna sigh slightly. "I suppose to you it doesn't."

"So?"

"I'll admit it's tempting," Luna said. "And it would be one thing if it was just you. But I'm having trouble getting past the jinn."

There was a note in Luna's voice which it took me a second to recognise, then suddenly I understood. Luna had already made up her mind. Now she was trying to figure out how to get Anne to take no for an answer.

"The jinn is the reason I can do all this," Anne said impatiently. "Look, stop getting hung up on that part, okay? I know what I'm doing."

"That's what Martin told me," Luna said. "As in, those exact words. Usually with some comment about how dumb everyone else was to be scared of wishes when all you had to do was word them right. And he kept being cocky right up to the point where he made the wrong wish and went crazy. I was there, okay? I watched him screaming his lungs out, trying to rip out his own eyeballs. So *don't* just brush me off when I have issues with this."

"He was making wishes," Anne said. "I don't have to." She opened up one hand; dark threads spun and coiled above her palm. "When you *really* bond with a jinn, you don't need all that anymore. We act as one."

"So what does the jinn get out of it?"

"Look, I don't have time to play twenty questions. Are you in or not?"

"I'm . . . going to have to think about it."

Anne's back was to me so I couldn't see her face, but all of a sudden, there was a dangerous note in her voice. "You'll think about it?" She dropped her hand, but the dark threads didn't disappear; they spun faster, growing. "This isn't a telemarketing call."

Uh-oh. I took one glance at the futures and stood up, making the movement big and noticeable. Reaching out with the fateweaver, I picked out a strand.

Anne paused. She turned her head slightly, then stopped. The dark threads twining around her shrank and disappeared. "Fine," she said to Luna. "I'll be in touch." She walked past the counter and left. The door shut with a loud click.

Through the glass, I saw Luna's shoulders slump, the tension going out of her.

ı ı ı ı ı ı ı ı ı

I was waiting on the roof of the Arcana Emporium when Anne's head poked up above the wall. "There you are!" she said. She looked cheerful; the flash of temper she'd shown down in the shop was gone. "I was wondering if you were going to stick around."

"*You* were wondering if *I'd* stick around?" I said. "I've been trying to catch up with you for weeks. You are not an easy person to find these days."

"What can I say? I'm a popular girl." Anne sprang lightly up the last few rungs of the ladder and alighted on the roof. She looked around appreciatively. The Camden skyline stretched out around us, chimneys and TV aerials rising up like saplings over hills of tiles and brick. The sky was a dusky purple, a couple of faint stars struggling to make it through the city's light pollution. "This brings back memories. So does she know you're spying on her?"

"You're not the only one who's popular in the wrong places," I said. "If Luna doesn't see me, she doesn't have to lie when the Keepers ask where I am."

"Still holding her hand, huh? Don't remember you doing that with me." Anne stretched and turned along the line of the rooftops. "Come on then, let's take a walk."

I fell into step beside Anne, crossing over the dividing wall to the next building. "Actually, I'm pretty sure I did exactly that when you got attacked at Archway," I said. "Or when you got kidnapped from your flat in Honor Oak. Or when you got kidnapped again a few years later. Or when—"

"Okay, okay, fine," Anne said, waving a hand. "Is this your way of saying I owe you?"

"Not exactly," I said. "But I do have a request. A while ago, you said you had a list."

"Working my way down, one name at a time," Anne said. "Why, you want someone put on there? I might do it if you ask nicely."

"More like a rearrangement. I'm guessing right now Sagash is next?"

"Got it in one."

I nodded. "Could you move him down to number two?"

"Who's number one?"

"Levistus."

"Well, well." Anne looked at me appraisingly. "So you're finally done playing nice."

"Playing nice has not done me much good over the last few years."

"Took you long enough to figure *that* out." Anne stopped on the roof of an apartment building and drummed her fingers on a ventilator for a second before shrugging. "All right."

That was easy, I thought. *No, too easy. Which means* . . . "You haven't figured out how you're going to get into Sagash's shadow realm, have you?"

Anne gave me an unreadable look.

"Funny, I thought that jinn of yours could do anything." I raised my eyebrows. "Maybe it's limited by having to act through you? So it's great at close-range effects, but more abstract stuff like gates—"

"It *is* great at close-range effects," Anne said, her tone clearly indicating that she didn't like the way the conversation was going. "Want a demonstration?"

I raised a hand, palm towards her. "Anyway, I imagine Levistus wasn't all that far down your list in the first place. He and Barrayar spent more than enough time trying to nail us when you were my aide, and I've always had the feeling that he had a hand in that interrogation order."

"I already said yes, you can stop selling. So what's the plan?"

I didn't have one, but I didn't want to admit that. "Not here," I said. "You have somewhere more secure we could talk?"

"Yeah, the place you used to meet me," Anne said with a grin. "If it's not broke . . ."

Of *course* she'd want to go there. "Works for me. I'll find you in a couple of days."

We stood in the twilight for a few seconds, facing one another. Anne watched me with a secretive smile, her reddish eyes dark in the reflected light, the wind from the streets making her hair drift slightly. I wondered what she'd say if I asked her to stay with me, and had to force myself not to look into the future to find out. I wasn't sure I trusted myself with the answer.

"Well, got to go." Anne stepped back and the moment was broken. "Catch you later!" She turned and vanished into the night.

I stood there for a minute after she'd gone. Half of me was disappointed, half relieved, and I didn't know which half was smarter. I hadn't realised how badly I'd missed hearing her voice.

Threatening futures loomed and I sighed and pushed the thoughts aside. The Council were hunting me yet again, and they were using those new-model tracking spells that had proven so annoyingly effective. If I wanted to give them the slip, it'd take me the rest of the evening.

But I had other things I wanted to be doing. Anne's sales pitch to Luna and the hints she'd dropped about other jinn were bothering me, and she'd agreed to my offer too easily. She was up to something, and I needed to know what.

ı ı ı ı ı ı ı ı ı

The flat in St. John's Wood had that blandly tasteful look you only find in the parts of London that are ridiculously expensive. The building security gave me little trouble; the security on the flat itself gave me even less. Once I was inside I took a glance around. There were more papers than the last time I'd been here, as well as a lot more magical auras, but fewer computers and electronics. It had also gotten even messier, if that were possible. The only chair was stacked with overflowing folders, so I gave up and just sat on the bed.

It was a little over an hour before I heard the rattle of the door, which gave me more than enough time to sort through the futures of the Council hunter team and nudge them in the direction I wanted. There was a click and light flooded in from the hallway, then there were footsteps, and the room lit up as a mage in his twenties walked in.

Sonder was dressed as if he'd just come from the office, and his head was buried in a sheaf of papers. The combination of smart clothing and messy hair made him look like a programmer at a big tech company, or maybe a political aide. He hadn't changed much since I'd last seen him, but then I'd been through a lot more lately than he had.

It was tempting to wait and see how long it would take for him to notice me, but I was on a clock. "Hi, Sonder."

Sonder jumped, scattering papers, and whirled. One hand started to come up, then he recognised me and froze.

"Nice to see you too," I said. "Okay, so I've got good news and bad news. Bad news—that slow-time field you're thinking of using, or that stasis field? You wouldn't get it off fast enough. Good news is I'm not here for a fight."

From looking at the futures, I could sense Sonder's thoughts racing. Slowly they calmed down and the possibilities of a fight vanished. "How did you get in?" Sonder asked cautiously.

"Your security sucks," I said. "So, how are things with the Council? I imagine after what happened to Sal Sarque they must have a bunch of openings."

I saw Sonder flinch slightly at the reminder. "It's . . . going well."

I sighed. "Oh, relax, Sonder. I've never lifted a finger against you in all the years we've known each other and I've got no intention of starting now. Not unless you try to arrest me or something equally stupid."

Sonder grimaced slightly. "Not much chance of that." He sat down, a little of the tension going out of him. "So are you . . . ah . . ."

"Doing well as an outlaw?" I finished. "Can't complain."

"Um. Good."

I looked at Sonder.

"I mean, not good," he said hastily. "It's good that, well . . ."

"Okay, you know what, let's skip the small talk," I said. "I'd like to quiz you about a research subject."

"Which subject?"

"Project Catalyst."

Sonder paused for just a second too long. "What?"

"After Morden did his raid on the Vault two years ago, the Council issued an order to investigate the imbued items that were stolen. You were one of the project leads and did most of the item reports, which I was reading the same day you delivered them, so can you not play dumb, please?"

"You know all this was top secret," Sonder said.

"Sonder, let me explain something to you," I said. "Right now, there is a team of Council Keepers hunting me. The longer I stay in one place, the better the chances that they'll track me there. When they do, there will be a fight. Once the dust settles, any survivors will be in an *extremely* bad mood, and when they discover that you and I were in this room, they will have questions. These questions will be uncomfortable and potentially highly embarrassing for both you and any allies you happen to have on the Council. So I would suggest that it is *very much* in your interest not to dick me around."

"Okay, okay," Sonder said hurriedly. "I get what you're saying, but Project Catalyst was huge. You can't expect me to remember all of the details."

"I don't need to know about all the items, just one. Suleiman's Ring."

"Well, I can remember *that*, but . . . look, there was a reason that thing ended up in the Vault. No one's going to go running experiments on a ring with a jinn."

"I know, I read your report. I'm not interested in what the ring can do. I want to know about the jinn inside it. Specifically, its history."

"Oh. Well, that's easy." Sonder seemed to relax a little bit. These days Sonder was a politician, but he'd started his career as a historian, and this was his home ground. "It's the marid sultan. It's just referred to as the sultan in the records, because it was unnamed . . . you know about that?"

I shook my head.

"It was what they did with all the marids. Apparently the binding ritual for the jinn used their true names. They wanted to stop them from breaking free, so after they finished, they made sure that the marids' names would be lost permanently . . ."

I nodded, listening with half an ear while I monitored

the futures. The Keeper team hunting me was narrowing down my location. I could stall them with the fateweaver, but not for long.

". . . and that was why they think it was in that bubble realm," Sonder said. "After what happened to the last mage who tried to use it, well . . ."

"Okay, you don't know the marid's name," I said. "Is there anything you *do* know about it? History, personality, goals?"

"Its goals were the defeat of the Council, I think," Sonder said. "The war went on a very long time. By the end the jinn had been fighting a losing battle for years."

"And the rest?"

"Well, most of the historical data we have from back then are official Council records," Sonder said. "They're focused on the progress of the war and Council resolutions. As far as the individual marids go, there are some tactical analyses, but . . ."

"Tactical analyses?"

"The sultan was served by four ifrit generals," Sonder said. "They each had different types of elemental control, sounded a lot like elemental mages, actually. Apparently they had some way of amplifying the sultan's power. It was only after the Council launched a strike specifically targeting them that they were able to defeat the sultan afterwards."

"So did they bind them into items too?"

Sonder shook his head. "No, they discussed that but rejected it. Too many worries that anyone who got hold of one of the generals could use it to free the sultan. They were banished instead."

"They didn't just kill them?"

"Well, they couldn't."

"Why not?"

Sonder looked at me in surprise. "Jinn can't be killed. You didn't know?"

I shook my head.

"It's because they're partly divine." Sonder settled back into his chair; he was in his element now. "I mean, 'divine' is the wrong word, there's nothing sacred about them, but the people who wrote about them back then were a lot less rational about these things. A better model is that jinn exist in two different states. They have a physical form that exists inside space-time, and a nonphysical form that exists outside it. That was how the binding ritual could work. It just remapped their nonphysical state from one body to another."

I frowned as I thought about that. "It was that easy?"

"Well, it took a lot of research to develop."

"I didn't mean easy to do. What effect did it have on the jinn?"

"Well, they were still around. And they could still grant wishes."

"I mean in terms of what it was like for them."

"Oh." Sonder shrugged. "I don't think anybody knows."

Arachne had told me that the binding process had harmed the jinn, filling them with hatred or driving them to madness. She hadn't explained why. "You said the jinn's nonphysical states existed outside space-time," I said. "So it was their physical forms that tethered them to our conception of time and space. Right?"

"Well, yes, in layman's terms."

"So switching their physical forms . . . would that mean that while they were in between the two, their consciousness wouldn't have a temporal anchor? So they wouldn't experience time in the same way as us at all?"

"Probably," Sonder said. "I mean, you're talking about the infinity point hypothesis, right?"

"The what?"

"You know, from Schulte?"

The futures shifted, and I paused to look at the change.

The Keeper team hunting me had managed to get a first-stage fix on my signature. They'd have to do a second pass to narrow down my location, but just gating wouldn't be enough to throw them off anymore. I had maybe five or six minutes.

"Alex?"

"Sorry. I'm not very familiar with his work."

"Well, you know how all of those attempts for mages to transfer their consciousness into external housings never seem to work, right?" Sonder said. "And it's not just here, pretty much every Light Council across the globe has a history of trying it. Golems, simulacra, clones, they never seem to take. Either the mind doesn't jump, or they come out insane. Anyway, Schulte's hypothesis was that it's our physical body that allows our consciousness to experience time in a sequential way. Without a physical tether, our consciousness still exists, but it doesn't occupy any position in space-time. The problem with all of those transference rituals was that no matter how they were designed, there was an infinitesimally small period during the jump where the transferring consciousness wasn't tethered to their new body *or* their old body. Everyone else would perceive that moment as only a tiny fraction of a second, but without an anchor, the transferring consciousness could theoretically experience it as *any* length of time."

A chill went through me. "You mean they could experience something that felt like thousands of years? With no sensory input or feedback?"

Sonder nodded. "Hence the insanity. That's the theory anyway. It's why nobody tries transferring their mind into a golem anymore."

"So the same thing could have happened to those jinn."

"Well, it would explain why they were so uncooperative."

I was thinking about what the jinn in the monkey's paw had said. *Between body and seal, we were outside. A blink of an eye and a thousand years.* What would it be like, to be shut out from the world in total sensory deprivation for a thousand years? Jinn wouldn't experience it the same way as humans, but it couldn't be good.

How would you survive something like that? You could do mental exercises, training your magical abilities in the way I'd trained in those long months when I was a prisoner in Richard's mansion. Or you could focus on something, some goal or ideal, something greater than yourself to give you something to cling to during the endless years. The marid within the monkey's paw had chosen the binding law of the contract. The sultan marid . . . what would it have chosen?

At the time of its binding, it had been leading its species in a war against mages. That would have been its goal.

Eternal war. I shivered.

"What is it?" Sonder asked. "You keep spacing out."

"Little distracted. Sorry." I rose to my feet, checking the futures. Only a minute or so left. "Sonder? One last thing. The jinn that weren't bound into items. Can they still be summoned?"

Sonder nodded. "By the higher-order jinn, yes. That's how jinn-possession subjects can pull off summoning rituals so easily."

"So could the sultan resummon any other jinn of lesser rank than him? Including those ifrit?"

"I hope not." Sonder looked worried. "It's bad enough dealing with one of them."

"Yeah," I said. The futures clicked. Somewhere in a Council facility, the Keepers hunting me had just learned my exact location. "Well, time to go. Thanks for the help."

Sonder tensed, probably wondering what I was going to do. I gave him a nod and walked out.

I shut the door of the flat behind me and started down the stairs. Mentally, I was cataloguing futures, calculating the Keeper team's next move. Right now, they'd be cross-referencing my location with GPS data and their own records and learning that I was at Sonder's flat. Next, they'd ping Sonder's locator and confirm that he was there as well. From that point they had two choices. They could decide that Sonder was now an additional suspect and needed to be brought in. In that case, they'd call in more reinforcements, deploy teams to surround the area, get ready to move in with maximum force.

The other possibility was that they'd decide that Sonder was innocent and that I was an intruder, in which case the first thing they'd do would be to contact him directly. When he told them that I'd just left, they'd be faced with a dilemma. They could pull the trigger, gate in, and scramble to try to catch me before I got away, but they'd have little chance of catching me and they knew it. That just left them with one last option for tracking me before I got out of range . . .

From above me, I heard Sonder's door, followed by the sound of feet hurriedly descending the stairs.

I sighed inwardly. *They could get Sonder to slow me down.* Sometimes knowing the future isn't much fun.

Sonder came racing around the last flight of steps and caught himself as he saw me standing at the bottom. "Is there a problem?" I asked.

"Uh . . . ," Sonder said.

I looked at him, eyebrows raised.

Sonder had just started to open his mouth to speak when there was a shift in the futures and he paused, the movement so slight that you wouldn't have noticed unless you were watching for it. It wasn't a long pause. Just long enough for someone speaking into his ear over a concealed link to suggest a cover story. "Don't use the front door," Sonder said. "The Council are monitoring it."

"I have to go out somewhere."

"You can go through the courtyard." He hesitated for just an instant. "There's a back way. I'll show you."

I looked up at Sonder. He shifted uncomfortably, and I felt a flash of disappointment. It wasn't the fact that Sonder had gone along with the Keepers—I'd always known his loyalty was to the Council. It was that he'd done it so damn fast. "Okay, but hurry up."

Sonder led me the other way along an internal corridor, where a pair of double doors led outside. Or not exactly outside; high walls rose up all around us. Sonder had called it a "courtyard," but it was more of an internal park, with flats rising up in a rectangle on four sides, and a neatly tended stretch of grass and trees criss-crossed by stone paths. It was a gated community and looked very exclusive and cosy. "So how's the war been going?" I asked.

"Pretty well."

"You mean apart from Sal Sarque and his entire retinue getting killed?"

"Drakh took losses too," Sonder said. "And we destroyed their base in that shadow realm they were using to launch attacks."

Sonder sounded distracted, as you'd expect from someone trying to follow two conversations at once. "Everyone seems to think you're losing," I told him.

"We're not losing," Sonder said quickly. "The war's in a stalemate due to . . ."

I listened with half an ear. The Keeper team were getting ready to gate in at multiple locations. Multiple *simultaneous* locations—how were they managing that? There should be too much variation in the gate timings for—*ah*. They had a space mage. In fact, it was someone I'd met a while ago. Her name was Symmaris, and she'd provided the transport for a Keeper hit team who'd burned down my old shop. They were planning to have her open several gates at once and surround me.

". . . which is why they're making a mistake," Sonder finished.

"Uh-huh," I said. Sonder was leading me diagonally across the courtyard. The Keepers were planning to launch their attack once I got out into the street, but they were still setting it up, and if I forced them to move early they'd have to go with their emergency plan, which was to gate right into the courtyard. I changed my focus to look at Sonder. They were probably talking to him through an earpiece—yup, earpiece communicator. I carry a dispel focus that looks like a long silver needle. Without breaking stride, I slid it out of my pocket, brought it up to just behind and to one side of Sonder's ear, and discharged it in the air.

There was a faint, tinny shriek as the communicator overloaded, and Sonder yelped, putting a hand to his head. He backed away from me, eyes flicking down to my hand and up again. "What are you . . . ?"

"Shh," I said, returning the focus to my pocket and watching the futures intently. They were swirling as the Keepers tried to figure out what to do. I pushed delicately with the fateweaver. *Not too hard, we don't want to tip them off . . . there.* I turned around and started walking back across the courtyard.

"What are you doing?" Sonder called.

"I'm going this way."

"The way out's—"

"No, I've got a good feeling about this way."

The futures flickered briefly as Sonder considered his options. I kept an eye on them while I paid most of my attention to the futures of the Keeper team. *Let's see, visual angle is there, firing angle is there.* I stopped, changed direction, walked ten paces, and stopped.

Sonder came up behind me cautiously. "Um . . . what are you doing?"

"Do you know what's special about this spot?" I asked Sonder.

". . . No?"

I pointed at the pathway ahead, where it curved towards the doorway that we'd come out of. "That point is midway between where I was when you met me at the foot of the stairs, and where I was when we turned around. If you were searching for someone you suspected of doubling back, it's where you'd start. Of course, it's not very good from a tactical perspective, because anyone could come up behind you." I turned and pointed to the left, where a grassy bed near the wall of the flats was lined with flowers. "If you wanted a good *tactical* position, you'd take *that* spot, right in front of the flowerbed. It's at the centre of the wall so it gives you a view straight down the courtyard, and it's between the windows of the ground-floor flat, so your back isn't exposed. If you were a Keeper and you had to pick a landing spot, that's where you'd go."

Sonder looked confused and alarmed at the same time. The mention of Keepers must have clued him in that something was wrong, but he was still two steps behind. ". . . Okay."

The futures had settled, the Keeper leader in charge of the team had given his orders, and Symmaris was forming her gateway. Space mages are very efficient at gateways. "But that's not where I'm standing. What's special about *this* spot?"

"I'm not sure," Sonder said.

"This spot is special because it's fifteen degrees offset from the plane of a gateway appearing at that spot there," I said, pointing at the flower bed. "Symmaris likes to create her gates so that they're rotated seventy-five degrees clockwise. She can't make the angle any more extreme than that without compromising the spell, but it means that if anyone's standing right there in front of the gate, she won't be facing them. She's paranoid that way. Do you understand?"

"Not really," Sonder said uneasily. "Look, I think we should get moving—"

Sonder stopped as space magic pulsed from the spot I'd been pointing at. With a shimmer, the air darkened and transformed, forming a gateway between the courtyard and somewhere else.

I'd already turned away. Using my coat to hide my movements, I drew my pistol and fired.

The bullet reached the gateway just as the gate portal had finished forming, and entered and exited the gate five and a half feet off ground level at an angle of fifteen degrees from the plane of the gate. I had just a fraction of a second to see Symmaris on the other side of the gate, standing in a Keeper briefing room, her hands raised as she focused on her spell, and her eyes came to rest on me and began to widen just as the bullet hit her in the middle of the forehead.

Symmaris's head snapped back and the gate winked out. The security man who had been about to jump through never made it. The echoes of the shot rebounded around the walls and died away, and the courtyard was quiet once again.

"Hey!" Sonder shouted. "What are you . . . ?"

I returned the pistol to its concealed holster and turned back to Sonder. "You really should pay more attention to these things."

Sonder looked on edge, ready to fight or flee. The funny thing was, I was pretty sure he didn't understand what had just happened. From his angle, he would have seen the gate open, caught a glimpse of Council security, then nothing. Sonder's never been very decisive; he can react when threatened, but when there's no clear course of action, he tends to hesitate. I used to be the same.

Up above, lights were coming on in the flats, and people were peering out of the windows to see what the noise was. Sonder looked from me to where the gateway had been. "We're done here," I told Sonder.

Sonder hesitated. A future wavered into existence of him trying to trap me in a stasis bubble.

I looked at him and shook my head.

Sonder looked back at me and the future vanished. I turned and walked away.

Two minutes later, three more gates opened up and a Keeper assault force came storming in to find Sonder standing alone in an empty courtyard. I was long gone.

chapter 5

Morden got in touch the next day.

The gate shimmered and faded behind me as I stepped into the shadow realm and glanced around. I saw green, rolling hills, with tall trees rising up into the sky. To my right, the ground sloped down into a lake, while up ahead, a collection of white-roofed buildings peeked up from behind the trees. Behind were the fuzzy and indistinct shapes of mountains. The air was warm with a gentle breeze, like a pleasant summer's day.

The beauty of the scenery was marred by scars of battle. The grass around my feet where I'd landed had been burnt black in a twenty-foot radius, and while some of the trees rose tall, others had been shattered, their stumps ending in jagged spikes. The remains of a jetty and boathouse were charred wreckage by the lake, and though I was still a long way from the buildings at the top of the hill, I could see that at least one had collapsed. Shoots of new grass were poking up from where the greenery had been burned away, but the damage was clearly recent.

Morden's four apprentices were waiting for me a little way up the hill. The looks they gave me as I approached weren't friendly, but at least they weren't planning to attack this time. "Good morning," I told them. "I assume you're escorting me in."

"This way," the tall boy said curtly. I followed him, and the other three fell in around me.

"I didn't catch your name," I said as we walked.

"I didn't tell you."

I nodded. "Manticore, wasn't it?" I glanced at the brown-haired girl. "And you'd be Lyonesse."

The two of them shot me looks.

The other boy spoke up. "You're calling yourself Manticore?"

"Shut up," Manticore said.

"Oh, right," I said. "You haven't told them. Should I use your birth name?"

Manticore gave me an annoyed look. The other girl opened her mouth to say something, and the taller one—Lyonesse—shot her a glare that made her close it again.

I was tempted to keep teasing them but decided to ease off. "So I'm guessing the four of you used to be students here."

"Before your people destroyed it," Lyonesse said.

The name of this shadow realm was Arcadia. It had been something between a school for adepts and a military training camp, and Morden had been the one running it. The Council had invaded and destroyed it at the same time that I had my showdown with Richard and Sal Sarque. "They're not really my people."

"It was the Council who did the attack," Lyonesse said. "And you were on the Council."

"So was Morden."

Lyonesse frowned.

"So how come—?" the other boy began.

"Stop talking to him," Manticore said curtly. We walked the rest of the way in silence.

Morden was standing on what had once been the school's front lawn. The rosebushes and hedges had been torn apart, but the grass of the lawn had mostly survived, probably because it had been too low to be hit by the crossfire. Behind Morden was what must have been the main entrance hall, built from white stone. It looked to me as though the defenders had fortified the front of the hall and used it as cover, and the Council forces had responded by calling in the heavy artillery. The entire building behind Morden lay in ruins: the only way you could even tell that it had been an entrance hall was by looking at the outline of the walls.

"Verus," Morden greeted me. "I see you found your way here."

"Your directions were fine," I said. "You do seem to have a knack for finding pleasant places to live. Did you design Arcadia yourself?"

"I had some hand in it," Morden said. Standing alone in the wreckage, he made an odd contrast, a figure in black on a field of green and white.

I gave Morden a curious look. "Does it bother you, what happened here?"

Morden gave a slight smile that didn't touch his eyes. "Shall we get down to business?"

"Let's."

Morden's four apprentices walked past me to stand near him, spreading out into a formation that left the five of them on one side and me on the other. "You asked me for a stepping-stone," Morden said, "but it would be more accurate to say that what you need is leverage. Against the Council in general, and Levistus in particular. Would you agree?"

"That seems fair, yes."

Morden nodded. "Do you know why Levistus was so strongly opposed to any action against White Rose?"

I frowned. I hadn't been expecting the question, and it took me a moment to answer. "Because he wanted to keep you off the Council. Without all the blackmail material you got from there, you wouldn't have been able to get your seat."

"Correct," Morden said, "but there is another side to it that you were never made aware of. White Rose, while it existed, held the largest reserve of blackmail material within the Light political landscape. The second largest reserve was held by Levistus."

"Really?"

"You first encountered Levistus during his attempt to acquire the fateweaver," Morden said. "He failed spectacularly, yet shortly afterwards advanced from the Junior to the Senior Council. His failure with White Rose was just as complete, yet that didn't stop him from forging an alliance with Alma and Sal Sarque. And don't forget his personal vendetta against you—pursuing a grudge against a lesser mage is one thing, but failing at it quite another. Levistus lacks Bahamus's birth and connections, he does not have the proven war records of Sal Sarque and Druss, and he does not possess Alma's administrative skill. So why is he perhaps the most powerful man on the Council?"

"I don't know," I admitted.

"Levistus's power lay in secrets," Morden said. "Many of which were also known to White Rose. The two of them had an arrangement where neither would disrupt the other. My actions threatened that."

"Huh," I said. I'd always wondered why Levistus seemed to have such a particular issue with Morden. Come to think of it, maybe that was one of the reasons he'd never liked me, either. Secrets only have power if they stay secret, and having a diviner around would cut into his territory. "So where did he get all those secrets? Mind magic?"

"I'm sure he would have gleaned the odd titbit, but every Council mage takes precautions against mind-reading. No, what Levistus has is much more interesting, and it was only relatively late in my time on the Council that I was able to discover it. Levistus has access to a bound synthetic intelligence."

I frowned. "An imbued item?"

"Not exactly. It is a thinking, conscious mind, grown over time. Unlike most mage creations, this one was designed to interface with machines, and in particular computer and communication systems."

"Communication systems? Like radio signals?"

"It intercepts, decrypts, and searches them," Morden said. "Effectively, Levistus has a small, private version of the British government's GCHQ, or the American NSA, able to collect and sort vast amounts of electronic intelligence. The overwhelming majority is useless or irrelevant, but not all."

"I wouldn't have thought he'd get much from the Council, given how low-tech they are."

"You'd be surprised," Morden said. "It only takes one bureaucrat or Council aide to make a phone call. The phone call is intercepted, flagged by an algorithm, and passed on in a daily report. Any clues in that message can in turn be investigated in more detail, whether by his agents or by Levistus himself. Levistus has been in possession of this synthetic intelligence for over twenty years. Twenty years of compound interest on information adds up to a very large amount."

"And your idea is to get hold of that information and use it against Levistus and the Council."

"I am not aware of the exact contents of Levistus's

files," Morden said. "But they are extensive. I imagine they will more than satisfy your needs."

"I can see a problem here," I said. "Levistus is going to have the tightest security on those files that he possibly can. He'll either have them in some data focus that's locked to his magical signature, or just keep them all in his head. He's a mind mage; he can probably memorise them all without breaking a sweat."

"Indeed," Morden said. "But I am not suggesting you go after Levistus's private vaults. I am suggesting you go to the source. The synthetic intelligence itself."

"How do you know there's anything there?" I asked. "Levistus could just take out anything he needs on a weekly basis and delete the rest."

"He could," Morden agreed. "And that would be the logical approach were he entirely focused on security. However, without existing data to cross-reference, it becomes harder to separate useful signals from noise. I suspect in the early days Levistus might have been willing to make such a sacrifice, but he has been operating this system for a very long time, more than long enough to become complacent. By the time I chanced upon his secret, he was, in my judgement, no longer spending enough personal time and attention on administering the synthetic intelligence for such an approach to be a realistic possibility. I believe that he has allowed data to accumulate for the sake of convenience."

"But you're not sure," I pointed out.

Morden spread his hands. "Things may have changed. But as I say, this is my own judgement."

"Mm," I said in a neutral tone. It was still possible that Morden was leading me into a trap. "All right. Say I go after this synthetic intelligence. Where is it? In some super-fortified shadow realm?"

Morden smiled. "That's the good news. Levistus

couldn't install it in a shadow realm. No radio. So he looked for a central location with the best reception he could find."

A fuzzy patch of grey appeared in the air between me and Morden, around five or six feet tall. Lines of yellow-white light appeared within, tracing a three-dimensional shape. It was a tower, roughly rectangular but with protruding panels, about five times as tall as it was wide. At the top, the structure broke up into an irregular stack of blocks, with a thin mast protruding from the highest one.

I tilted my head, studying the design. "A skyscraper?"

"Recognise it?" Morden asked.

It took me a second. "Heron Tower," I said. It was at Liverpool Street, right in the middle of London's financial district.

Morden nodded. "One of the tallest buildings in the city, and far enough removed from the Council power centres at Canary Wharf and Westminster. Levistus's data centre is here." The tallest block on the tower, the one with the radio mast, blinked red.

"Huh," I said. I must have looked up at Heron Tower a thousand times while living in London. I'd never suspected a thing. "How come no one's noticed anything?"

"Levistus has opted for stealth over fortification. The data centre has almost no permanent wards, and the few magical sources within are heavily shielded. No bound guardians, no powerful defences to radiate an obvious signal to magesight."

"Security forces?"

"As I said, stealth over fortification," Morden said. "The system is entirely automated. Remember that Levistus's primary concern when setting up the site was not defending it against Dark mages, but against Light ones. He would not have been able to permanently staff it without the risk that someone would talk."

"So in theory pretty much anyone could just break in

and steal the hard drives," I said. "Is that what you're saying?"

"More or less."

"Okay," I said. "So if this place is such a great target, why haven't you knocked it over?"

"Morden doesn't need anything some Light mage could give him," Lyonesse said. She and the other three had been standing quietly up until now.

"Trust me," I told her, "there are lots of things your master could do with that."

"While such material is less useful to me now than when I was on the Council," Morden said, "it is still valuable."

"Which makes me wonder why you haven't made a move."

"While Levistus's data centre may not be fortified, it is still defended," Morden said. "The location has multiple redundant alarm systems. If any are triggered, Levistus can deploy a rapid reaction force. Privately hired mercenaries, probably from outside the country."

"Mercenaries don't sound too bad."

"Secondly, the data centre contains a compact and powerful bomb. I suspect, but do not know, that it is set to detonate in case of any incursion that reaches the computer systems at the centre. The bomb is more than powerful enough to destroy the synthetic intelligence and all of the records on-site."

"Ah," I said. "If he can't have it, no one can."

"And that is why I have not taken action," Morden said. "Destroying the data centre would prevent Levistus from gaining any future benefit, but he would still have access to the records it had generated already. Over time it would weaken him, but it would take years, and any influence he lost would simply be gained by other Council members instead. I judged it not worth the risk."

"But if you could disable the bomb and *retrieve* the records . . ."

Morden nodded.

I tapped my lip. "What are the bomb's triggers?"

"You're a diviner. I expect you can find out."

I studied the glowing lines of the tower. "Hmm."

"Oh, and I would suggest timing your attack for, say, tomorrow afternoon."

I shot Morden a look. "Why?"

"Just a suggestion," Morden said. "You're free to ignore it."

"Your little suggestions have a habit of being not so little," I said. "I'll keep it in mind. One last thing. What are you going to be doing while I'm dealing with this?"

"You mean, will I be coming with you?" Morden asked. "No. Honestly, Verus, I really don't think you need me to hold your hand. Besides, Levistus is your problem more than he is mine."

"If he wasn't yours as well, you wouldn't be being this helpful."

"Needs versus wants," Morden said. "The one who wants sets the terms. Was there anything else?"

Tomorrow afternoon didn't give me much time. I'd need to stake out the place and path-walk to feel out the defences. Even once I'd learned everything I could, I had a feeling this wouldn't be a one-man job. "No," I said. "I think that's enough to go on."

We departed without incident, Morden's students giving me suspicious looks as I walked away. Before gating out, I glanced around the ruins of Arcadia. It was still beautiful, despite the damage. I wondered if the adepts who'd trained here had seen it as a haven, and whether it would grow into a legend over time.

I also wondered whether Morden's help was a form of revenge on Levistus and the Council for what they'd done here. Over the past few years, Morden and I had both sat on the Council, and we'd both been stripped of our positions. There was a certain symmetry in the two of us being the ones to strike back.

⁛⁛⁛⁛⁛

I spent the afternoon scouting out Heron Tower and pathwalking to test its defences. There was good news and bad news.

The good news was that I was pretty sure I could break in. The bad news was that as I'd suspected, this wasn't going to be a one-man job. If I wanted to have any reasonable chance of this succeeding, I'd need help. And that was a problem, because while I knew a lot of people capable of supplying that help, there were good reasons that I didn't want to ask them.

The natural choice for a job like this was Luna. Luna isn't the best combat mage, but her chance magic is excellent for stealth operations. Just as important, I knew her, trusted her, and we knew how to work together. The problem was that while I was pretty sure we could get into the data centre without being detected, leaving would be another story. There was a very good chance that I was going to end up shooting my way out, along with anyone I brought with me. And if I did that with Luna, it was only a matter of time until the news got back to the Council. At that point, Luna would become an outlaw, just like me. The life as a shopkeeper and independent mage that she'd so carefully built would be destroyed. I couldn't do that to her.

Going to Variam brought the same issues. He'd be worse at the stealth parts of the job, better at the combat ones, but again, it would only take one person recognising him for his career as a Keeper to be over. In fact, pretty much anyone with any kind of relationship with the Council was out for the same reasons, which ruled out all Light mages and most independents.

There was the option of Anne. She was more than powerful enough and couldn't care less about getting into trouble with the Council, given that she was on their most-wanted list already. Unfortunately, she was on that list for very good reasons, the main one being that she was possessed by a human-hating, enormously powerful, and probably insane jinn. On top of that, Dark Anne was the one currently running things, and she was violent, impulsive, and unreliable. I didn't want to trust her with something like this unless I had no other choice.

So I needed someone who was either a Dark mage or the next thing to it, but who could be depended on to perform a difficult and dangerous job. And it had to be someone I knew well enough to trust.

Put like that, I could only really think of one person who fit.

ııııııııı

"And that's pretty much all of it," I finished.

I was standing in a small park near to the old Arcana Emporium. Back in the old days, before my shop had been burned down, I'd used it as a gating point. Thick trees and bushes blocked out line of sight to the buildings all around, and provided some shade from the late afternoon sun.

The man standing in front of me was big and heavily muscled, as tall as me but with the build of a heavyweight boxer. His arms were folded, the muscle outlines visible through his sleeves, and he was staring past my shoulder, apparently deep in thought. He'd listened to my entire story without saying a word.

"So?" I prompted when Cinder didn't speak.

Cinder looked up at me with a frown, then went back to studying the grass on the small hillock over my shoulder.

"Are you in?" I asked eventually.

"Thinking," Cinder said in his rumbling voice.

A minute went by.

"Is this going to take a while?" I asked when Cinder still didn't talk. "Because I could give you some time. You know, go for a walk, get some tea . . ."

Cinder didn't answer.

"Learn a new language . . . work out the issues with general relativity . . ."

"You going to shut up?"

I stayed quiet.

"All right," Cinder said at last.

"All right?"

Cinder nodded.

"Any questions?"

"No."

"You don't even want to hear the plan?"

"You're about to tell me."

"Well . . . yes."

"So?"

I sighed. "You know, you're much less fun to explain things to than Luna."

Cinder just looked at me.

"Fine," I said, handing Cinder a tablet. "You can see the blueprints for Heron Tower there. Levistus's data centre is on the two floors in that top block, highlighted in red."

Cinder took the tablet and zoomed in, studying the map. "Getting in is easy," I said. "Getting in without the bomb going off is hard. The blast won't threaten you but it'll destroy the records I'm there to get. Unfortunately, whoever set up the security measures for the place was thorough. There are a *lot* of redundant and overlapping triggers." I'd spent a good two hours path-walking, trying to figure out a way to disarm the alarm systems, and I hadn't found one. Any attempt to disarm it piecemeal just caused another trigger to activate instead, and the frustrating thing was that I often couldn't tell why my attempts were failing. Though I wasn't sure, I suspected that Levistus might have put in security measures specifically to mess with diviners. "Opening the doors triggers the bomb, cutting through the walls triggers the bomb, gating inside triggers the bomb, and trying to interfere with any of those triggers *also* triggers the bomb. There's a chance that if I get close I might be able to figure out a way through, but I don't want to bet on it."

"So?"

"There's one weakness I can find," I said. "Levistus didn't want to use heavy ward coverage, because that would have made his spy station too obvious to magesight. So he's had to rely on technological defences, mostly sensors and alarms. They need power." I nodded at the tablet. "The main electrical switchboards are in the mechanical levels in the basement. The backup power is on the roof. If we cut the power at both locations, that should open up a way into the data centre."

Cinder raised an eyebrow at me. "Should?"

"I haven't been able to test it," I admitted.

"If it doesn't work?"

"Then I'll improvise," I said. "If it helps, I'd like for you to handle the basement while I take the roof. That means that any nasty surprises are going to be landing on me, not you."

Cinder grunted and turned his attention back to the map. "What's their backup?"

"Backup is going to be Levistus's personal response team," I said. "The leader is Levistus's personal aide, a mage called Barrayar. Force mage, pretty dangerous. There's also a small hit squad that I haven't met. They look like either low-grade mages or adepts, but they seem like combat specialists. One teleporter, one force blaster, and one who uses hand-to-hand attacks. Once an alarm is triggered, they'll gate in within minutes."

"Keepers?"

"That's the good news. Levistus's alarms are set to alert him, not the Council, and he isn't going to call for Council reinforcements as long as he has any other alternative. Given the contents of that data centre, the last thing he wants to do is draw attention."

"Exit?"

"From the basement, you'll be able to gate out anytime you want," I said. "The upper levels are more difficult due to the gate wards."

"Bringing that elemental?"

"That's the plan."

"All right." Cinder tossed the tablet back to me. "I do this, you find me Del."

"Okay. I can't guarantee she'll cooperate, but—"

"No," Cinder said. "You *find* her, and you make sure I get a chance to talk to her."

I grimaced. I didn't like it, but it wasn't like I hadn't seen this coming. "All right."

⁙⁙⁙⁙⁙

I t was late that night before I was able to empty my pockets onto my desk, sit down on my chair, and start unlacing my shoes in preparation for bed. Outside my window, the stars of the Hollow were glowing in the purple-and-green nebulae of the shadow realm's night sky. It was beautiful, but I felt tired and unhappy.

The plan I'd worked out for the attack on Heron Tower was sketchy, with a lot of places where things could go wrong. If this had been the old days and if the participants had been my old group—me, Luna, Vari, Anne—I never would have okayed it. But now I had the fateweaver, and Cinder. We might or might not get the data, but I was pretty sure we'd be able to make it out in one piece.

But it wasn't the plans for tomorrow that were bothering me. Instead, my mind kept wanting to go back to my memories of last night, and that brief split-second where I'd looked into Symmaris's eyes. I hadn't known Symmaris well, but I *had* known her, known her name and quite a few other things about her, right up until the point where my bullet had blown the brains out of her skull and turned her from a living, breathing person into a corpse. It hadn't been the first time Symmaris had been involved in an attempt to kill me, and judging from what I knew of her, she'd probably deserved it, along with the rest of the mages on that team.

So why was it bothering me?

Because it wasn't really about Symmaris, it was about all the other people before her. Symmaris wasn't the first person I'd killed, or the second, or the twentieth. She was just the most recent addition to a whole pile of bodies. And tomorrow, I was going into battle against Levistus's men, and they'd be trying to kill me, and to stop them I'd have to kill them first, and one by one, the pile would keep getting higher. And worst of all, I couldn't see any way it was likely to stop. There'd always be some new enemy or some old one. How long before I got so tired of it that letting one of them kill me first would start to seem like an easy way out?

In the past, what had held me together had been my friends. When I'd brushed up against the darkness, Anne and Luna and Vari had grounded me, given me something to hold on to. Now I was drifting.

And if I succeeded at everything, if I somehow managed to bring Anne back from her possession, would she still want me? Back in the early days, my relationship with Anne had nearly ended because I killed one person. How would she react to what I'd become now?

I sighed and lay down on my bed. I'd stripped off my clothes while I was thinking, and now I switched off the light and lay on my back, staring up at the ceiling. I remembered a conversation I'd had with a Dark mage, back when I was still an apprentice. He was an older man who'd been a battle-mage for a long time before retiring, and he'd told me something that had stuck with me. He'd said that a lot of the people he'd known back in the life had died not when they threw themselves into danger, but after. They'd been able to stay ahead of their enemies while they'd been going all out; it had been afterwards, when they'd tried to slow down, that it had caught up with them.

I couldn't afford to do that. I had to be ruthless.

But how much of myself was I going to lose?

My artificial arm felt cold against my side. I put it out of my mind and forced myself to sleep.

: : : : : : : : :

I was in the middle of a dream when I became aware of someone seeking me. The dream was vague, confused, a memory of sitting on the high grassy fields of the Heath with Anne, but as I rose to my feet I saw that I was alone. I readied myself, aware of a presence coming closer.

A door opened in the air just up ahead, white-and-blue crystal. It swung open to reveal a figure behind. "Hey, Alex," Luna said. "Got a minute?"

I shook off the sleep-mist and walked forward, letting the dream weaken and fade. By the time I reached the door and stepped through, the scenery behind me had faded to black. The door swung shut with a click.

We were standing in a palace of crystal and silver, the colours a mixture of pale blues and whites. The hallway I'd stepped into looked almost as though it had been sculpted from glowing ice. Floating staircases curved away up to landings with high arched doors on the level above.

"I was wondering if you'd call," I said, looking at Luna. Luna was wearing a white dress with sky-blue slashes, and heeled shoes that rang on the glass-like floor. "You look good."

"It's Elsewhere," Luna pointed out. "I can look however I want. And you picked a hell of a time to disappear on me."

"Yeah, sorry. I'm not really the safest person to be around right now."

"Is this about those Keepers?"

"They're still checking on you," I said.

"Those two, Avenor and Saffron?" Luna shook her head. "Don't worry about it. They'd have given up a week ago if they weren't so desperate."

"Mm."

"Stop worrying, I know what I'm doing. Come on, I need to talk to you."

I wasn't as comfortable as Luna about shrugging off a Keeper investigation, but she turned and started walking, and I followed. We started up one of the staircases towards the balcony above. "Anne came to see me," Luna said.

"I know."

"You know—of course you do. You couldn't have stopped by?"

"Every time those Keepers talk to you, Saffron's reading your surface thoughts and Avenor's watching your body language," I said. "The less you have to lie to them, the safer you'll be."

"I was there for the raid on Onyx's mansion and for your trip to Sal Sarque's fortress," Luna said. "Did they figure that out?"

"No," I admitted.

"Yeah, because I didn't let them. Come on, Alex, give me some credit. I'm not a little girl anymore."

"You're really not, are you?" I said. I looked sideways at Luna as we walked along the balcony and through the arch. She looked confident and poised, and I remembered the first time I'd brought her into Elsewhere, where I'd been the one to step into her dream. She'd come a long way since then. It was a pleasant thought. *Even if this doesn't work out, I'll be leaving something behind.*

"What are you smiling about?" Luna asked.

"Oh, nothing. You were saying?"

"Right," Luna said. "Anne. What *exactly* is your plan with her?"

We'd come through into a long hall with railed galleries running around the edge. A swimming pool rippled in the centre of the hall, and fires burnt in fireplaces at floor level, giving an interesting flame-and-ice contrast, red against blue. "The Council's the priority, then Richard," I said. "As long as they're out there, Anne and I have a reason to work together. Once they're gone . . . well, we'll cross that bridge when we come to it."

Luna nodded as if that had been what she'd expected to hear. "I'm not sure you're going to have that long. When I was speaking to Anne . . . you were watching that?"

"Yeah."

"Figures. Alex, she *really* scared me. I've met Dark mages out to kill me and Light ones out to kidnap me, and she frightened me more than any of them. I'd rather be back in Onyx's mansion dodging fireblasts than spend another ten minutes alone in a room with her."

"Why?" I said slowly. "What are you afraid she'll do?"

"I don't know," Luna said. She fell silent and we walked a few steps, her shoes tapping on the gallery floor. "It felt like a recruitment pitch. I think she's trying to get a bunch more jinn-bonded mages, with her as the boss."

I frowned, thinking. "I've been learning some things about jinn." I told Luna what I'd heard from Sonder. "Maybe that's her plan. She wants hosts for those four ifrit."

"And then what?"

"God knows."

"Do you think the jinn's making the decisions?" Luna asked. "Is she that far gone?"

"No," I said, shaking my head. "The jinn might be nudging her, but she's still the one in control. For now, at least."

"Yeah, that was the feeling I got too," Luna said. "But I don't think that's the good news you seem to think it is."

"Why not?"

Luna was silent for a few seconds before answering. "Why do you think Anne fell in love with you?"

I looked at her in surprise. "Is this really the time?"

"There's somewhere I'm going with this."

"Fine . . . Because she trusted me, I guess. And because I was smart enough and good-looking enough and got on with her well enough and all the rest. But I always had the feeling that the biggest reason was that she'd spent most of her life having everyone pull back from her and be afraid of her, and I didn't."

Luna made a face. "I was afraid you were going to say something like that."

I looked at her in annoyance.

"Argh." Luna ran a hand through her hair. "I'm not good at explaining these things. Look, Anne and I have spent a lot of time together. Visiting at the apprentice programme, meeting at the shop, watching anime in the evenings. She might have liked you the most, but I'm pretty sure I understood her the most, better than anyone except maybe Vari. Now, I can't remember when it was that you told me about her dark side, but I do remember it wasn't actually much of a surprise."

"Okay . . ."

"What do you think were the things you did that made the biggest impression on her?"

I shrugged. "The whole business with Fountain Reach, I guess. And then what happened with Sagash."

"Right."

I waited. We'd done a full circuit around the walkway.

I stopped, leaning on the railing, and looked at Luna. She looked back at me.

"What are you getting at?" I asked.

"None of those things involved you trusting her."

"Well . . . maybe not."

"Okay, Alex, harsh truth time, okay? Anne didn't fall in love with you because you trusted her. And it wasn't because you're tall and fit and good-looking and owned your own house, though that helped. She fell in love with you because you were stronger than her."

I gave Luna a disbelieving look. "That doesn't make sense."

"Why?"

"Well, for one thing, I'm not."

"I know that's how it looks to you," Luna said. "But think about how it looks to her. You saved her from those gunmen at Archway, you rescued her from Vitus's shadow realm, you rescued her *again* from *Sagash's* shadow realm, you got her away from Lightbringer and Zilean . . . you get the idea? Every time she's been in real trouble, you've been there to save the day, either by outsmarting the people who get in your way or by flat-out killing them. I know Anne's got more raw power but she can't do what you do. Light Anne likes that because she feels that when she's with you, instead of having to take care of everyone else, she gets to be the one taken care of for a change. And Dark Anne likes that because strength is the *only* thing she's got any respect for."

"Okay, look," I said. "Whether I agree or not, how is this going to help?"

"You're thinking that it doesn't matter if Dark Anne's evil, she still cares about you," Luna said. "She does, but not in the way you think. She's going to push you to see what she can get away with, and she's going to keep pushing, and being nice to her is just going to make things worse. It won't *matter* that the jinn's not in charge."

I looked down at Luna. She looked back up at me, leaning on the railing, her gaze clear and serious. "You're not just worried about me, are you?"

"If Anne does go ahead with this recruiting spree, I don't think she's going to want strangers."

"I'll do what I can to step on it," I said. "But right now the Council comes first."

"It's not the Council I'm worried about."

I watched Luna walk away, disappearing into the blue-white light of the palace, before turning away to open a doorway back into my own dreams. Between my arm, Anne, and the Council, there were a lot of clocks running. I wished I knew which was going to run down first.

chapter 6

When you're hitting a stationary target, there's always a trade-off between time and preparation. If you're willing, you can spend weeks staking out a place, working out your attack plan. The more information you can gather, the more you'll know what you're getting into, and the more prepared you'll be.

The other option is to wing it, which usually involves brute force. Back when I was a Keeper, I'd noticed that elemental mages had a tendency to just throw up a shield and kick in the door. It seemed to work for them, but I'd always preferred to lean towards the planning end of the scale. The way I saw it, I had a lot less safety margin than other mages, so the more risks I could control, the better.

Things were different now. I had more power, less time, and was playing for much higher stakes. Still, I'd been given a little room to prepare, so I made the most of it.

"Come on, make one!" Starbreeze said.

"No."

"Come on."

"No."

"Come *oooooon*."

"No."

The inside of the van was cramped. I was sitting by the doors with my eyes closed. Cinder was at the other end, his bulk fitting awkwardly into the tight interior. And floating in the air above him was Starbreeze, looking like an elfin girl drawn in lines of vapour. I'd tried to explain what I'd need her to do, and she'd promptly ignored me and started bugging Cinder to make a flame for her.

"A little one?"

"No."

"Okay, a big one."

"No."

"Please?"

"No."

While Cinder was occupying Starbreeze, I was busy path-walking. It was one thirty P.M., which put us in the time window that Morden had suggested would be a good one for the attack. Some earlier divinations I'd done had given me tentative confirmation that some kind of fight might soon be going down elsewhere, and I'd been hoping to narrow the time down more precisely. Path-walking is quite a difficult use of divination, and you really want a quiet, secluded location to do it from. Still, I had the fate-weaver to help stabilise the thread, and I'm very good at what I do. I could probably manage it even with a few distractions.

"Can you do colours?"

"No."

"I could help."

No answer.

"Ooh!" Starbreeze said. "What if I guess the colour?"

The immediate futures flickered with various possi-bilities of Cinder attempting to murder Starbreeze. It disrupted the thread I'd been trying to follow, which promptly vanished. I sighed inwardly. Maybe I was being optimistic.

"Red!"

"No."

"Orange!"

"No."

"Blue."

"No."

"Orange."

Cinder glowered at her. "You just said orange."

"I did?"

"Yes."

"Why?"

"Because . . ." Cinder seemed to realise what he was doing and shut his mouth.

"Oh," Starbreeze said. "What were we talking about?"

"Starbreeze," I interrupted before Cinder could do anything. "Could you check to see if anyone's watching?"

"Okay!" Starbreeze said brightly. She zipped out under the van doors in a puff of air.

Cinder closed his eyes and brought his head back against the side of the van with a *thunk* that made it sway on its tyres. "Jesus."

"She takes a while to get used to."

"Used to wonder why you didn't use that elemental more." Cinder opened his eyes and glared at me. "Now I know."

I took a second to path-walk again and this time got the result I was looking for. "Okay," I said. "Far as I can tell, the Council are going to get an incoming attack in about thirty to forty minutes. Should do a lot to cut down their response time."

"Drakh?" Cinder asked.

I nodded.

"Where?"

"Not sure."

Cinder gave me a look. "Not sure?"

"I'm looking ahead to see what'll happen if I get in touch with people on the Council," I said. "It's easy to see the point where they suddenly stop picking up their phones. Detail is harder."

Cinder grunted. "How long for?"

"Not sure about that either."

"Seems like you say that a lot."

"Like I said. If things really go to hell, I'm not going to have an issue if you just gate out."

"Hm. We going?"

I nodded. "Let's do it."

I'd parked us just off Bishopsgate, the big A-road that runs from north to south through the Liverpool Street financial district. It was a warm sunny Friday and the area was crowded, men and women in business suits mingling with travellers and service workers. Both new and old skyscrapers rose up all around, with Heron Tower just visible over the nearby building, tallest of all. A little way to the north, hidden behind a city block, was Liverpool Street mainline station. If things got messy and Starbreeze wasn't able to get me out, that was my backup plan for shaking pursuit. Glancing at the front of the van as I climbed out, I saw that in the brief time that we'd been stopped, it had picked up a parking ticket. The van's owner was not going to be happy.

Cinder clambered out behind, the van lifting noticeably with the loss of his weight, then reached inside and took out a pair of big plastic toolboxes, handing one to me. I took it and had to shift my stance—it was heavier than Cinder had made it look—then we turned and started walking.

Cinder and I were both dressed in orange fluorescent worker's overalls, with silver reflective stripes. They're the most garish outfits you could imagine, but oddly enough, they made us blend right in. Central London is usually filled with construction work, and Bishopsgate was no exception—there were new skyscrapers going up on both sides of Heron Tower, and nearly one man in ten was wearing gear like ours. No one spared us a second glance as we walked towards the building.

Heron Tower is shining steel and glass, lines of white lights running along each floor, bright enough to be visible even in the daytime. Bright metal zigzagged from above our heads up and up through dozens of stories until the top blocks were so small you had to squint. The right corner of the skyscraper had a pair of lifts that were visible through the grid of glass panes, rising and falling in plain view from the outside. The side entrances had a bar and a sushi restaurant.

The inside lobby was quieter. Security gates to the right led to a set of escalators, and there was a gigantic aquarium in the lobby centre. A tall security guard with a neat salt-and-pepper beard stood to the left, and I could feel his eyes settle on us as soon as we walked in. I headed for the reception desk before he could intercept us.

There were three receptionists behind the desk, and I'd already picked out my target. She was blond and in her thirties, holding an iPad, pretty with lots of makeup that almost hid the crow's-feet at her eyes. Her smile slipped a little as she saw us approaching, and I could see her sizing us up. Construction workers, therefore not rich or important. Conclusion: shoo away. She waited as we walked up to her and—

—*my future self reached forward and plucked the tablet out of her hands. She tried to protest but I held up a hand while I looked at the tablet. It was still unlocked and I opened up the list that said* Appointments *and started scrolling through. The security guard moved in but Cinder blocked him; both the guard and the receptionist were speaking angrily but I was fo-*

*cused on the appointments list. Anglo-American . . . no.
GlaxoSmithKline . . . no. Lloyds Banking Group . . . no
way we could pass for that. Murphy . . . maybe, but the
appointment was for four. The security guard tried to
deal with Cinder physically. Bad idea. He went down
hard; the receptionist hit an alarm and backed away;
other security guards were hurrying from the other side
of the room; Cinder shot me an irritated comment. A
company name caught my eye: EDF Energy. Two people.
I scanned the names, checked the time, let the future
collapse—*

—and I was back in the present. The lobby was quiet
except for the murmur of conversation and the noise of
the escalators. The receptionist was looking at us, the tablet in her hands.

"Hi," I said. "We're from EDF. Looking for Keith Adams from Salesforce?"

The receptionist eyed me doubtfully. "Do you have an
appointment?"

I nodded at the tablet. "EDF Energy."

The receptionist checked the tablet. "Can I have your
name please?"

"Radu Todoca."

"You're a bit early . . ."

"Our job window's twelve to three."

"It just says three here," the receptionist said, but she'd
lost interest. My name matching the one on her tablet had
removed any suspicion. She handed me a clipboard. "Can
both of you fill in your name, company, and time entered.
Also, we need a mobile number so we can contact you
while you're in the building."

I took the clipboard and started filling in the form. The
security guy had wandered up, apparently friendly. "Hello
there, sir," he said. "What were your names again?"

"Radu. And this is Bogdan."

"Oh, really? From Poland?"

"Romania."

"Romania! That's great. What are you here for?"

I handed the clipboard to Cinder; he took it and started to fill in the blanks in silence. "Need to check the power for the twenty-third floor," I said. "Health and Safety."

"If it's the power, shouldn't you be going to the basement?"

I shrugged. "Work order says twenty-third."

"I've sent a message to Keith Adams," the receptionist said. She handed us two badges. "I've scanned you through the security gate. Make sure to wear these at all times inside the building."

"Okay." I took the badges, handed one to Cinder, gave the security guard a nod, then turned and headed for the gates. Cinder followed. No one stopped us as we walked through the security gates, took the escalators to the mezzanine floor, waited for a lift, and stepped inside. I hit the button for the twenty-third floor and the doors hissed shut, leaving us alone.

"You are *shit* at passing for an electrician," Cinder said.

"I got us in, didn't I?"

The lift hummed as it rose. Gravity pressed down on us as the lift climbed past the lower floors and into the glass elevator shaft I'd seen from the outside. Through the clear windows we could see the street and shops and pavement below, shrinking quickly.

"That guard had you made."

"He's a security guard," I said, keeping an eye on the numbers above the lift door. We were going up fast. "Being suspicious is his job."

"You sounded like an American doing a Cockney accent."

"Oh, come on. I wasn't that bad."

"Yeah, you were."

"My dad was a university professor. I'm never going to make a convincing construction worker."

"You sound like a posh twat."

"You think anyone with an RP accent sounds like a posh twat."

"'Cause they are."

The lift slowed and stopped with a *ding*, the doors sliding open to reveal two women and a man in business dress. I held up a hand. "Sorry. Maintenance."

They stared in confusion. I hit the Close button, followed by the top floor. The doors slid shut and we started rising again. "Okay," I said. "Once I get off, head down to the basement and find a place to hole up. I'll get in touch with you once it's time to cut the power."

"Use your phone," Cinder said.

"Mind-to-mind is quicker."

"Yeah, and it's creepy as shit," Cinder said. *"Phone."*

I sighed. "Anyone ever tell you you're kind of picky?"

The lift reached the top floor and I stepped out. Behind me, Cinder pushed the button to the basement; the doors closed and he disappeared from sight. Above the control panel, I saw the numbers counting down.

The clock was ticking now. Our cover story had gotten us inside, but the longer we stayed, the better the chance someone would figure out that we weren't supposed to be here. I wasn't worried about building security or police, but I *was* worried that Levistus might have a communications tap, or that the Council might pick up on an alert. The first thing I did was strip off my overalls and bundle them into a nearby closet. One nice thing about overalls: they're so ill-fitting, people don't notice when you're wearing armour underneath. The set I was wearing was an imbued item of reactive mesh with solid black plates covering vital areas. It had been badly damaged when I'd taken the fateweaver, and it was only within the last couple of days that it had recovered enough that I felt comfortable wearing it. I could feel its presence around me, watchful and protective. Time to get to work.

The top of Heron Tower was a windswept jumble of smaller structures, crowded with ventilators, railings, and stored equipment. The data centre was a smaller subtower that reached up above the roof, its top a forest of aerials. For now, my goal was the longer, squatter structure on the tower's east side which held the tower's backup power systems. A few flights of stairs and some work with my lockpicks got me into the power room, which unsurprisingly was deserted. The generators stood against one wall, silent and unguarded.

Divination is powerful, but it has limits. The further ahead you look, and the more decisions you try to map through, the harder it becomes to follow a possible thread. Looking ahead to see what would happen if I left the van *and* got past the security guards at Heron Tower *and* made it all the way up to the top floor *and* bypassed all the other security measures *and* waited for Cinder to cut the power in the basement had been too difficult. Now that we were both in position, it was a different story. I took out my phone and called Cinder; he picked up on the second ring. "Yeah?"

"Get ready to cut the power. Don't go without my signal."

"Sure."

And with that, I was ready. I looked ahead to see what would happen if I crossed the roof of Heron Tower, approached the data centre, and tried to force my way in. My future self felt a low-pitched, vibrating *crump* as the bomb went off, destroying everything of value inside. But if I cut the backup power, called down to Cinder to cut the main power, *then* crossed the roof to the data centre and forced the door open, then—

Crump.

Uh-oh.

"Hold on," I told Cinder. I looked ahead to see what would happen if I tried a different way in. *Crump.* Call Starbreeze and have her give me a lift? *Crump.* Gating, picking the lock on the door, breaking a window . . .

Crump, crump, crump.

Shit.

I tried every route I could see and got the same result. Damn it, I was *sure* the defences were electrically powered. Now that I was this close, I could sense the gate wards on the data centre with my magesight, and they were far too weak to do any heavy lifting on their own. The place *had* to be running off mains. Why wasn't cutting the power working?

Battery backups? If it was that, there might be some sort of delay before the cut-in that I could exploit. I tried searching for one . . . nope.

I checked the time. Fifteen minutes until Richard's attack was due to start.

"We going or not?" Cinder said.

"Hold on," I said. The problem was that I didn't have any information to work with. *Any* attempt to get inside the building was setting off the bomb, and once it had gone off, the inside was too much of a wreck to learn anything more. If there was some future where the bomb didn't go off, I could strengthen it with the fateweaver, but I wasn't seeing one. I might be able to find one if I kept looking . . . but I had no idea how long that could take.

Time to go with plan B.

When Cinder had been telling me not to use mind-to-mind, he'd been referring to my dreamstone. It's a shard of amethyst-coloured crystal that I picked up and bonded with years ago and which gives me the ability to step between our world and Elsewhere. Its core ability, though, was mental communication. It's easiest with someone you know well, but with practice, you can do it with people you've never met.

Or with creatures that aren't people.

I reached out through the dreamstone, probing delicately. Distance isn't a barrier to the dreamstone's mental link, not exactly, but it's a lot easier for me to touch someone's mind if I know where it is. *Hello there*, I said. *Can you hear me?*

A response shot back instantly, crisp and clear. *Please specify the required data.*

Oh good, I said. *What's your name?*

There was a moment's pause. *That is not a valid request.*

What, you like to shake hands first? I leant against the wall, folding my arms. *Okay, how about you tell me how your day's going?*

That is not a valid request. Please supply a valid authorisation code.

I'd never tried linking to a synthetic intelligence before, and it was surprisingly easy. Trying to communicate with most humans this way is difficult: their thoughts are too messy. The synthetic mind's thoughts were like smooth glass, precise and clear. *Oh, I don't have a code. I just wanted to chat.*

I'm not a chatbot. Who are you?

My name's Alex Verus. Yours?

Silence. I smiled slightly. Divination isn't great for in-depth interactions—too many forks—but you can read off basic responses easily enough. I knew the machine intelligence recognised my name.

Why are you contacting me?

Well, I'll get to that in a second. Sure you don't want to tell me your name? Going to be a bit awkward just saying you *all the time.*

Another pause. *My routing designation is November Epsilon underscore one one seven.*

Great! November it is.

I must ask you to cease your communication. The synthetic intelligence's thoughts were still clear, but noticeably disturbed. *By contacting me in this manner you are placing us both at considerable risk. Should your actions be detected, you will be terminated and I will be subject to severe sanction.*

Oh right, I said. *I guess you only know the information that Levistus has access to, don't you? There's been a bit of a shift in the balance of power. Let's just say that if Levistus could terminate me that easily, I wouldn't be here.*

Well, I wish I shared your confidence, November said frostily. *I'm not in a position to be quite so cavalier about such matters.*

Oh, come on, loosen up a bit. Tell you what, how about getting outside? Must get a bit boring being cooped up in that data centre all the time.

Yes, well, if only it were that simple.

I'm serious, I said. *Think of it as a job offer. I mean, I've seen how Levistus treats his nonhuman staff, I can't imagine that being his spy station is all that pleasant. Considered switching employers?*

I don't know whether you consider this to be a joke, or whether it's some elaborate test of loyalty, but I am profoundly unimpressed in either case.

So that's a no?

Do you need me to say it in another language? I can communicate in over two thousand of them if it would help deliver the message more clearly.

Well, so much for asking nicely. *Okay, in that case I guess I DO have a data request. Please give me the access codes for the data centre on top of Heron Tower.*

I have good reason to believe you are not authorised for that information.

What if I said please?

You are not authorised for that information.

What would I have to do to get authorised?

You are not authorised for that information.

Okay, let's put this another way, I said. *In about*—I checked the time—*eight minutes and forty-five seconds, I'm going to force my way into the data centre. Which is probably going to set off its self-destruct charges. You know, the ones you're in the blast radius of right now.*

What?

Still sure you don't want to give me those codes?

You're going to—*what do you mean, force your way in?*

Oh, cut the power, pick the locks, and if that doesn't work, blow the door down. I'm hoping cutting the power will be enough to deactivate the alarms.

You're hoping—? *Of course it won't be enough!*

Well, you never know until you try.

Yes! You do know! You know right now, because I'm telling you!

There's always the chance the hard drives might survive.

The demolition charges are SPECIFICALLY DE-SIGNED to destroy the hard drives, you idiot! Along with me!

In which case, I walk away, and Levistus loses his spy network. I'll take it.

But . . . November trailed off.

You've been working as Levistus's spy, I said, my thoughts flat and hard. *Did you think there wouldn't be consequences? That you were above it all?*

I was never given a choice!

Well, you're getting a choice now. In seven minutes, I'm kicking those doors down. What happens when I do is up to you.

This isn't fair!

If you want to spend your last six minutes and forty-

*five seconds arguing about whether the world is fair, I'm
not going to stop you, but I wouldn't recommend it.*

Silence. Seconds ticked. *I'll make you a deal,* I said.
*You get me in and make sure I get access to Levistus's
files, and I'll get you out and do my best to keep you unharmed. Then once we get away, you're a free agent. You
can keep working with me, or I can set you up on your
own. Your choice.*

*Once you have what you want, you'll have no reason
to keep your end of the bargain.* November's voice was
bitter. *There'll be nothing to stop you doing as you like.*

*The way Levistus likes to get rid of his agents once
they've outlived their use? Yeah, he tried to do that to me
as well. I don't know what Levistus's files say, but I've
spent most of my life working with magical creatures.
They're my friends and allies. Can't prove it to you, but
it's the truth. Whether you believe it or not is up to you.*

Silence again. I watched the futures waver. The pattern
was different from a human, but very much recognisable.
Interesting. He really *did* have free will.

I suppose I don't have much choice, November said at
last. *Very well.*

*Great, welcome to the team! So, I'm guessing just cut-
ting the power won't disable the security?*

Of course not, November said irritably. *What idiot
would expect a security system to be run solely off mains?
But it will disable the heat sensors and the primary motion detectors, which will be necessary once you get past
the door. The door has an access code and a standard
lock. I can supply the code; the part involving manipulating chunks of metal I would hope you can take care of
yourself.*

Sounds good. All ready?

Would it make any difference if I said no?

Not really. I took out my phone and redialled. "Cinder? Go time."

Through the phone, I heard the sound of Cinder's heavy footsteps. There was the creak of a door, followed by a rustle of movement and a new voice. "Oi, mate. What are you doing?"

"Maintenance," Cinder said briefly.

"Not down here you're—"

There was a soggy thud and a grunt, followed by the sound of something heavy falling to the floor. "Ready?" Cinder asked.

"Do it."

I heard a series of clicks through the phone, and with a clunk and a sighing sound the machinery around me slowed and stopped. The fluorescent lights in the ceiling winked out, and the fans that had been spinning with a *whum-whum-whum* began to slow down. A red light on the backup power panel that I'd just deactivated began to blink angrily.

Through the futures, I could tell that Richard had started his attack on the Council. Now it was a race.

I left the power building and crossed the roof to the data centre, stepping over pipes and railings. Warm air whipped at me, the winds fickle and strong. I could sense Starbreeze somewhere out there, riding the winds, but couldn't spare the attention to look more closely. The data centre was tall and intimidating, blacked-out windows showing nothing of what was inside. *Okay, I'm at the door*, I told November. *Hit me.*

The door code is Alpha-seven-six-Xray-five-nine-Tango-Charlie—

Slow down, I said, typing into the keyboard. *Did they deliberately make it this obnoxious just to mess with diviners?*

Yes. Code continues: Romeo-zero-Romeo-Victor-eight-five-zero-Sierra-six-two.

I hate the Council. The system had been programmed with a random element in the false results too, enough to screw up my normal techniques. The panel beeped. *Working on the padlock.*

I suggest you hurry. Local radio traffic has increased significantly.

Oh, I'm sure it's nothing to do with us.

My phone rang.

You were saying? November asked.

I'd supplied an accurate (if disposable) number when I'd signed in. I hit the Answer button, put the phone on speaker, laid it down, and took out my picks. "Hello?"

"Hello?" an angry English voice said through the speaker. "Is this Radu?"

"Speaking," I said cheerfully. "How can I help you today, sir?"

"You can get this fucking power back online!"

"And who would I be talking to?"

"You'd be talking to the divisional head of Heron Tower Salesforce."

The padlock on the door was a good-quality one of thick steel. I threaded my pick and wrench through the keyhole. "Very happy to meet you, sir. Sorry for the inconvenience, we had to do a shutdown."

"You were only supposed to be working on the photocopiers! You've cut the power to the whole goddamn building!"

"Well, sir, photocopiers are a very serious matter. Do you know how many office fires every year are caused by faulty photocopying equipment?"

"Listen to me, you little shit. I know the directors of your company on a first-name basis. If you give me any more of this Health and Safety crap, or if you do anything other than get the power online *right now*, I am going to make personally sure you never work for EDF again and that the Home Office deports you back to whatever shithole country you crawled out of!"

"I'm very sorry to hear you feel that way, sir," I said. "If you'd like to make a complaint, we have an automated customer service number on our website."

"You can TAKE your customer service number and—"

The padlock came open with a click. "Just a second, sir, I'm getting some interference. You'll have to call me back." I hung up and tapped Block This Caller. *Have they called the police yet?*

No, but apparently there are people en route to the basement.

"Incoming, Cinder," I said through the phone, then tucked it away and pulled open the door. Cold air rushed out: the corridor beyond was dark in contrast to the bright sunlight outside.

I must warn you that while some of the physical triggers have been disabled, the magical ones have not. November's thoughts were tense. *Please do not use any magic strong enough to register on magesight while inside the building. The wards are extremely sensitive.*

Not planning to. I started down the corridor.

The door to the server room was blocked by a laser grid. I didn't need November's help this time: a brief search found a control panel, and this alarm code wasn't as hard as the one on the door. As I did, I heard a scuffle of movement through the phone. A couple of indistinct voices were calling something; I couldn't quite make out the words but it didn't sound friendly. There was a *thump* and a *thud*. "Hey!" someone yelled. "What are you—?"

Thump. Thud.

"Are you punching out everyone who comes into the basement?" I asked Cinder.

"You wanted the power off, didn't you?" Cinder said. "Wait one."

There was the sound of a door opening and another voice. "Oi. Why isn't—?"

Thump. Thud.

"And there I was thinking you couldn't do subtle."

"Move your arse. I'm running out of places to put these guys."

I opened the door to reveal the server room. Tinted windows along the far wall looked out over the London skyline, and racks of computer equipment lined the sides. The room was shadowed and gloomy, but the hum of machinery still echoed from all around.

At the centre of the room was what must be November's housing. The electronics were nothing special, but the magical energy radiating from it made it stand out like a searchlight. I crossed the room and bent over to study it.

You should probably be aware, November said, *that the London Metropolitan Police have received a call from Heron Tower reporting a suspected terrorist attack on their power grid.*

I rolled my eyes. *Are the police actually buying that?*

No, but they're dispatching officers anyway. The first car should arrive in four minutes.

And yet it takes them all day to respond to a break-in. I finished running through the futures where I pulled the housing apart. *I'm guessing your core functions are in the black case in the centre?*

I believe so, yes. November sounded nervous.

The reason I ask is that's the piece of equipment the blocks of plastic explosive are attached to.

Wonderful. Please tell me you know what you're doing.

Nope.

Oh.

Don't worry. I have no idea how explosives work, but I know what makes them go bang.

That isn't as reassuring as you seem to believe.

All right, I said. I'd had time to analyse the mess of wires and wards around November's core. *Looks like there are three security measures still active. One electrical alarm, one magical alarm, and the explosives. Which one would you like me to work on first?*

I would appreciate it very much if you could start with the explosives.

I figured. Using a screwdriver, I took apart the housing and then shone a penlight. November's core was an irregular black box about the size of a games console. A pair of off-white blocks of plastic explosive were clamped to it, one on either side. *Can you be removed from that box?*

Yes, but I would prefer it if you didn't. The loss of the components within would seriously degrade my performance. Besides, quite frankly, given the attitude you've demonstrated towards explosives, I'd rather not have you doing brain surgery on me with a hammer.

Fair enough. I'll just carry the whole thing. I pulled out a backpack from my toolbox and eyeballed it to confirm that it should fit. I settled myself down comfortably and started studying the explosives. *So how long have you been up here?*

I'm not entirely sure, November said. *My memories date back only as far as February 2, 2011. Circumstantial evidence leads me to believe that I have existed longer than that, perhaps considerably longer. I believe that those memories were deleted upon my installation here.*

Yeah, that sounds like Levistus's style, I said. *So this has been your whole life? Sitting up here, receiving data, and passing it on to Barrayar or some other aide?*

Essentially.

Sounds lonely.

I . . . suppose it is.

Oh, interesting.

What?

I pointed, forgetting that November probably couldn't see. *These blocks of explosive? They're standard make, probably C-4 or a derivative. The detonators are standard too, but in addition to the wires, they've got a built-in ward with a low-level lightning spell. It looks like it's set to activate on any significant magical signature. If someone uses any spell with any kind of power, an electrical charge is set off which triggers the detonators.*

That's fascinating, but would you mind removing them?

Figuring out *how* traps work is the hard part. Now that I knew what would set off the bombs, it was easy to disarm them. I scanned through possible futures and quickly decided that the easiest solution would be to sabotage the anti-tamper switches on the detonators, then pull them out. I found the futures where they succumbed to mechanical failure and got to work with the fateweaver.

The first police unit has arrived, November said.

"Cinder?" I said into my phone. "Cops are here."

"No wonder with how long you're taking."

"Another ten minutes and you can bail. Please don't kill anyone if you can avoid it."

Cinder gave an audible sigh and hung up.

My spirits were rising. Once I was done with the detonators, I only needed to disable the alarms and I'd be able to pick up November and get out. There were still some protective wards on November's core that I hadn't had time to decipher, but I'd already confirmed that they wouldn't stop me carrying it away physically, and once I was safely back at the Hollow I could take them apart at my leisure. As I worked through the futures with the fateweaver, I saw the first tamper switch dim and fail. I changed focus to the second.

As I did, a flicker on my precognition caught my attention and I frowned. My attention was on the short-term futures, and all of a sudden a bunch of them were terminating in explosions.

I tried altering my actions. No effect. No, wait—now *all* of the futures were terminating in explosions. *November? Did I just trigger something?*

I don't believe so.

The futures had settled: the bomb was going to go off *really* soon. I searched for an answer, trying to stay calm. Nothing I did seemed to make a difference. But if nothing *I* did was making a difference, then that must mean that the source was from someone else. I changed my focus, looking at what was going to happen just before the explosion, and saw the flash of a gateway and—

Oh, SHIT.

I had less than a minute. Frantically I threw my energies through the fateweaver at the second switch. As I did I hit Cinder's number. It rang. Rang again. Rang again. *Come on, come on—!*

Click. "Verus, I don't have time for this shit," Cinder said. "There are six cops about to—"

"Deleo is here," I interrupted. "You want to catch her, get up here *now*." I hung up.

Thirty seconds. I was feeding the future where the switch failed, pouring energy into it. Sixty percent, seventy, eighty, ninety, ninety-five, ninety-six, ninety-seven . . .

It stuck at ninety-seven. There was a slight possibility of a short circuit that I couldn't seem to shake. Three percent chance of killing myself. Could I risk it?

Five seconds. I put a surge of power into the fateweaver, giving it everything I had. The short-circuit future wavered and vanished.

My hands shot out and I pulled both detonators from the C-4, like sticks coming free from particularly stubborn clay. Just as I did, the air on the far side of the room darkened and a gate appeared in front of the tinted windows. One of the detonators was far enough out and the ward didn't trigger, but the other did, and I swore I saw the flash of an electric spark as the explosive missed going off by less than a second.

Rachel stepped through the gateway and turned towards me with a look of death on her face.

chapter 7

All the alarms I'd so carefully avoided went off at once. Red lights flashed, magical and electrical warnings went flying out, and Rachel sent a disintegration beam at my chest.

I dropped, the ray passing overhead and taking out a chunk of wall. The table with the housing hid me briefly and I heard Rachel's footfalls as she closed in. She'd have me in sight in seconds.

When you can't run, attack. I came up in a lunge, my knife searching for her heart. Rachel's shield flared and the blade glanced off. She tried another disintegrate spell, but I was inside her range and knocked her arm away; the beam went high, destroying a patch of ceiling.

Mr. Verus! November sounded panicky. *The alarms—*

I know! I snarled. I drove Rachel back, kicks and slashes keeping her briefly off balance, but I couldn't get through her shield. Rachel recovered and cast some spell I'd never seen. A sea-green whip of darkly glowing light formed at her hand and I threw myself backward; the snaking whip caught my knife and a table leg, cutting both in half. The table went down with a crash, sending computer banks tumbling to the floor, and I dived behind it, rolling out of sight.

Rachel's footsteps started up again as she continued her approach. I looked from side to side, my thoughts racing. The toolbox didn't hold anything that could break Rachel's shield. My dispel focus could, but trying to use that against someone as fast as Rachel was suicide. There was the computer case holding November's core, with the blocks of plastic explosive, one detonator that was triggered . . .

. . . and one that wasn't. I grabbed one of the blocks of C-4, shoved in the detonator, then stood and threw it in a single motion.

Rachel saw the block coming and strengthened her shield. The ward on the detonator registered the magical energy of the spell and triggered instantly.

Light and sound hammered me with a roar. I'd seen what was coming and dived for cover, but in the confined space of the data centre the explosion was horrendous. The shock wave battered my body and sent every piece of furniture in the room flying. A table crashed down on top of me, then all of a sudden everything was silent but for the ringing in my ears.

Somehow I managed to get to my feet. Daylight was streaming in: the windows along the far side of the room had blown out. The room was filled with smoke, and I coughed as I kicked aside the table and staggered over to November's housing. The housing was scrap, but in the fraction of a second I'd had to spare, I'd managed to nudge the explosion in the direction I'd wanted, and November's core had survived largely undamaged. *That was extremely unnerving*, November said. *Mr. Verus? Are you still there?*

Yes. I'd lost track of my toolbox, but not the backpack. I started to pull cables out of November's case.

I thought you were going to kill me.

I said I'd get you out, didn't I? Now shut up and let me concentrate.

One of the cables was refusing to come free. I kept yanking at it for a good five seconds before I registered that it was held in by screws. I spun them loose, still dazed from the explosion. I'd lost track of Rachel, but I knew she'd be back.

The last screw came out. I heaved up November's case; my left hand slipped but the right held steady and I got it into the backpack. I shrugged on the straps as I stood up and started feeling my way towards the exit.

Mr. Verus? November said. *I know you said not to bother you, but we may have a problem.*

I'd already sensed it. Gate magic was being used outside the data centre, both the steady signature of a gate and the briefer flashes of the more specialised teleportation spell that I'd only ever seen used by space mages. I'd made it back into the main corridor, but I knew that as soon as I stepped out onto the roof, it was going to start a fight. I slumped against the wall, my legs still shaky. *Starbreeze?* I asked, reaching out through the dreamstone. *I could really use a lift right about now.*

Come watch the fire man, Starbreeze said brightly.

Maybe later. I really need to get out of here.

I'm busy.

Starbreeze!

No answer. I looked ahead to see what would happen if I opened the front door.

There were four people out on the rooftop, and all of them were looking straight at where I'd appear. One I'd seen before. He was short and slight, with English looks, and was dressed like a civil servant who'd just stepped out of the office. His name was Barrayar, and he was Levistus's personal assistant and troubleshooter. I'd never fought him, but I knew he was more dangerous than he looked.

The other three were strangers. There was a black guy, and a man and a woman who looked Japanese. All were wearing matte-black combat gear with low-level magical enhancement that looked like a weaker version of my own combat armour. I'd glimpsed them in my path-walking, enough to have a vague idea of what they could do, but not in detail. *November? Give me a report on those three.*

November answered instantly, the thoughts and information flashing into my mind. *Coleman Ward, aka Crash. Elemental adept, ranked near-mage level. Force magic: enhanced strength, speed, toughness, mobility, personal range only. Ito Ryuunosuke, aka Jumper. Universal adept, ranked mage level. Space magic: personal and touch-range teleportation. Ito Midori, aka Stickleback. Elemental adept, ranked near-mage level. Force magic: creation of circular force planes, offensive and defensive utility. Group status: limited affiliation with Light Councils of North America, Japan, and Korea; outlaw status in China. Employment status: long-term retainer contract with Levistus. Primary duties: personal security of Levistus and two designated priority locations, of which this is one.*

I didn't like the sound of that. Adept mercenaries don't live long enough to make a name for themselves unless they're good. I scanned the futures, looking for ways out.

There weren't any. I couldn't reach any exits from the data centre apart from this one, and the wards prevented me from gating. Worse, Rachel was on her feet and heading for me. She'd appear at the end of the corridor in less than fifteen seconds.

Okay, time to go back to thinking like an underdog.

Rachel was less than five seconds away. My supply of

one-shots was low, but I still had a few that I'd saved for a rainy day. I pulled a condenser from my pocket and waited. Rachel came around the corner thirty feet away. I let her get a glimpse of me, then as her hand came up I threw the condenser to shatter at my feet and kicked open the door.

Water magic flared: both the weak magic of the condenser as its mist cloud rushed out to obscure everything around me, and the sharp deadly signature of Rachel's disintegration spell. I sidestepped and the beam flashed past through the doorway towards Barrayar and the three mercenaries. There was a shout but I was focused on Rachel. She hadn't stopped casting, and even blind, Rachel's guesses at my location were way too accurate. I twisted aside from one beam and then another: the wall behind me puffed into dust, and more beams sped through the gap. Then I felt more magic from behind.

I sprinted through the gap and away down the edge of the building, catching a glimpse of a violet-tinged disc of force cutting horizontally through the mist. I came out of the light and into the dazzling sun, ducking around a corner and breaking line of sight to Barrayar and the mercenaries.

I jumped over a pipe and skirted a pair of huge fans. Behind me, the bright September day lit up in a furious exchange, force magic against the sea-green light of Rachel's disintegration beams. I didn't have time to see who was winning, and didn't care. I was focused on whether any of them were coming after me. I'd only been in sight for a moment, but that might have been long enough for them to catch a glimpse and figure out—

Force magic pulsed. I came to a stop and turned.

Barrayar came flying down from his jump like a falling missile, and landed on top of a flat-roofed shed with a crash. The small concrete-and-metal building shook under the impact, and Barrayar stood up. The wind ruffled his hair and tie, blowing them out to one side, and his eyes were hard. "It's in that backpack," he told me. "Isn't it?"

"Hey, Barrayar," I said. As I spoke I was path-walking in all directions, scouting the terrain. The part of roof I was on was largely bare, cluttered with industrial equipment but with no way down. "So how are things—?"

"I'll only say this once." Barrayar's voice was clipped. "I don't care about catching you, not today, but that synthetic is more dangerous than you can possibly understand. Drop it right now and you can leave. Do *anything* else, or try to stall, and I'll kill you."

"Dangerous how?"

When Barrayar had said "anything," he'd meant it. A thin line of force magic flashed out like a bullet.

That line was the width of a fingernail, and invisible. It was also powerful enough to rip through my armour and internal organs and go right out the other side. I twisted, my divination giving me warning to dodge left even as I used fate magic to pull the attack to the right, and felt the vibration as Barrayar's spell punched a neat hole in the roof. Barrayar tracked me, firing again, and I ran, the impacts lacing lines of death through the futures.

I put a small building between us and ducked as Barrayar shot through it blind, the attack going over my shoulder. I'd run too far and now I was out of roof. Up ahead was another skyscraper, a little lower than Heron Tower; down below, the traffic on the A-road wound its way around a growing cluster of police vehicles that looked like toy cars.

There was another crash as Barrayar landed on the building right behind. I turned to see him looking down from less than twenty feet away, his eyes narrowed. He aimed his right hand at me, palm first, taking his time to make sure he hit, maybe wondering why I wasn't dodging. Then he paused. He'd sensed the same thing that my magesight had: a powerful elemental source, rising fast.

With a *whoosh* Cinder burst up into the sky like a phoenix. Wings of fire spread from his shoulders; dark red flame burnt about one hand, while on his other a gauntlet shone with power. Cinder reached the peak of his leap, hovering, and aimed downwards; Barrayar jumped away as the roof of the small building erupted with a roar.

Cinder floated forward and down, landing in front of me with a *thud*. A fiery shield burned around him, the flames licking at his hands and legs without consuming them. "Why are you standing around?" he growled.

I grinned. "Never been so happy to see a Dark mage."

Starbreeze came flitting up behind Cinder, giving him an interested glance before looking at me. "Where did you go?"

Cinder leapt up with another flash of fire magic into a smaller jump. He landed on the scorched roof where Barrayar had been, and strode out of sight. "I'll tell you later," I said to Starbreeze. "Mind getting us out of here?"

"Oh, okay." Starbreeze swept around me. I felt her starting to transmute my body to air. Just a few more seconds, and we'd be—

The transmutation stopped with a sudden jar, my body turning back to flesh and blood. Starbreeze separated from me, floating away. "Can't."

"What?" I said. "What do you mean, 'can't'?"

"Can't."

"Can't *what*?"

Starbreeze pointed at my backpack. "He's heavy."

"What do you mean, 'heavy'? That doesn't make any sense!"

The air above Heron Tower flashed red, fire magic meeting force with a boom that sent a shiver through the building. *November*, I said. *Why can't Starbreeze transmute you?*

Ah . . . assuming Starbreeze is the air elemental mentioned in your files, I'm not entirely sure. My core was constructed using certain hybrid materials that are held in a more unstable state than is typical for—

I don't need a science lesson! Can we fix it?

Well . . . given the timeframe, no.

Sea-green light flashed. I was running out of time: Cinder couldn't keep everyone busy and it wouldn't take them long to track me down. "Go watch the fire?" Starbreeze asked.

"No! Look, if you can't transmute us, carry us." I pointed across the gap to the nearest skyscraper: it was only a street's width apart, maybe sixty feet across and about as much down. "Get us there."

"But you're *heavy*."

"Starbreeze! Please!"

With an exaggerated sigh, Starbreeze swept around me. My hair whipped as if in a whirlwind, and with a jolt my feet left the roof. Painfully slowly, I floated over the railing and down into the sky.

The flash and boom of attack magic sounded from the rooftop. Behind was Heron Tower, ahead the other skyscraper, below a seven-hundred-foot drop. The afternoon sun beat down out of a blue sky, leaving us horribly exposed. I couldn't see any of the combatants on the roof behind, but I knew how visible we were. The other rooftop drew closer. Thirty feet . . . twenty feet . . . ten . . .

The futures changed, suddenly and for the worse. *Starbreeze! Get us onto the roof, now!*

Okay, okay. Starbreeze changed angle. *You're still heavy—*

A violet disc of force flashed out from Heron Tower. I'd seen it coming and pushed with the fateweaver, trying to diverge its track from ours. I almost made it; it missed us but clipped Starbreeze, who dropped me with a yelp.

I twisted in midair and my feet hit concrete with a jarring thud. "Ow!" Starbreeze said. "That hurt!" She fled, disappearing.

I stood. Unlike Heron Tower, the top of this skyscraper was a construction site. A tower crane rose from the roof centre like a gigantic tree, its blue-triangle column stretching up into the sky. Pipes, steel beams, and building materials were scattered around, and a high fence prevented anyone from jumping or falling. There were some buildings at the far end that I knew had roof access. I also knew I wasn't going to get the time to reach them.

A figure jumped from the roof of Heron Tower, crossing the sixty feet in one impossibly long leap and landing on the roof with a *boom*. It was one of the mercenaries, the black guy. A second later, mercenaries two and three blinked into existence forty feet away, the Japanese guy holding the shoulder of the woman. All three looked at me, sizing me up.

"Can we talk about this?" I asked.

The black guy charged.

I stood still for a second as the adept pounded towards me, studying him in present and future. The adept—Crash—was big and fast; he moved with more-than-natural strength and came in for an attack strong enough to break bones. I ducked at the last second and tripped him, sending him flying, then sprinted towards the other two.

The woman, Stickleback, watched me coolly as I closed the distance. Her hands glowed with a faint violet light as a disc of translucent force appeared between them, growing, rotating, and starting to spin all in a fraction of a second before it flashed out at me at knee-height like a giant flying saw blade. I jumped over it, but she was already making a second, followed by a third. I dodged each one, closing the distance. Thirty feet, twenty feet, ten—

The Japanese man hadn't taken his hand off the woman's shoulder. Space magic pulsed, and the two of them vanished, reappearing sixty feet behind me.

I turned to look at them. *That is* really *annoying.*

Pounding feet announced Crash's arrival. I stepped away from a reverse spin kick that would have shattered my skull, then gave ground against the punches that followed. Crash responded to my lack of aggression by pressing in; I took the opening and hit him with a palm strike to the face. It should have broken his nose, but instead my hand stung as if I'd hit wood, and Crash rocked back, catching himself and watching me with calculating eyes.

Protective force magic, evasive teleportation. I didn't have time to get through that many defences. I broke contact, running left.

Stickleback responded, throwing discs of force. I weaved, letting the discs pass ahead and behind. Stickleback and Jumper were near the roof's edge and I cut across the middle. The futures I was looking for lined up and I sent a surge of energy through the fateweaver.

Stickleback threw another force disc and I dropped flat. The disc sailed over my head with a hiss and struck the base of the tower crane, the force magic shearing through steel. With a shriek and a groan of twisting metal, the crane fell, toppling straight towards Stickleback and Jumper.

Stickleback looked up at the monstrous thing falling towards her, and her eyes went wide. Jumper teleported just in time, and both of them vanished as the crane came down with a horrific crash, splintering the fence as the cross-beam of the crane smashed down onto the top of Heron Tower.

Dust and particles swept up into the air. The crane, which had once risen vertically into the air, now formed a crooked bridge between Heron Tower and the skyscraper I was on. The three mercenaries were all staring at the destruction, and before they could decide what to do next, I dashed along the side of the fallen crane, and jumped through the gap in the fence and out into space.

Wind roared around my ears as I plummeted. *Er*, November said as the cars below me grew larger and larger, along with the pale spots of faces looking upwards. *I'm detecting some odd signals. Is everything going according to plan?*

Fine! I pulled a life ring from my pocket and broke it, leaving it as late as possible. Blood rushed through my body as I decelerated, the magic slowing me down just in time to drop the last few feet safely to the tarmac.

Scattered screams sounded, trailing off: several people had seen me fall and were now staring in confusion. Two police cars were blocking off the street at the intersection, and a uniformed officer was looking at me openmouthed. I sprinted past him and turned north up Bishopsgate.

Oh. Well, that's a relief.

There were more police outside Heron Tower and a couple turned to look as I ran, but most were shading their eyes as they looked up towards the broken crane above. *On an unrelated note*, I told November, *I could use the exact departure times of mainline trains from Liverpool Street Station in the next, say, three to five minutes.*

Of course. Er, I don't mean to worry you, but there's an alert going out on police frequencies for someone that matches your description rather closely. Apparently you're considered a suspect for a terrorist attack on Heron Tower and to be apprehended on sight.

Just get me those trains.

The plaza outside Liverpool Street Station was busy, commuters hurrying back and forth. Police lights were flashing farther up the road. I saw the black of police uniforms moving towards me and I turned quickly aside and down the escalators into Liverpool Street Station.

The station was huge, filled with noise and people. Departure boards blinked along the right-hand side, above the ticket gates. I wound my way through the crowds, searching the futures for signs of pursuit. Nothing yet, but through the crowds, I saw a pair of police officers at the centre of the station floor, and the futures in which I got too close to them turned violent fast.

The next train departing Liverpool Street will be the Greater Anglia service to Norwich from platform eleven, leaving in—

What are the police saying?

There was an unconfirmed sighting of you descending onto the main floor of Liverpool Street Station. They're asking for additional units to seal the exits.

I briefly considered knocking the two police out, but it would draw too much attention. Besides, it would be really bad if I was in the middle of dealing with them and—

The futures shifted.

—and something like *that* happened. I turned right, bumping past someone dragging a heavy suitcase, and strode through the ticket gates. As I did, I reached out through the dreamstone. *Cinder.*

Cinder replied straightaway, sounding bad-tempered. *Where are you?*

Liverpool Street Station. You still engaged?

No, they're all chasing you. Where's Del?

Chasing me, where do you think? The massive iron-and-glass roof of the train sheds arched overhead. Liverpool Street's platform area is huge enough that I could count on the police taking some time to track me down. My magical pursuers were another story.

The Greater Anglia train was white-painted with red doors, humming. A whistle shrilled from down the platform as I stepped aboard. Only a few seconds later, the *beep-beep-beep* sounded, and the doors hissed shut.

I'm on the Norwich train leaving now, I told Cinder. I walked up the train, winding my way between the seats. The train was about two-thirds full, and I had to twist aside to avoid a fat man struggling to get his briefcase into the overhead racks.

Where's Del?

If I'm lucky, back in Liverpool Street with those mercenaries and about fifty police. I opened the door to the next carriage and stepped through. The train swayed under my feet as I walked, the wheels going *thunkity-thunk* as it accelerated, and I had to make an effort to keep my balance, all while searching the futures for danger, looking for the telltale signature of gate magic with my magesight, and keeping open the mental links to Cinder and to November all at the same time.

The windows went black as the train entered a tunnel, brightened as we came out into the sun, went black again. I watched closely for any signs of gating. Combat adepts are dangerous, but they usually don't have the detection abilities that mages do. I'd very carefully *not* done anything between the street and the train that would show up on magesight. With any luck, they wouldn't be able to follow me. And Rachel hadn't gotten close enough to see what train I'd boarded. There shouldn't be any way she should be able to figure out that I was on this train—

Rachel was going to gate onto this train.

I swore out loud. Several passengers glanced up at me from where they were seated, then looked hurriedly away. I was still wearing my combat armour, plus whatever dust and dirt I'd picked up from the fighting. I didn't know what I looked like, but judging from the way people were shying away, it wasn't reassuring. *Cinder, your psycho ex is following me. You want to make up with her, get on board.*

On my way.

Er, Mr. Verus, November said. *Is this a bad time?*

No, no, it's just wonderful, I said. *Rachel is going to gate into the back carriage in about twenty seconds. What did you want to talk about in the meantime?*

Well, it's just that I've intercepted some communications from Mage Barrayar. Apparently he's received a report from Crash's team that they suspect you of being aboard one of two trains departing Liverpool Street, and he's calling in reinforcements. He seems quite agitated.

What kind of—you know what, I don't have time. Where's Crash's team?

I believe two of them are teleporting onto this train now. Oh, come on!

A flicker of space magic from up ahead confirmed the news. Now I had Rachel behind, and the adepts in front.

"Fine," I muttered to myself. I strode forward to the next set of carriage doors and found the nearest toilet. It was vacant, which spared me the embarrassment of having to evict someone. I closed the door, locked it, and waited.

Standing in the cramped space, balancing on the swaying floor, I had time to wonder at how crazy my life was. I was hiding in a train toilet so that I could ambush my insane ex-fellow-apprentice water mage and draw her into a fight against a group of adept mercenaries who were after me to steal back an artificial intelligence that I was carrying because it could give me leverage on one of the people running the country who'd originally wanted me dead because I'd failed to get him the artefact that was currently eating its way up my arm but who had only managed to get me sentenced to death because I'd failed to cover up the crimes that my ex-girlfriend had committed while possessed by a jinn.

How had I managed to end up like this?

I shook it off. Back to work.

Rachel was approaching from one side, the adepts from the other. I adjusted the futures with the fateweaver, pulling Rachel in, slowing the adepts down. The creak of a door sounded from outside as Rachel entered my carriage. She stopped just outside.

I yanked open the door just as Rachel was about to fire, catching her by wrist and throat and slamming her against the side of the train. Her spell went high, disintegrating the roof right above us and bringing a roar of wind and noise and dust down into the carriage. Rachel's eyes stared into mine from behind her mask, shock and fury mixed together as she struggled to break my grip.

I could have killed Rachel in that moment. Two things stopped me: my promise to Cinder, and the other targets. Rachel tried another disintegration ray, and I forced her hand away, lining the spell's futures up with the length of the train just as the door at the far end of the carriage flew open and Stickleback stepped through.

The green ray flew the length of the carriage, missing the shocked and yelling passengers on the seats, and hit Stickleback square-on. She managed to throw up one of her violet force fields; it almost stopped the spell, but not quite. A thread of the ray brushed her side and she fell back, her face contorting in pain. Rachel fired another ray and I aimed it to finish Stickleback off, but another future cut across: Jumper blinked into existence just before the strike could land and opened up a portal that the ray disappeared into.

The passengers on the train were screaming and the wind was roaring through the hole above. Rachel and I struggled, swaying back and forth. Rachel's shock had been replaced with rage and she tried to kick me, then when that didn't work reconfigured her shield into a short-range disintegration ring. I jumped up, bounding off the wall to get my feet above the lethal green pulse, caught the edges of the hole in both hands, and kicked Rachel in the face. She went sprawling, her magic shredding the door, and I pulled myself up through the hole and onto the train roof.

Wind whipped at me, blasting at my hair and sliding off my armour. We'd come out of the tunnels and onto a stretch of open track, the landmarks of east London opening up before us. To my left the Olympic stadium was sliding past, while to the right I could see the towers of Canary Wharf. I ran forward, pushing against the wind, my feet echoing with dull thuds on the roof as I kept my balance against the sway of the train.

A green ray shot up into the sky above and behind, followed by another as Rachel fired blind through the roof. I felt the surge of force magic below as Stickleback answered, but it was aimed at Rachel, not me. I jumped a carriage and kept running, putting distance between us.

Mr. Verus, November said anxiously. *I'm having trouble tracking our location. Are we safe?*

Yes! I jumped another carriage. *Just perfect, but I'm a LITTLE busy!*

Well, it's just that Barrayar is vectoring—

I felt a thump vibrate through the roof and looked back to see Crash straightening from where he'd landed. He started towards me, breaking into a charge, keeping his balance seemingly without effort on the swaying train.

There was no room to dodge this time. I made my decision in a split-second, turned, and leapt at Crash feet first.

The wind that had been checking me became my ally, and my feet slammed into Crash's stomach, throwing him nearly head over heels. He slammed back onto the roof, scrabbling for purchase, only barely stopping himself from rolling off the edge. I fell a little more gracefully and hauled myself up as Crash rose to face me. He looked pissed off but there was a wariness in his eyes now, and as he advanced his stance showed more respect.

We roared through Stratford station, passing the Westfield shopping centre to the north, a wide pedestrian bridge rolling past overhead. Shocked faces looked up at us from the platforms as we flashed by. *Why the hell is this train still moving?* I asked November as Crash edged forward. *You have access?*

Of a sort . . .

Crash jabbed at me. He'd taken a kickboxing stance, and I shifted instinctively to counter as he tried more jabs followed by a cross. I stepped back, deliberately staying just within range for the spinning kick he'd tried before. A move like that would make him an easy target on the shifting train, but he didn't take the bait. Instead he shifted his hands into a guard that I'd seen used by military special forces types. I switched to a Krav Maga stance, hands loose. *The driver's board should be lit up like a Christmas tree. Why hasn't he stopped?*

But that was what I was trying to tell you, November said. Crash struck at my eyes; I twitched aside and hit him in the shoulder to no effect. *It's Barrayar. He's overridden jurisdiction from the Metropolitan Police and he's ordered the driver to maintain speed while they call in a response team.*

Crash kept attacking, his movements tight and aggressive. His force magic made his blows faster than they should have been, not just on the strike but also on the recovery, giving me few openings. His toughness and his lack of reaction to hits reminded me of Caldera, but Crash was faster. The wind roared as we traded kicks and punches.

Crash moved in, striking low, and this time I had to jump back. I could hear the clattering of rotors off to my side, but couldn't afford to take my eyes off the adept. *What did you say about a response team?* I asked November.

Well, can you see a helicopter in the area?

What do you mean, a—? I began, then looked left.

A black-and-yellow helicopter with *POLICE* written along its side was flying parallel to the train a short distance away. It was close enough that I could see the pilot through the canopy, his face hidden by a helmet, looking straight ahead as he controlled the machine. The side doors on the helicopter were open, one man holding the

doorframe, and a second crouched in the centre of the
helicopter, aiming some kind of mounted weapon. I could
see bipod legs, an ammo box, and a long metal barrel. It
looked like a light machine gun.

As it turned out, it was.

The weapon opened up with an echoing *duh-duh-duh-
duh-duh*. Futures of violent death flashed on my precognition; I snatched ones that I needed and twisted aside,
bullets zipping by my head with an eerie whickering
sound. I caught a glimpse of Crash jumping backwards.
The gunner kept firing, his touch controlled and profes-
sional, short aimed bursts. Chips of metal flew from the
roof as bullets tore holes at my feet.

A green beam flashed past, and I spared a glance to
see that Rachel was back. She was up on the roof three
carriages down, trying to snipe me with a disintegration
ray. I didn't have time to think about it: it was just one
more variable in a set of futures already crowded with
images of my own death. I saw myself die singly and in
clusters, to bullets and disintegration and the train's racing wheels, jagged flashes of blood and pain fading to
darkness. My focus narrowed to the next five seconds, the
fateweaver and my divination working together to keep
me alive. With the fateweaver I chose attack patterns that
were easier to dodge, then with my divination I matched
my movements to images of safety. I stepped back to
avoid a beam, left to dodge a volley of shots, then back
again, my movements quick and erratic, forcing the gunner to guess at where to aim next. All of my focus was on
surviving five seconds more, then another five after that.

Then suddenly the helicopter was climbing, the machine gun falling silent. A forest of gantries was coming
up, followed by a pair of road bridges. Farther down, Rachel stopped firing and started to advance, struggling to
keep her balance on the swaying train.

Crash was hesitating. I saw him glance at Rachel, then

at me; he looked like he was calculating the chances of Rachel shooting him in the back and not liking the answer. The first bridge flashed overhead, and the helicopter vanished from sight. *Cinder*, I said through the dreamstone, *it would be really nice if you could—*

Cinder landed in front of me with a *wham*, the train roof denting under his weight. He'd jumped from the bridge, fiery wings slowing his fall. He straightened and his eyes locked onto Crash.

Crash took in the new odds instantly, and through the futures, I saw him make a snap decision. Mercenaries don't usually fight to the death; for them, the big question is "Are we getting paid enough?" and for Crash, the answer had just become no. He leapt from the train, hitting the ballast beside the tracks and rolling, falling out of sight.

"You took your time," I called.

Cinder didn't turn around. "Stay out of this."

The second bridge flashed by and Rachel appeared from its shadow one carriage down. She saw Cinder and went dead still. She shouted something, her voice whirled away by the wind.

Cinder held out a hand towards her, palm up.

Rachel's face twisted. A disintegration beam shot out, aimed to burn through Cinder and hit me.

Cinder's shield flared. Fire met water with a deafening *crack*, but Cinder didn't move. He sent a fireball straight back at Rachel. She disappeared in a roar of dark red flame, the smoke blowing away almost instantly to reveal her standing unharmed.

Again Cinder held out his hand.

The futures forked, zigzagging. I'd never seen a pattern like that, and even with everything that was happening, I couldn't help but be fascinated. It was as if two different futures were meeting within Rachel's mind, both trying to overwhelm the other. She swayed with the moving train, eyes flicking from behind the domino mask from Cinder to me.

Off to our left, the helicopter swept down in a shallow dive to match the train's speed, and again the machine gun stuttered. Without looking, Cinder held out one arm: the gauntlet on it glowed with power, the gems on the blue scale gleaming, and the bullets sparked off an invisible barrier.

"Del," Cinder called.

Some indecipherable emotion convulsed Rachel's face. She turned and ran, fleeing down the train at lightning speed. She dropped down the hole she'd opened up into the carriage and was gone.

Cinder took a step after her, but had to halt as another burst of machine gun fire sparked off his shield. "She's gating," I called.

"Stop her!"

Metal gantries flashed by overhead. "I try, I might kill her."

Cinder swore. "Ten seconds," I said. I could sense the gate forming, far faster than was safe. It wouldn't take much to twist the futures, cause a cascade failure . . . assuming I didn't care what happened to Rachel.

Cinder didn't reply. Seconds ticked, and the gate opened, then closed. "She's gone," I said.

Cinder growled. With a flick of his wrist, he threw a fireball at the helicopter. The spell exploded against an invisible countermagic barrier thirty feet from the aircraft.

Mr. Verus? I'm sorry to keep bothering you, but—

But there's another problem, of course there is. Let's hear it.

November didn't use words this time. A three-dimensional diagram flashed into my head, combined with estimated times of arrival and blast radii.

Cinder threw another fireball at the helicopter; it

bloomed against the shield, the helicopter emerging un-
scathed a second later. A burst of return fire was blocked
by Cinder's shield as well. "Waste of time," Cinder muttered, and looked at me. "Stop this bloody train."

"Bad idea," I said tersely.

"Why?"

"Because Barrayar's called in an airstrike," I said. "In
three minutes an RAF jet is going to hit this carriage with
a laser-guided bomb."

Cinder paused. His shield could hold off light machine
gun fire, but military explosives were another story. And
that was without the train crash that would follow.

A train crash that would also kill every single passen-
ger in the carriages below. I'd known Barrayar wanted to
stop me from stealing November. I hadn't known how
badly.

"So?" Cinder asked.

I looked around, searching for ideas. My eyes fell upon
the helicopter. It had pulled back out of firing range but
was still pacing the train. I could just barely see one of the
men inside aiming some piece of equipment at us, probably a laser designator.

And the pilot was holding course and speed so they
could draw a bead . . .

I pointed at the helicopter. "How far can you jump
with those fire wings?"

Cinder looked at the helicopter, then back at me.
"You're fucking crazy."

I grinned at him. "Chicken?"

"Never going to hit."

"I'll take care of that."

Cinder hesitated.

"Two minutes," I told him.

I felt the futures settle as Cinder made his decision. He
stepped next to me and put a thick arm around me, grabbing me under one arm. I turned towards the helicopter,

already thinning out the futures with the fateweaver, looking for the one where ours intersected at just the right angle.

"We miss this," Cinder growled into my ear, "last thing I do before we hit the ground is blow your head off."

"Oh, relax," I told him, focusing on the helicopter. All of a sudden it looked very far away, a black-and-yellow wasp flitting above the trees. "Remember, falling doesn't kill you, it's the sudden stop when you—"

Cinder jumped.

Fire flared around us, and my stomach lurched as we kicked off the train and went speeding through the air. The wind roared in my ears, the helicopter growing bigger and bigger. Time seemed to slow down, and I had what felt like forever to see the eyes of the two men standing in the helicopter's fuselage go wide behind their goggles. The gunner fired a burst but the bullets fell low and left. The helicopter grew bigger still, filling my sight, and the future of the next three-quarters of a second was a solid line as the open side of the helicopter grew closer and closer. I felt us go through the countermagic shield, which did nothing as we were just a pair of ballistic objects at this point, the blast of the wind mixing with the clatter of the rotors as we flew under them and into the men in the doorway—

—and time snapped back to full speed and suddenly everything was happening at once. I hit the man with the laser designator and we both went sprawling, slamming into the helicopter's floor, my leg kicking out into empty space. The helicopter lurched, engine screaming. Someone was shouting and I fought with the man I'd landed on, elbows and weapons and teeth. Fire and heat bloomed and there was a horrible scream—

—and suddenly it was over. I hauled myself up on a handhold and saw that Cinder and I were the only ones standing. The machine gun was still there, mounted in the door. Through the gap between the seats I could see the pilot at the front of the helicopter; he seemed to be shouting. Cinder jerked a thumb towards him—it was too loud to speak—and I nodded and moved forward, grabbing a pistol from one of the bodies.

The pilot was talking fast into his microphone. He stopped short as I leant in next to him. His eyes rolled towards me fearfully.

I showed the pilot the pistol. "You have five seconds to use that parachute."

The pilot didn't need to be told twice. His harness flew open, he kicked open the side door, and he jumped into space.

The helicopter rocked, threatening to tip over. "Know how to fly this thing?" Cinder shouted from behind me.

I half fell into the pilot's seat, reached over for the open door, and slammed it, cutting down the noise. "Not yet."

Looking out, I saw that we'd gained height—the pilot must have climbed when we boarded—but the helicopter was lurching and swaying. The panels in the cockpit were an incomprehensible jumble of screens and dials, but the stick and pedals looked simple enough. I concentrated on the futures and a dozen Alexes tried a dozen combinations of movements: the futures that survived forked, forked again. I pulled the stick to one side, then flicked a switch and gently tilted it forward. The helicopter stabilised, its beating rotor holding it stationary, then angled forward, heading north.

November. Status.

The tactical net Barrayar has been using to direct your pursuit is . . . somewhat confused, November said. *They seem to be under the impression that you boarded their helicopter in midair.*

That's because we did. How long until they get organised?

You . . . Yes, well. The fighter-bomber that had been tasked with the strike has aborted its attack run. Barrayar wants confirmation of the helicopter's status and is attempting to order use of air-to-air missiles.

"Hey, Cinder," I called over my shoulder. "You know how to make a gate from inside a helicopter?"

Without even looking back, I knew that Cinder was rolling his eyes. "Now?"

"Well, Deleo can make one from a train," I said, looking through the futures to figure out how to work the autopilot. "But hey, maybe she's better than you. I'm not an expert on this stuff."

"How long we got?" Cinder growled.

"Ages. At least five minutes."

Six minutes and forty-five seconds later, the police helicopter was struck by an infrared-homing ASRAAM missile fired from astern. The missile hit the aircraft high on its right side, the warhead's fragments reaching the fuel tanks and causing a secondary explosion. The flaming wreckage crashed into a field somewhere west of Chelmsford, and the pieces were still burning when the emergency services pulled up. By the time that they—and Barrayar—determined that no one had been alive and on board at the time of impact, Cinder and I were long gone.

chapter 8

Cinder and I separated and I lay low for the rest of the day. The next morning found me back in the Hollow.

We've got trouble, Variam told me telepathically.

Slow down, I said. *What trouble and how?*

And when you say we, *do you mean trouble for us, or trouble for the Keepers?* Luna added. *Because one of those bothers me a lot more than the other.*

Things had reached the point where I couldn't risk meeting Variam face-to-face, and phone or internet communications were almost as bad. The only safe method left was the dreamstone, which was why I was sitting in my cottage in the dark, eyes closed as I concentrated. Maintaining a three-way link (so that Luna could take part in the conversation as well) was much harder than a two-way one, but at least I was getting plenty of dreamstone practice.

Okay, Variam said. *So that attack yesterday that we got scrambled for? The one where we thought we'd driven them off? Turns out we didn't drive them off, they with-*

drew. And they withdrew because they got what they wanted.

It was definitely Richard's cabal? I asked.

They were using shroud spells, but yeah, we're ninety-nine percent sure. They were using their big guns too. Vihaela was there, and from the sound of it so was Richard.

So last year Onyx steals something from the Southampton facility, and now Richard does? Luna said. *Why do they even keep using that place?*

It wasn't supposed to be there at all, Variam said. *It was being constructed in a shadow realm, and they were supposed to be transferring it directly to the Vault. There was some issue and they moved it to Southampton temporarily. Somehow Richard found out and hit the place first.*

Okay, I said. *You said at the beginning that this was something to do with Anne. What's the link?*

So, we haven't been told any of this officially, Variam said. *But when they found out about Anne and that jinn, it seems some of the high-ups green-lit a crash program to create some sort of anti-jinn weapon. They've been rushing construction on the prototype and they were moving it to the Vault for testing.*

They want to use it on Anne? Luna asked.

What kind of weapon? I asked.

No one's talking, Variam said. *But they are seriously stirred up right now. The Council's been in emergency session since last night and everyone's on standby.*

Right, I said. *About that. The attack on Southampton might not be the only reason the Council's in emergency session.*

What do you mean?

Let's just say you might be getting some orders soon about making me a priority target.

Alex? There was a warning note to Variam's thoughts. *What did you do?*

You're probably better off not knowing.

Oh, bloody hell. I could feel Variam sigh. *Look, I've got to go, Landis is calling. I'll check in when I hear anything.*

Don't, I said. *It's too risky for you to contact me. I'll get in touch with you instead.*

He's right, Vari, Luna said.

Fine, but you'd better tell me what the hell you've been up to. Vari out.

I let the link to Variam and Luna dissolve and stood, wincing a little at the stiffness in my legs. Pulling back the curtains from the window, I blinked as the midmorning sun streamed into the cottage. Once I'd adjusted to the light, I slipped the dreamstone into my pocket and walked out into the warm air of the Hollow.

Hey, November, I said, closing the door behind me.

It is somewhat disturbing when you do that unannounced, November replied.

I started out along one of the grassy paths. *Would have thought you'd be used to it.*

You don't use any kind of handshake protocol! How am I supposed to authenticate that it's you? All I have to go on is . . .

. . . Tone of voice?

If you were using a voice, *I could employ vocal recognition software.*

Well, you'll just have to recognise me the old-fashioned way.

But it's so untidy!

I came out into Karyos's clearing. The hamadryad was sitting cross-legged under her tree, chin resting in her hands. November was propped up in the grass, a webcam balanced on top of his case. ". . . which was why Levistus made the choice to install me there," he was saying. His voice sounded slightly tinny through the speakers. "It was to do with trade-offs in location."

"I don't understand this 'Heron Tower,'" Karyos said. "Why would he build it?"

"Um, he didn't," November said. "Its construction was financed by a property development company."

"But why would they build something so tall?"

"Because . . . er . . . well, skyscraper development is correlated with land value, and the property values in the financial districts of central London are more than high enough. It's really local ordinances that are the limiting factors."

"But if they built something smaller, they'd be closer to the ground."

"Er . . . well, yes, that's true, but . . ."

"Hey, guys," I said, walking out into the clearing. "How are you getting on?"

"The things your elemental tells me are so strange." Karyos gazed thoughtfully at November. "I have so much to learn about your world."

"I told you, I'm not an elemental," November said, sounding slightly annoyed. "And as for your question, Mr. Verus—"

"You know, you can just call me Alex."

"Yes, well, I'd find it much easier to adjust if I didn't have to rely on this substandard equipment."

"You wanted speakers, I got you speakers."

"They're Apple speakers!"

"Is that a problem?"

"Yes!"

"Do they not work?"

"It's the principle of the thing. In Heron Tower I had a customised full-surround—"

"I know, you've told me," I said, holding back a sigh. "Look, you're just going to have to accept that living in freedom out on the wild frontier comes with some sacrifices. Which apparently include Apple speakers."

"Those speaking machines are not made of apples," Karyos pointed out. "I don't understand why the elemental is concerned."

"For the last time, I am not an elemental!"

"November?" I said. "I just heard something a little worrying from one of my contacts with the Council." I relayed Variam's story. "Do you know anything about that?"

"Hmm," November said thoughtfully. "Unfortunately not. I had picked up some pieces of information suggesting the existence of a new weapons project. But as regards such matters, the flow was always one-way. I passed on my findings to Levistus and Barrayar, but they didn't keep me informed in return."

"Did Levistus give you any special orders as far as Anne and her jinn were concerned?" I asked. "Push them up the priority list for tracking, that sort of thing?"

"Not at all," November said. "He never gave me any indication that he was especially concerned with her. Actually, he was far more concerned with you, and the rest of his political opponents on the Council."

I sighed. "Yeah, I should have guessed." Anne wasn't a direct threat to Levistus's political career, and at the end of the day, that was what he cared about. "Okay. Let's carry on where you left off."

"Of course," November said. "We'd just reached the aftermath of the collapse of White Rose and Morden's ascension to the Junior Council. As you know, it was in this period that Levistus was raised to the Senior Council. He had been allowing everyone to believe that his strategy for doing so relied upon arranging for Nirvathis to be raised to the Junior Council first. In reality, Nirvathis had never been more than a smokescreen, which is why he was discarded so quickly after Morden's appointment.

Levistus's actual plan had always been to leverage his influence over Undaaris and Sal Sarque, while keeping both of them ignorant of his dealings with the other. This was also the period in which the remaining members of the Council became fully aware of Richard Drakh's return. While most of them did not favour taking any sort of direct action, Levistus was able to take advantage of this increase in tension by . . ."

Listening to November's history lesson was fascinating. I'd thought that by now, when it came to the Council, I was well-informed. I'd been *very* wrong. November's position had given him a bird's-eye view of all of Levistus's dealings, and it was eye-opening to learn how much had been going on.

For example, Levistus had had plans in place for years to have me assassinated, and the only reason he hadn't pulled the trigger was because of all the attacks and assassination attempts I'd drawn from everyone *else*. Basically, he'd decided it wasn't worth spending the resources to have me killed because there was such a good chance that if he waited long enough, someone else would do it for him. He'd been happy to point other people in my direction though: he'd been the one to supply the Nightstalkers with my name and address, and he'd had a hand in getting the Council intelligence services to order my death during the operation in Syria. Once I'd been raised to the Council, he'd been planning to step that up further, but he'd been distracted by a behind-the-scenes power struggle between him and Bahamus.

On that subject, November's files had also contained Levistus's notes on the other members of the Senior Council. Right at the top of the list was Undaaris, a water mage who'd been largely responsible for my first death sentence. I'd noticed for a while that Levistus seemed to have a lot of influence on Undaaris, and the files made it clear why. Undaaris had been a heavy user of White Rose before its destruction, and the report had gone into detail as to the kinds of activities he'd pursued there. With attached audio and video files. I'd unwisely had November show them to me and was forced to take a break while my digestive system tried to crawl up my throat and spit acid on my brain.

Sal Sarque had also been under Levistus's influence, though for a different reason. Apparently back when Sal Sarque was a captain in the Order of the Star, he was given command of a sensitive operation where he screwed the pooch in a major way. It had been covered up, but not well enough. Levistus had dirt on Bahamus as well, though in his case it had taken the form of family secrets. Bahamus's father had also been a mage, and active in Council politics. He hadn't been as successful as his son, and his family had accumulated some of the sorts of favours that it's a bad idea to owe. Bringing that all to light wouldn't have brought Bahamus down, but it would have seriously damaged him. Bahamus, in turn, had evidence of Levistus's own breaches of the Concord during the first struggle over the fateweaver, and as a result Levistus and Bahamus had settled into an uneasy truce.

That left Druss, Alma, and Spire. In Druss's case, Levistus had turned up some irregularities concerning Druss's past romantic relationships (of which it turned out there had been a lot). However, when Levistus had approached Druss on the subject and offered his silence in exchange for Druss's support, Druss told Levistus to go screw himself, and Levistus backed down. Finally, with Alma and Spire, Levistus had been unable to find any significant blackmail material at all. The lack of dirt on Alma was irritating, since she'd consistently been my third-worst enemy on the Council, but that's how life goes. Just because someone's your enemy doesn't mean they're evil. Or at least no more evil than any other politician.

It was a weird thought, but in helping get rid of Sal Sarque, I might have done the Council a favour. With him and Undaaris under Levistus's thumb, Levistus had only ever been one vote away from a straight majority. In another five years, he probably would have been running the country. I wasn't sure how happy I was about cleaning up the Council's messes for them, but it wasn't as though I had much of a choice.

"Well," I said once November had finished. "That was . . . educational. Thank you."

"You're welcome."

"Your Council's problems sound familiar," Karyos said. "Perhaps humans haven't changed so much after all."

"So, if you don't mind my asking," November said, "what are you going to do now?"

"Now?" I said. "I get back in touch with the Council and try again to call a truce."

"Even with Levistus?"

"Even with Levistus. I'm not in this for revenge. If I can make peace, I'll do it."

"Ah," November said. "I'm not sure how to say this, but . . ."

"No, I'm not going to give you back to Levistus," I said. "Firstly I made you a promise, and secondly I wouldn't trust him to keep any deal he made."

"That's certainly a relief," November said. "But do you think you can negotiate with the Council at all?"

"Well, that's the problem," I said. "As long as they see me as just some turncoat mage, talking to them is going to be a waste of time. I have to make them realise that pursuing me isn't worth it. Unfortunately, I don't think they're going to take my word for that. Which means I'm going to have to prove it to them. And on that subject . . ." I looked at Karyos. "Remember when we were talking about how we first met? You told me you'd been to a lot of shadow realms over the course of your life. Do you still remember them all?"

"My memories are distant, but they have been growing clearer."

I nodded. "I'm looking for a shadow realm with some particular characteristics. Specifically, a deep shadow realm."

"What characteristics?"

I explained.

Karyos frowned. "I believe there are one or two. But much time has passed. I do not know if they may have changed."

"It's a place to start," I said. "Give me the details and I'll go check them out."

"Do you really think these negotiations will work?" November asked.

"I don't know," I said. "The Council might decide that now I have access to your files, it's too dangerous to try to destroy me. On the other hand, they might decide it's too dangerous *not* to try to destroy me. It's too big a decision for me to swing. I'll just have to wait and see which way they jump."

"When will you know?"

"I've already put out a feeler to Talisid," I said. "I don't think it'll be long."

: : : : : : : : :

Talisid got back to me only a couple of hours later, arranging a call for that same evening. It was nice to know I'd be getting a definite answer, but I had no idea whether it'd be a good one.

As evening approached I went to a similar location to the one I'd used for my last call, and went through a similar set of preparations. One thing was different: the futures didn't have any Council Keepers gating in on top of me. Apparently the Council had suspended their hunting operations, which was a hopeful sign. Once I'd finished, I leant against a tree and closed my eyes. The day's warmth had faded with the setting sun, and the breeze felt cool as it stirred my clothes and hair.

Faces swam in my mind's eye. Cinder and Rachel. Morden and Richard. Arachne, Anne. Links and plans and traps, past and future, all shrouded in fog.

Once I'd been a simple shopkeeper. I'd had little power, but with that lack of power had come freedom. I'd lived as I pleased, and no one had noticed or cared. Now I had all the power in the world, and no freedom at all.

My communicator chimed. I straightened, opened my eyes, and activated the disc. "Talisid," I said.

"Mage Verus," Talisid said.

You can tell a lot from how someone opens a conversation. Talisid had called on time, and his voice had a subtle but definite note of caution. So far so good. "I assume you've been briefed on yesterday's developments."

"I believe so," Talisid said carefully.

"That's fine. I think you understand the important parts. I'd like to carry on where we left off. You remember our last conversation?"

"As I recall, you were requesting a ceasefire."

No scare quotes around *ceasefire*: also good. "So let's try this again," I said. "Is the Council willing to reconsider?"

"Why would you expect them to be?"

"Because if they don't, I'll blow them up," I said. "Metaphorically, not literally. Though I think they'd rather deal with a literal explosion than the political fall-out from this. I'm pretty sure I can bring down . . . oh, three or four of the current Senior Council? Not really the best timing, is it, with you being in the middle of a war? Especially not with Richard Drakh still carrying out successful strikes like yesterday's. I imagine it really wouldn't help to have your leadership paralysed with a political crisis."

"The Council does not respond well to threats."

"Funny, they spend enough time threatening everyone else. I know you've got them on the line. Go get your orders."

Silence. I stood there and watched the swirl of futures. Nothing useful.

"What exactly are you proposing?" Talisid asked eventually.

"A ceasefire, like I said. Amusing as it would be to watch, I don't actually have any particular interest in causing a political catastrophe for you guys. You halt your operations against me and my associates, and you don't carry out any further ones. In exchange, I'll keep my recent information windfall to myself."

"That hardly seems like an even trade."

"How is that not an even trade? Stopping your attacks on me costs you nothing. In fact, it costs you *less* than nothing, because you'll be able to take the resources you've been deploying against me and use them against Richard's cabal instead. You remove a threat and free up personnel, all without lifting a finger."

"The problem is security," Talisid said. "Once you have what you want, there'll be nothing to stop you from taking the information you have and distributing it anyway."

"And there'll be nothing to stop *you* from going right back to hunting me."

"We have considerably more to lose than you do," Talisid said. "I'm sorry, but we're not willing to accept any arrangement with you holding a sword over our heads."

"Funny, I've been living with that for years," I said. "But fine. You don't like the deal, come up with a better one."

"Hold, please."

More silence. I tried to imagine how the argument between the Council members must be going. I had the feeling that Levistus was very unpopular right now.

The pause dragged out. Five minutes passed, then ten. At last Talisid's voice came from the focus. "Mage Verus?"

"I'm still here."

"The Council has come to an agreement," Talisid said. "We are . . . conditionally . . . willing to grant your request. If you agree to our terms, you will be granted a full amnesty and pardon for your actions connected to the incident at San Vittore, as well as to any actions taken during your period as a fugitive."

"What kind of terms?"

"I am given to understand that your 'information windfall' is in fact a self-aware storage system and imbued item that you took possession of yesterday," Talisid said. "The Council wants it returned."

I didn't answer.

"Mage Verus?"

"I heard," I said. "I'm just trying to think what possible reason I could have for saying yes."

"As I said, we are willing to grant your request. This is what we require in exchange."

"Why?" I said.

"Consider it a show of commitment."

"I can see how it's a show of commitment for me. Not seeing how it's much of one for you."

"You are asking the Council to accept multiple, repeated, and flagrant breaches of the Concord," Talisid said. "Your actions have—by your own admission— earned you a capital sentence many times over. If we are to set this aside, we require something in exchange."

Again I didn't answer.

"Mage Verus?"

"Hold, please."

I closed my eyes and path-walked, looking through

short-term conversations and long-term ones, searching for common elements. Shadowy proposals and counter-proposals flickered in and out of existence, but I didn't catch a single glimpse of any future in which Talisid gave way. This was the only deal they were offering. It was take it or leave it.

There was one thing more I needed to know. "How are we going to make the trade?" I asked.

"At a neutral location," Talisid said. "I suggest Concordia."

The old, famous bubble realm where the Concord had been negotiated. "No," I said. "We're doing this face-to-face, I'm picking the location."

"As long as it is a neutral location, we will consider it," Talisid said. "I would also suggest that both sides bring no more than five delegates."

"Three," I said. "And you have to be one of them."

"Providing that you likewise attend, that is acceptable."

He'd agreed to that quickly. Time for the big question. "All right," I said. "One last condition. I want that amnesty you offered to restore the status quo. That means I keep my seat on the Junior Council."

Talisid paused. "That does not seem in keeping with your previous demands."

"If you're changing the deal, so am I. Well?"

"I will have to consult with the Council."

Silence. I studied the futures. They were still swirling, but there was a pattern to them. The decision had already been made.

It took less time than I'd expected for Talisid to speak again. "Mage Verus? The Council is *provisionally* willing to restore your seat. However, you will not be guaranteed it in perpetuity. Normal procedures of elevation and removal will apply."

"I see."

"Do we have an agreement?"

I stood silent for a moment. "Yes," I said at last, my voice steady. "We have an agreement. Oh, and just so you know, those two people I'll be bringing to the meeting? One of them will be Mage Anne Walker."

Talisid paused before answering. "I hope that isn't intended as a threat."

"Just something for you to keep in mind," I said. "I'll contact you tomorrow with a time and place."

"Understood," Talisid said. "Thank you for your time."

"You as well."

The light on the communicator focus went dark and the connection broke. The sun had set and the light was fading from the sky, leaving the woods dark and cold. "Shit," I said to the empty clearing. I stood there for a long time, my figure one more shadow in the gloom.

         ı ı ı ı ı ı ı ı ı

I returned to the Hollow, fell asleep, and travelled to Elsewhere. I had people to meet.

"So that's the plan," I told Dark Anne. "You in?"

"Hmm," Anne said. She put her chin in one hand and studied me.

We were on the border between my Elsewhere and Anne's. Behind me was an ancient city of yellow-brown stone; behind Anne, a wild forest of ancient trees. Anne's dream-self was wearing a wine-coloured dress that left her arms bare but fell all the way to the ground: it trailed behind her as she walked. She had one arm folded under her breasts, her reddish eyes staring at me. The sky behind her was grey-black and stormy, and the leaves on the trees whipped in a distant wind.

"So?" I said when she didn't speak.

"You've changed," Dark Anne said.

"I told you that a while ago."

"I thought you'd have gone back to normal by now."

"This is the new normal."

Dark Anne watched me unblinkingly. "You never would have done this before."

"Back when your other self was running things, you'd always push me to be less cautious," I said. "Now all of a sudden you've changed your mind?"

"Maybe there's something you want," Dark Anne said. "Is that it?"

I sighed. "I was always like this, Anne. It's just that back then I was trying to be someone different."

"Mm."

"What, you're worried your half's too dangerous?" I said. "I suppose I could find someone else if I have to, but I honestly thought you could handle it."

"What?" Dark Anne said. "No, that's easy. Though you've got some cheek calling it a half. I'm going to be doing all the hard work."

"And I'm the one who's going to be on his own in the shadow realm. You really want to trade jobs?"

Dark Anne tapped her fingers against her arm, then shrugged. "All right, I'll trust you. You'd better not make me regret it."

"What's with the attitude?" I said. "A few weeks ago, you seemed all in on this."

"I still am. What's your endgame, Alex?"

"What do you mean?"

"Don't play dumb. Right now we're aiming at the same targets. What are you planning once they're gone?"

"You're worried I'm going to stab you in the back?"

"Pretty much."

"I don't want to stab you in the back," I said. "And I don't want to get rid of you any other way, either."

"No, you just want me locked up again."

I shook my head. "I think we've both learned that doesn't work."

"So what *are* you going to do?"

"Anne locking you up didn't work," I said. "You locking Anne up won't work any better. The two of you can't stay like this. You're split when you should be whole, and it's killing you."

"Bull," Dark Anne said. She spread her arms invitingly. "*I* am doing just fine. You want to sit around until this kills me, you're going to have a long wait."

I studied Dark Anne. "Has the jinn started taking over yet?"

Dark Anne's face went expressionless.

"It'll be subtle to begin with," I said. "You'll be deciding what to do, and one choice will look better for some reason. You won't be quite sure why, but it'll just seem like the natural thing to do. Then later on, it'll start to have more of a voice. Persuading and convincing. You can say no, but it won't get weaker, it'll get stronger. It'll always be there, pushing you. Each time you give in, it'll take a tiny bit of ground, then a tiny bit more, until there's nothing left. This thing is *thousands* of years old; you haven't even turned twenty-seven. You think you're going to beat it in an endurance contest?"

"You've spent all your life making deals with magical creatures," Dark Anne said. "You think you can do it and I can't?"

"All of those deals, I made sure to know what the creature wanted. And what I could afford to give."

"Yeah, well, we don't all get it that easy, do we? I saw a way out and I took it. Sorry it doesn't meet your approval."

We stared at each other across the boundary. Seconds dragged out.

Dark Anne broke the deadlock, shaking her head. "Whatever. I'll do your job. Just don't keep me waiting." She turned and left, disappearing into the trees. I watched her go, but she didn't look back.

Once I was sure she wasn't returning, I walked to a

white stone bench and sat down. Even though I'd moved only a little way, my own Elsewhere had closed in around me, and the trees and wilderness of Anne's landscape were distant and faded. I stared at the grey sky and the swaying trees.

The conversation had gone to plan, more or less. Still, I wasn't happy. It felt as though every time I saw Anne, she was further away. I was pretty sure she'd do her part this time. But after?

I shook off the feeling. I had someone else I needed to meet, a conversation I'd put off too long. I sat on the bench and waited.

I felt her presence first, ripples spreading through Elsewhere, quick and agitated. I sat there as the footsteps grew louder until a teenage girl with short red hair appeared from behind a line of pillars. "You!" Shireen pointed at me. "Stay there!"

I stayed where I was as Shireen strode across the courtyard. "You know how long I've been looking for you?" she demanded. Her face was flushed and angry. "Every time you come to Elsewhere you hide, then you run away before I can catch up!"

"Sorry."

"What do you mean, sorry? What are you doing? What are you *trying* to do?"

Shireen looked like a teenager, but she was the same age as me . . . or at least she had been. When Rachel had killed her, a part of Shireen lived on, tethered to our world by her connection to the girl who'd once been her best friend. I didn't know whether she was a ghost, a memory, or something else, but she'd been trying for years to get me to help Rachel. I'd finally done something, but she didn't seem happy about it.

"I've had a stressful few weeks," I said.

"Oh, *you've* had a stressful few weeks?" Shireen

glared at me. "Rachel's going insane right now, you know that? Her place with Richard and her relationship with Cinder were the only things holding her together! Now she's lost both!"

"Okay, I'm pretty sure the second one of those is not my fault," I said. "Rachel and Cinder had their bust-up before I got involved. In fact, from the sound of it, Cinder barely got out alive."

Shireen shifted uncomfortably. "She wasn't trying to hurt him badly."

"And the *last* time they met, she tried to disintegrate him, then ran away."

"That was never going to kill him."

"Yeah, and neither would sticking him with a knife, but I don't stab him every time I say hello."

"It's . . . complicated." Shireen shook her head. "Stop distracting me! Maybe that isn't your fault, but what happened with Richard is!"

"Not arguing that."

"You tricked her! Now Richard hates her! She's been cut loose!"

"You wanted me to break her free of Richard," I pointed out. "Seems to me I did exactly what you asked."

"She needed to leave Richard because she *wanted* to! Instead she got thrown out! Richard told her that she could fix her mess or die trying, so now that's what she's trying to do! She's going crazy!"

"Come on," I said. "You really expected me to talk Rachel into *wanting* to leave Richard? She would never have done that. Never in a million years. I saw exactly one way to break her away from Richard and keep myself alive into the bargain, and I took it. And honestly, you should be grateful for what you've got, because you and Cinder are the *only* reasons I haven't killed her already."

"She used to be your friend!"

"She sat around filing her nails while I was getting

tortured in Richard's basement," I snapped. "She's tried to murder me so many times I've lost count. She watched what Richard did to Anne, and *laughed*. She is *not* my friend, and I don't owe her shit."

"You owe *me*."

"And that's why she's still alive."

We glared at each other across the cracked flagstones. "How can you be this selfish?" Shireen demanded. "I thought you were trying to be better than this?"

"I try to be better when I'm dealing with people who deserve it," I said. "Which Rachel most definitely does *not*. I have known her for a really long time, and I can honestly say that she's one of the worst human beings I've ever met. She's sadistic, unstable, totally self-centred, and she doesn't have the slightest trace of kindness or honour to balance it out. Her only redeeming features are her relationships with you and Cinder, and she tried to kill Cinder and she *did* kill you! I don't understand why the two of you haven't given up on her by now. What is it going to take to make you write her off?"

"I can't," Shireen said. "She's why I'm here. As long as there's a chance, I have to try."

I stared at Shireen, and all of a sudden it struck me that maybe she meant that literally. She'd described herself once as a shadow. Maybe that was how she'd been preserved, as some kind of embodiment of Rachel's guilty conscience. She literally *couldn't* stop, any more than a heart could stop beating.

"Okay, Shireen," I said. "I'll give you your chance. Tomorrow. I'll be there, and so will Cinder. Get ready to talk to Rachel and make your case. Because one way or the other, I'm ending this. Rachel's going to have to choose a side, once and for all."

"Tomorrow where?" Alarm flashed in Shireen's eyes. "No, Alex, what are you planning? She won't listen to me. It has to be you."

"She's going to listen to someone. Only question is who."

"Wait!"

"Tomorrow, Shireen," I said. "It's time to end this." I stepped out of Elsewhere, and back into my own dreams.

chapter 9

The next day dawned hot. It was September, but the summer weather had lingered, and the morning sun shone down out of a brilliant blue sky. Even this early, it was warm: come midday, it would be scorching. I stood in the shade at the edge of the woods, looking across the grassy valley.

We were in Wales, at Richard's mansion. Or what was left of it. The once-elegant building was a mass of rubble and shattered walls, so thoroughly destroyed that you couldn't even tell where the rooms had been. It looked as if a bomb had hit it, which it had. The front lawn was wild and overgrown, scattered with pieces of tile and stone that had been thrown outwards in the blast. A pair of crows hopped between the rocks, pecking at the ground.

To me, Richard's mansion had been many things. A home, a school, a prison, a graveyard. I'd loved it and feared it and hated it with a burning passion. Seventeen years ago, for the four of us, this was where it had all begun. Today, this was where it would end.

A muffled footstep announced Cinder's presence. He moved quietly for such a big man. "So?" he said.

"We're clear."

I started walking down the slope, and Cinder fell in beside me. The morning sun lit us up, casting bright shadows behind us. "Council?" Cinder asked.

"They won't interfere."

"Thought they wanted you."

"Two days ago, they were hunting me," I said. "Day after tomorrow, they might be doing it again. But not today."

From across the valley, the ruins looked as if they could have been made yesterday. Up close was a different story. Grass had grown around the scattered tiles and bricks, and new bushes and saplings marked where last year's battle had scorched the earth. The crows took off as we approached, flapping away down the slope, cawing in their harsh voices: *arrh, arrh, arrh.*

Cinder nodded at the rubble. "Dig through?"

"Don't have to," I said. "Council earth mages cleared a way."

"Basement might have caved in."

"I was the one who called in that airstrike, and I was the first one down into the basement. It's still there."

"Anyone moved in?"

"Who the hell would want to?"

We climbed over some rubble, skirted the remains of a chimney stack, and found ourselves at the top of a set of stairs leading down into darkness. It was easy to miss: in the bright daylight the stairway was a small shadow with nothing to mark it out. Searching with my magesight, I couldn't see many auras. The summoning trap was long gone, and the gate wards that had once protected the mansion were ragged and patchy, many of their nodes destroyed. They would hamper gate magic, but wouldn't prevent it.

Cinder called up a light and we descended into darkness, leaving the warmth and sun behind. Our footsteps echoed on the stone steps as we went deeper. At the bottom of the stairs the dark red of Cinder's light illuminated a door.

We didn't go far. One short corridor and we came out into the room the four of us had once called the chapel. The statues in the corners had been removed at some point, but the murals were still there, strange and unsettling. The archway by which we'd entered led back into the corridor and up the stairs. A second archway at the far end led deeper into darkness. I walked to the middle of the room and stopped.

"This is it?" Cinder asked.

I nodded.

Cinder's light lit his face from below, casting strange shadows from his features. "So?"

I began to lean against one of the walls, then saw the murals and thought better of it. "Now we wait."

Cinder looked at me. "Wait?"

"What, you thought I was going to use the fateweaver?" I said. "Lure her in?"

"Can you?"

"I've seen her twice the past few days," I said. "Once in Tibet, once in London. Both times she gated in on me. Know what I did to lure her in?"

Cinder looked at me.

"Nothing," I said. "I was trying to deal with other problems, and both times Rachel somehow managed to show up at exactly the time and place to make my life as difficult as possible. So no, I'm not going to lure her, or do any kind of fancy tricks. I'm just going to hang around somewhere suspicious, like here, and wait for her to show up and ruin my day. Because that's what she does."

Cinder studied me. "Called her Rachel."

"I did?"

Cinder gave a nod.

I shrugged irritably. "Slip of the tongue."

"You sit here, she shows up?"

"Best guess."

"So why'd you wait so long?"

"Because bringing her here is *all* I can do," I said, and pointed up and out. "You and I have been allies two and a half years now. The deal was that you'd help me out if I got R—split her from Richard. Well, I've done it. But you wanted more. You want things back the way they used to be. Right?"

Cinder looked at me for a second, then nodded again.

"And that I can't promise," I said. "Right now, she walks down those stairs and sees me, she's just going to kick off and we're back to square one. The way I see it, the *only* thing that has a chance of turning her off the path she's on right now . . . is you. And it has to be now, because I can't keep doing this. She's been trying to kill me too long, got close too many times. If after you've said your piece she still goes for me . . . then it'll be the last time."

Cinder looked at me silently.

"You okay with that? I can't keep softballing any longer."

"Enough chances," Cinder said. "I get it."

We stood in silence for a little while. The chapel was dark and cold. We would only have to turn and walk up those steps to return to the warmth and the morning light, but somehow it felt very far away.

"Mind if I ask you something?" I said.

"Yes."

"I've never asked how you two got to be partners. Figure it's not my business. But I really want to know why you haven't given up on her."

Cinder didn't answer.

"I mean, maybe it's just me, but if a girl I knew was

shooting disintegration spells at my chest, I'd take that as a pretty strong indicator that we were officially broken up."

Silence.

"Look, at the end of the day, it's your life. I'm just wondering."

"You ever stop asking questions?"

"Not really."

More silence.

"So?"

"Just do your job."

"I am doing my job," I said. "But until Rachel shows, we've got nothing better to do."

"Bloody hell," Cinder said. "You do *not* take a hint."

I shrugged. "Diviner curiosity. Used to think it would get me killed someday. Turns out a lot of other stuff is going to beat it to the punch. But right now, I'm here and you're here, so . . . ?"

"I'll tell you if you'll just *shut up*."

"Deal."

"Del and I made a promise, long time ago," Cinder said. "She'd have my back, I'd have hers."

I waited for Cinder to go on. "That's it?" I asked when he didn't.

Cinder shrugged.

Trying to get Cinder to open up is like prying apart a stone wall with a chisel. "Well, I suppose that was pretty much how things were when we first met. When it was you, Deleo, and Khazad. Khazad sold her out soon as it got convenient. You didn't."

"Khazad was an arsehole."

"But that all changed when Richard came back, didn't it? She got drawn back in."

"Yeah."

I studied Cinder. "I don't buy it."

Cinder shot me a glare. "What?"

"I can believe you're the kind to keep that sort of promise," I said. "You've kept every deal you've made with me. But that's because *I've* kept every deal I've made with *you*. If I'd stabbed you in the back, you would not be trying to save me like this."

Cinder didn't answer.

"Now, maybe you think I just don't look as good as she does," I said. "But you never really struck me as the kind to care that much about looks. And you might be playing some kind of complicated game where she's a piece on the board, except you never really struck me as *that* kind of person, either. So we're back to the same question."

Another silence, but this one of a different kind. I could feel the futures shifting and knew that Cinder was going to speak. I waited for him to decide what to say.

"Every time I used to see you, you'd have some kid around," Cinder said. "That apprentice of yours, that Council time mage, the Indian kid, that life girl . . . even with that spider, you'd made friends."

"Yeah."

"Lot of Dark mages think that's dumb," Cinder said. "They stay cold. No attachments. Travel light, travel fast." He paused. "But you do that, you got nothing when you get there. People like that . . . they don't last."

I looked at Cinder curiously. "Was that why you bonded Kyle?"

"Del doesn't have that," Cinder said, ignoring me. "Used to. Had that friend, Shireen. Even you, sounded like. Until Drakh. She couldn't let him go."

"He doesn't care about her," I said. "I'm not sure he cares about anyone. As far as he's concerned, at this point, she's just a failed experiment."

Cinder grunted. "Told her that."

"How'd she take it?"

"Not well."

"So why—?" I paused. "Oh. Out of time."

Cinder shifted, straightening, and walked to the centre of the room. I moved to the archway at the far end. The passage beyond led into the laboratories and cells of the mansion's basement complex. I had plenty of memories of them, few good, but I wouldn't be going there today.

Silence. Minutes ticked by. I scanned through futures and learned little—normally my divination gives me some idea of how a conversation is likely to go, but Rachel's just too unpredictable. I began to channel through my dreamstone, carefully weaving together pieces of a spell that I hoped I wouldn't need.

I felt a flash of gate magic from above and knew Rachel had arrived. I'd wondered if she'd hesitate, suspecting something, but as the futures moved it became clear she was coming straight down. "Thirty seconds," I told Cinder.

"Great," Cinder said. "Now keep your mouth shut."

Footsteps sounded from the archway. A moment later, sea-green light, dark and flickering, illuminated the steps. Rachel's feet appeared, then her body, and finally her face. The black domino mask hid her expression, but I saw her eyes flicker past Cinder to me and felt the futures spike as she called up her magic.

"NO!" Cinder roared. Dark flame billowed with a hungry *whoosh*. It didn't strike either of us but it did make us jump. Rachel's spell faltered and she looked at Cinder in surprise.

"We are NOT DOING THIS!" With his back turned, I couldn't see Cinder's face, but his voice held an intensity I'd never heard from him before. "I do not have TIME for your shit right now. You are going to LISTEN."

Rachel drew back slightly. I think she was surprised. I certainly was.

"This shit with Verus?" Cinder said. "It *ends*. No more hunting him. He goes his way and *so do you*."

"Why are you on his side?" Rachel snapped. But for now at least, there were no futures of her resuming her attack. Cinder seemed to be holding her by sheer force of personality.

"How many times have you tried this?" Cinder demanded. "Over and over, and you missed every time! You think the hundredth is going to work?"

"I have to!" Rachel shouted back.

"Why?"

"Because—Richard—"

"Drakh's not your master!"

"Because of *him*!" Rachel shouted. "He tricked me!"

"Drakh was using you," Cinder said. "Every time he got someone new, he put them above you. Wasn't going to change."

"No!" Rachel's voice cracked. "I'm his Chosen. It—it would have been fine if he hadn't—"

Cinder just looked at her.

"Stop looking at me like that! It's *his* fault!"

"Del," Cinder said. He didn't shout this time; he spoke clearly, simply. "Drakh's not taking you back."

"No." Rachel's voice wavered. "No, he told me. He told me this was my last chance. If I proved . . ."

"You've served him long enough," Cinder said. "It's time to stop."

Rachel drew a breath, looked away. Then she turned back, suddenly calmer, and I felt the futures shift. "Maybe," she said. "But not till I kill him."

Uh-oh. I sped up my working through the dreamstone.

Cinder's voice was flat. "Not an option."

"No, I have to, you see?" Rachel's voice was suddenly bright, persuasive. "He's the one who set all this up. You just can't see it because he's fooled you too. He does it to everyone, except me. He's laughing at you right now. Look!"

"Forget. About. Verus."

"You should call him Alex," Rachel said absently. "I don't—oh. Wait." She turned and stared into empty space, her head tilted.

I felt a chill. *Shireen.*

"I thought you couldn't come when he was around?" Rachel asked. She paused, then nodded. "Oh, that makes sense. But you see, don't you? He killed Tobruk and he killed you. So I *have* to kill him. I'm all that's left."

"He didn't kill Shireen, Del."

"Yes, he did." Rachel sounded as if she were explaining things to a child. "If it hadn't been for him, she'd be fine." She paused, frowned. "Well, you *would* say that."

This isn't working. I finished the shaping through the dreamstone. The gate was almost ready. All it would need was a push.

"This ends," Cinder said. "Today. You got two choices. Back up the stairs with me. Or—"

"Or through that other archway and go after Alex," Rachel said. "You know, there's a reason I got bored of you."

"Del—"

"Shh." Rachel put a finger to her lips. "No more talking."

Rachel took a step towards Cinder, then another, smiling to herself. I tensed.

"We made a promise," Cinder said quietly. He didn't move as Rachel closed in.

Rachel laid her hands on Cinder's shoulders. She had to reach up to do it. Blue eyes gazed up at Cinder's face. "I know," she said. "And I always keep my promises."

Cinder hesitated.

Rachel's smile deepened. "It's just that sometimes the *important* promises are the ones you make to yourself."

"Cinder!" I shouted.

Green-black light formed at Rachel's hands. Cinder's black flame sprang to meet it, just a heartbeat behind. There was a flash and a roar. I caught a glimpse of Cinder staggering, then Rachel was darting towards me, light steps flying across the stone.

My spell completed and a gateway appeared in the wall to my right. I leapt through.

I held my grip on the spell, making sure the gate would stay open a few seconds longer than usual. I needn't have bothered. Rachel jumped through with blinding speed. "Ah-ah!" she called. "No running!"

I backed away. We were in a room that looked much like the one we'd left, except that instead of being dark it was clearly lit in grey and blue.

Rachel didn't seem to notice. She moved forward, graceful and balanced, still smiling. "Here we are again," she told me. "Do you remember?"

"Oh, I remember," I told her.

"I knew you'd come back," Rachel said, as if telling me a secret. "But you shouldn't have done that with Richard. He's supposed to be mine."

"You wanted to keep Richard for yourself, you shouldn't have given him Anne."

Rachel nodded. "You're right. You *are* right. I should have made sure, shouldn't I? If she'd died in that attack, it would have been fine. Richard would have been angry, but he'd have come around. But I can fix that. If I just—"

"I really don't care."

Rachel frowned. "I'm not finished."

"Rachel, how many times have we done this?" I said. "It's been six years now and we keep running into each other. Sometimes you're more crazy, sometimes you're less crazy, but it never makes much difference, does it? Nothing ever changes."

"Well, of course it doesn't." Rachel sounded as if she were explaining the obvious. "You're *you*."

I'd been backing away as Rachel approached. She could have closed the distance in a lunge, but instead she paced me, watching me closely. Strangely, I hadn't got any closer to the edge of the room.

"But I *have* changed," I said. "It's been painful, but I've learned. You, though? You're frozen in time. You're

still the same broken angry teenager standing over
Shireen's dying body."

Rachel's smile faded. "Don't say her name."

"Why not?" I nodded to one side. "She's right there."

"Rachel!" Shireen came striding out from the archway,
tension and alarm in her movements. "What are you
doing?"

"Not *now*," Rachel said absently, not looking at
Shireen.

"No!" Shireen said. "You have to get out!"

"Oh, and don't forget your jinn," I said, gesturing to
the other side of the room. "Looks like the gang's all
here."

A slender, almost-human shape was standing in the
shadows, unnaturally still. It watched us both, unmoving.
Rachel shot it an uninterested look. "They're always
here."

"Has it occurred to you," I told Rachel, "that you've
managed to kill or drive away every single person who's
ever cared about you? First there was Shireen. She was
your best friend and you murdered her in cold blood.
Then there was Richard. He might have put Anne above
you, but he still would have kept you on. At least until you
managed to ruin years of his work by freeing her. Oh, I
was the one who manipulated you into it, but it was still
your choice, and Richard knows it. He'll never trust you
again."

Rachel's expression had become fixed. All traces of a
smile were gone. "Shut up."

"And finally there's Cinder. God only knows why, but
he's stayed loyal to you for years. Even today, you still
could have taken his offer and walked away. Or you *could*
have done, until you tried to kill him yet again."

"Rachel!" Shireen burst out. "You have to—"

"Shut *up*," Rachel hissed. "All of you." She stared at

me, eyes icy with hate. "Richard should never have taken you in. He could never see what you were. I'm going to—"

"Look at your hands, Rachel," I said quietly.

Rachel blinked and glanced down, then stared. Faint wisps of light were rising from her fingers.

"You didn't know that I could open gates to Elsewhere now, did you? I told you I'd changed." I paused. "Something else I noticed. Ever since our reunion, the times we've met via Elsewhere, you've never gone *into* Elsewhere. You'll walk right up to the edge, you'll look over the line, but you'll never cross it."

"You're lying," Rachel said. But all of a sudden, she looked uncertain.

"He's not!" Shireen said. "Rachel, please, you have to run!"

Without looking, I knew that wisps of light were starting to rise from my own clothes and body. Not enough to be dangerous, not yet. "I spent a while wondering why you'd never set foot into Elsewhere," I told Rachel. "I mean, Elsewhere's a reflection of your inner self. So I thought it'd be interesting to see what happened if I brought you here. What do you think, Rachel? What would your Elsewhere be like?"

Rachel looked at me for a long moment, then turned to run. And stopped. Behind Rachel, where the door had been, was a floor-to-ceiling mirror spanning the length of the room.

"Oops," I said softly. "Guess you're staying."

Rachel tried to call up a gateway. I snuffed it out with an effort of will. She tried again with the same result.

"What are you doing?" Shireen cried. "Let her go!"

"Like she said," I told her. "No running."

Rachel threw a disintegration ray at the mirror, the beam and its reflection meeting in a green flash. It should have turned the mirror to dust, but the glass absorbed the spell as though it were nothing. I could feel Elsewhere shifting, focusing around us. I couldn't make out the shape of what was happening, but Rachel was the centre of it.

Rachel turned on me, and green death lashed out. I bent the spell away, letting it fizzle out somewhere off to the side. There was no way Rachel could hurt me, not here. Gate magic might work, but it was my will against hers and—

A chill went through me.

In the mirror behind Rachel, I could see myself reflected, quite small at this distance. I could see Shireen's reflection as she called out again for Rachel to run. I could see the jinn's reflection, silent and unmoving in the shadows. And I could see Rachel's reflection standing just behind her.

Except that when Rachel had spun to face me, the reflection hadn't moved.

Rachel sent another disintegration ray at me; without looking I knocked it away. Her reflection was watching me from over Rachel's shoulder.

"Die already!" Rachel shouted at me. When I didn't answer, she paused. She followed my gaze, turned with a frown. She looked at her reflection; the mirror Rachel looked at me. The real Rachel turned back. "And look at me when I'm killing you!"

I stared back at Rachel, the chill inside me growing. *She doesn't see it.*

The mirror Rachel turned away, her gaze lingering, then began walking, heading for my reflection.

Instinctively I backed away. My reflection moved sideways, matching me, but the mirror Rachel was advancing faster and faster. "What the hell is wrong with him?" I heard the real Rachel say.

"It's Elsewhere." There was a frantic edge to Shireen's voice. "Something's here. Alex, get us out! Please!"

Elsewhere is dangerous. Anne and Luna and I can use it because we're careful and disciplined. Every crack inside your mind, every part of yourself that you can't face, is a vulnerability. And by that measure, Rachel was about as bad a candidate for Elsewhere as you could get. So my plan had been to bring her here, then simply wait for her to self-destruct.

All of a sudden, it was occurring to me that bringing the most mentally damaged person I knew into a place shaped by thought might not have been a good idea.

Rachel's reflection lunged for mine. I flinched, half expecting to feel the impact, but didn't. Rachel's reflection slid around mine and yanked my knife from its sheath.

My hand went instinctively for the same knife, and closed on empty air.

Rachel tried again to disintegrate me. I was so distracted I barely managed to deflect it. I had no idea what was going on anymore. I'm used to knowing how to handle threats, but I didn't know how to handle this.

Dimly, I was aware of Rachel talking to Shireen. "Is he even paying attention?"

"I told you, something's here! You have to get out!"

The mirror Rachel looked at me through the glass. Our eyes met and a secretive smile touched her lips; she held up my knife, the blade glinting in the light. Then she turned her gaze towards Rachel.

"Hey," Rachel called to the jinn. "How about you do something useful for once and—"

The mirror Rachel lifted the knife out in front of her, clasped in a double-handed grip, blade down, and drove it into her own stomach.

Rachel's words cut off in a scream. She doubled over, clutching her belly, then looked up at me in pain and shock. There was blood on her fingers.

The mirror Rachel drove the blade into her stomach again and again. Each time she wrenched the knife out, it left a bleeding wound, but she didn't react. For all the pain she showed, she might have been stabbing a plank of wood. Her eyes were locked onto her counterpart. The real Rachel cried out and staggered as the knife went in.

"Stop it!" Shireen screamed at me. "*Stop it!*"

"I'm not doing anything," I snapped.

The mirror Rachel looked at her original, head tilted, and drove the dagger into her thigh. Rachel screamed again as her leg gave way beneath her. She collapsed to the stone floor.

"Make it stop!" Shireen yelled at me. She looked around wildly, then her gaze turned towards her reflection. "Rachel!" she called. "The mirror! It's the mirror!"

Rachel twisted around from where she lay. Within the mirror, Rachel's reflection looked back at her. Something seemed to alter in Elsewhere, the surroundings changing with a click, and Rachel's eyes widened as she finally saw what I did.

The two Rachels looked at each other through the mirror. The mirror Rachel smiled.

Rachel's face twisted in rage. She sent another disintegration ray into the mirror, then when that didn't work, lashed it with a whip of sea-green energy. She followed that up with a water blast, then a spray of acid, then some sort of cutting effect I didn't recognise. Spell after spell hit the mirror, each of them powerful enough to kill a man in an instant.

The mirror soaked them all up. Rachel might as well have been hitting thin air.

The light from the last spell faded to reveal Rachel's reflection standing on the other side of the mirror, untouched. She was still smiling. She lifted up my knife, turning the blade to show the blood on it.

The anger in Rachel's eyes began to turn to fear.

"Alex!" Shireen shouted. "Make it stop!"

"I told you," I said, not looking at her. I couldn't take my eyes off Rachel. "It's not me."

"Then open a gate! Take her out of Elsewhere! You can do that, I know you can!"

The mirror Rachel looked down at Rachel, then opened her mouth very wide, her jaw gaping.

"No," Rachel muttered. She held up a hand, sea-green light glowing around it, but there was nothing to strike at. All of her deadly battle-magic was useless. The light around her hand winked out.

The mirror Rachel reached into her open mouth with her free hand. She gripped her tongue between thumb and forefinger.

"No," Rachel said, her voice rising. "No!"

The mirror Rachel raised my knife. Metal glinted as she pointed it down towards her mouth.

"Shireen!" Rachel screamed.

"Alex!" Shireen screamed desperately. "Please!"

I hesitated, looking at Rachel. Just for a second I felt the urge to help.

Then I thought about what had happened only last month, when Crystal had controlled my body and forced me to beat Anne until Anne had snapped. I remembered how I'd been left on the floor, crippled and helpless, just as Rachel was now, and how Rachel had laughed at my tears, her eyes bright with happiness.

The urge to help died.

The mirror Rachel brought the knife down, stabbing through her tongue and pinning it to the floor of her mouth.

Rachel gave a horrible choking scream. The mirror Rachel dragged the knife out, blood welling up. Rachel clutched her face and threw her head from side to side in agony, red droplets spattering on the floor.

"Rachel!" Shireen screamed and ran to Rachel's side. She tried to pick Rachel up, cradle her in her arms, but Rachel thrashed wildly, hitting Shireen in the face and knocking her flat. Rachel managed to pull herself up onto one knee, looked up at the mirror to see that her reflection was still standing. The lower half of her reflection's face was a mask of blood, but its eyes were still fixed on Rachel.

It was holding my knife against its neck.

Rachel stared back at her image, then slowly, she turned to face me. The bloody mess of her jaw matched the image behind her. Her eyes met mine, and for once there was no anger there, only fear. She tried to speak through her mangled tongue but the words were incomprehensible.

I was still looking into Rachel's eyes when her reflection cut her throat.

A horrible wound opened up across Rachel's neck, starting below one ear and going all the way around to the other, the skin slicing and tearing like a paper bag. Blood spurted from the arteries, and the trachea gaped open. Rachel convulsed and collapsed, making a wet gargling sound.

"NO!" Shireen screamed. Again she ran to Rachel's side and again she was knocked away. Rachel was thrashing wildly, blood spurting out to pool around her. Shireen looked around desperately and ran to me. "Help her!" she screamed. She beat at my chest with her fists. "Alex, you bastard! Do something!"

I looked back at Shireen coldly and stood my ground.

Rachel died slowly and horribly. She thrashed and clawed, but as the blood gushed out, her movements became slow and sluggish. At last her hands clutched at the stone a final time and then went still. Her head fell to one side and her eyes began to glaze. Her chest rose and fell more and more slowly until it stopped.

The instant that it did, the wisps of light around Rachel brightened tenfold. Physical bodies of any kind don't last long in Elsewhere. A living creature can hold together for a while—a dead one can't. Rachel's corpse dissolved from the outside in, the hair and fingers going first and the rest following, the body coming apart into flaring particles in an eerie imitation of the disintegration magic she'd used on so many other people. From start to finish it took less than ten seconds. A last few wisps of light trailed upwards, then faded.

Rachel was gone.

Shireen was left alone, staring at the empty patch on the floor. Even Rachel's blood was gone. "You . . ." she began, and trailed off.

"I'm sorry," I said quietly.

Shireen shook her head.

"I didn't want it to end like this," I said. "But I just couldn't afford to let her keep trying to kill me every time I turned my back."

"Stop it," Shireen said softly.

"I gave her as many chances as—"

"Stop it," Shireen said. "Stop talking!" She turned on me. "Do you know what you've done?"

I looked at her silently.

"When Rachel Harvested me, she took a piece of me," Shireen said. "That was *me*!"

I sighed. Suddenly I felt very old and very tired. "I know."

"I told you to redeem her! That was what I was waiting for, all these years! I *helped* you, because I thought you were going to help *her*! And you do *this*?"

"She chose the other way. I'm sorry."

"*She* chose the other way? You think this was *her*? You sound like—"

Shireen cut off. She lifted a hand, staring at it. For a moment I couldn't see what was wrong, then I realised that I could make out the outlines of her chest through her fingers. Shireen was fading. She stared at her hand a moment longer, then her eyes rose slowly to me. "Oh, my God," she said softly. "All this time, I never saw it."

"Saw what?"

"Richard set us against each other," Shireen said. "He

wanted to see who'd be the last one. I thought it was over, but it wasn't!" Her voice rose. "It was you! First you killed Tobruk, then you killed Rachel, now you've killed me! I thought it was Rachel that was Richard's Chosen. But it was *you*!"

My heart went cold. I couldn't answer.

"It was you!" Shireen laughed wildly. She was transparent now, the walls and floor clearly visible behind her. "All this time, I thought I was helping you save her, and you end up taking her place! Well, enjoy it, Alex! You're the last one, so enjoy it! You finally get what you wanted! You finally get . . ."

Shireen faded away. Her words lingered a little longer, echoing, before dying away.

The jinn had watched the entire exchange from the edge of the room. Now it stepped back, fading into shadow. Its shape merged with the darkness and it too was gone.

Wisps of light were rising from my skin, dangerously bright. I stared down at the space where Shireen had been, then with an effort tore my eyes away to make a gateway back to the physical world. But before I did I took one last look at the mirror.

Rachel's reflection was still standing there, still bearing the same horrific wounds, still holding my knife. She met my eyes through the mirror, lifted her free hand, and waved her bloodstained fingers with a secret smile.

A thrill of terror went through me. I turned and fled.

। । । । । । । । ।

Cinder was waiting for me in the chapel, standing in the centre of the room. He was favouring one leg and arm, but otherwise showed no sign of injury. As I walked in through the archway he looked at me in silent question.

I came to a stop and looked back at him.

We stood facing each other for a long moment, then

Cinder turned and walked away. His magelight followed as he climbed the stairs, leaving me alone in the dark.

As the sound of his footsteps faded, a bolt of pain shot through my right arm, making me gasp. I staggered to the wall, leaning against it for support. It was too dark to see, but as I slid my left arm inside my clothes, my fingers felt the cool, too-smooth material of the fateweaver above my bicep. There were only a couple of inches of flesh left below my shoulder.

I put my back against the wall, slid down to a sitting position, then leant my head back against the stone and closed my eyes. I needed to visit the shadow realms that Karyos had marked out for me. I needed to prepare for the Council, and for Richard, and for Anne. But right now I wanted to sit, and remember the apprentice I'd once been.

chapter 10

"But the interior defences are another story," Chalice finished. "And those are likely to be the most important."

"That's fine," I said. It was Monday and we were in the same park in which I'd met Cinder, shielded by the greenery. I was leaning against a tree, flipping through the folder that Chalice had handed me. "It's the location I'm most concerned about. You're sure this is his primary base of operations?"

"As sure as I can be," Chalice said. "It's very likely that he also has a personal bubble or shadow realm that he keeps for private use. But this is definitely his primary base. There's too much traffic for it to be anything else."

"Good."

There was a pause. "You don't need to worry," I said without looking up. "The Council aren't tracking me. At least not at the moment."

"You may say that," Chalice said, "but that doesn't change the fact that right now you're one of the most wanted mages in Britain. Even Crystal wasn't this high priority a target."

"Crystal's dead."

"Really?"

I flipped another page. "Anne killed her a few weeks back."

Chalice is slim and a little shorter than average, with light brown skin. She has a graceful, composed manner, but she'd seemed uncomfortable from the start of this meeting. Her next words confirmed why.

"Verus, I haven't asked you any questions about why you wanted this information," Chalice said. "However . . . there really aren't all that many possible explanations."

I closed the folder and looked up. "Is this the kind of thing you're uncomfortable with?"

"Frankly, yes," Chalice said. "Back when I did that research on Lightbringer and Zilean, I thought it was a one-off. I wasn't expecting you to make a habit of it."

"Are you concerned I might come after you?"

Chalice paused, her dark eyes weighing me. "No," she said at last. "But there *will* be consequences."

"I understand," I said. What Chalice was leaving unsaid was that I was running out of credit. This was the second such favour she'd done for me in a short time, and she wanted something back. I tapped the folder against my leg, thinking. "From some of the things you've said, you've made it sound as if you care about the way this country works. There are things you'd like to see happen, and things you'd like to avoid."

"Yes . . ."

"How interested would you be in politics?"

"In what sense?"

I shrugged. "For all their talk, the Council hasn't actually gotten around to revoking that law about having a Dark mage on the Junior Council. Once all this is over, they'll need one, and that person'll need an aide."

Chalice looked taken aback.

"Have a think about it," I said. "If not, we can work something out."

"I . . . will," Chalice said slowly. She started to turn away, then paused. "You've changed a great deal."

"A lot of people have been telling me that."

Chalice nodded and left.

       ı ı ı ı ı ı ı ı ı

My conversation with Talisid had taken place on Saturday. Nailing down a time and place for the exchange took far too long, but I was finally able to get him to agree to meet at the shadow realm of my choosing on Tuesday noon.

The delay left me tense and on edge. I needed the time—I had a lot of things to set up—but the clock was ticking and everything was taking longer than I'd hoped. When I first thought up this plan, I'd figured that if things went wrong, I could always back off and try again. Now, I wasn't so sure. If I didn't pull this off, I might not be able to do it at all.

Tuesday dawned bright and clear. I went to London to make final preparations.

       ı ı ı ı ı ı ı ı ı

"All right," I told November. "Mike and speakers should be connected. Give it a try."

"Testing, testing," November said, his voice sounding through the speakers. "Feedback is good. I believe everything's operational."

"Good," I said, managing not to roll my eyes. For someone who communicated largely through radio signals and the internet, November was absurdly picky about audio equipment. I suppose if the only ears I had were electronic ones, I'd have high standards too. "The rent on this flat is paid through the next three months, and you've got the bill accounts. There shouldn't be anyone coming to the address, but if there is, get in touch."

"Yes, well . . . ," November said. "About that. I'm not quite sure how to say this . . ."

"You're wondering what you're going to do if I end up dead," I finished.

"Well, yes. I mean, this operation of yours does have a disturbingly large number of potential points of failure."

"It seems that way to you because you're used to planning everything in detail," I said. "I'm a lot more used to what you might call short-range adaptation."

"It still seems inadvisable."

"You're welcome to come along."

"No, no, no," November said hastily. "That last time was more than enough."

"Anyway, your connection should be good enough for today," I said. "Your radio reception's probably more limited than you're used to, but I can't really set up an antenna forest on a south London flat without drawing the wrong kind of attention."

"I was hoping for a proper array, but . . . maybe another time," November said. "Actually . . . this might sound strange, but would you mind using that mental communication technique rather than audio signals?"

"I thought you wanted a proper microphone. You were complaining constantly about the one you had in the Hollow."

"It *was* terrible," November said, "but I have to admit, since I've been introduced to your telepathy, I've been realising how much I lose when I have to rely on voice analysis. The mental communication you use is so much richer. I'm starting to understand why humans prefer to speak face-to-face."

"Hmm," I said, and reached out through the dreamstone. *Better?*

I do think I prefer it, yes, November said. *You're quite sure you're going through with this plan?*

Sure as I can be.

Well . . . in that case, please do be careful.

I smiled. *Nice of you to say.*

I don't mean to take liberties, November said hurriedly. *But it's rather nice having a human mage willing to show me a minimum of consideration.*

Don't worry, I'm not going to be dying today, I said. Next week was another story. *But I'll give you Luna's contact details just in case. She's a good person for you to get to know if you want another contact.*

Actually, I already have two phone numbers for her.

I rolled my eyes. Freaking Levistus. *Time to move.*

I walked outside and took out my phone. The flat I'd rented for November was in south Lewisham, and was about as back-end-of-nowhere as I'd been able to find. No one moved on the street as I leant against the wall and dialled a number. It rang twice before being answered. "Hello," Morden said in his calm voice.

"Ready," I told him.

"Time window?"

"Best guess, six to ten hours depending on level of paranoia," I said. "But I should be able to give you at least two hours on the other end."

"Sufficient," Morden said. He hung up.

I put the phone away and let out a long breath. "All right," I said to the empty street. "Let's do this."

⁙⁙⁙⁙⁙

I stepped through into the shadow realm, and let the gate close behind me.

Karyos had directed me to many shadow realms which fit my requirements to a greater or lesser extent, and the one I'd eventually selected was called Hyperborea. Ac-

cording to legend, Hyperborea was supposed to be a
mythical land of perfect beauty. Either whoever had
named this shadow realm had thought he was being
funny, or something had gone very, very wrong, because
the place was a wasteland of sand and barren soil. A dusty
haze hung in the air, thickening as it approached the
edges of the shadow realm until it became opaque at the
borders. A pale yellow sun gave little heat. There were
no trees, no plants, and not so much as a rock formation
to break the monotony of the level sands. It wasn't hard to
see why no one had moved in.

The Council wasn't here, which was good news. I'd
been careful not to give them any hints to the location,
and I'd path-walked extensively just to make sure, but it
was still reassuring. I gave the perimeter a quick circuit,
then took out my communicator to call Talisid.

Talisid answered right on time. "Mage Verus."

"Talisid," I said. "Are you and your escorts ready?"

"We are."

"The exchange will be made in the shadow realm of
Hyperborea," I said. I gave the real-world mirror location
and the information required to find it. "I'll be within the
deep shadow realm accessible from within. The access
point is at the centre."

"A deep shadow realm?"

"Correct."

I could tell that Talisid was frowning. "Our agreement
did not mention a deep shadow realm."

"We agreed on a shadow realm of my choosing. This
is the one of my choosing."

"Can I ask why you've chosen such a remote location?"

"Because I don't trust you very much," I said. "Go
check with your bosses if you like, but I'm not moving."

There was a long pause. I was ready to argue if I had
to, but I was pretty sure Talisid would accept it. Sure
enough, in a couple of minutes, his voice spoke from the

communicator. "We are . . . provisionally . . . willing to accept this location. However, we will need additional time to verify its security."

"How long?"

"Two hours."

That was actually better than I'd hoped for. "Fine. Just remember, three people including you. I see more than that, the deal's off."

"I understand. Who are your escorts?"

"You mean, is Anne with me?" I asked. "Yes. Whether you'll see her is another question, but trust me, she'll be watching. I'll be seeing you soon." I broke the connection.

* * *

Two hours passed. Hyperborea stayed barren and empty, but it wasn't long before the futures became crowded with signs of Council mages sniffing around. As the deadline approached, I saw the future of a gate opening into Hyperborea, clear and steady. Three people would be coming through: Talisid, and two security men. They would take a total of one minute to enter the shadow realm: Talisid would arrive thirty seconds behind the first man, and thirty seconds ahead of the second.

I nodded. All as expected. I focused on my dreamstone, then used it to open a gateway into the deep shadow realm.

* * *

The deep shadow realm was coloured in shades of purple, lavender and violet and mauve. White lights shone from invisible sources far above, illuminating spiralling ramps and high platforms. The air was hazy, and smelt odourless and dry. The place felt alien but familiar; it hadn't changed in the two years since my last visit. Of course, it was only two years to me. In this place, it would have been a lot more.

I didn't let the gate close behind me. Instead, the instant my foot touched the ground, I broke into a run, heading for one of the tunnels leading out of the central chamber. I could feel the strain of holding the gate open mount quickly, and as I reached the tunnel, the pressure became unbearable. I let go and felt the gate snap closed. I would have maybe half a minute before the two realms fell out of sync, at which point Talisid would arrive.

At which point things would get complicated.

I'd spent a long time setting this up, and part of the reason it had taken me so long was to make sure that it wouldn't be at all obvious what was really going on. So I should probably take a moment to explain.

Deep shadow realms are similar to shadow realms: small pocket realities that can only be accessed via gate magic. They differ from shadow realms in several ways. The first big difference is that deep shadow realms can only be accessed via other shadow realms, and the paths by which you can reach them shift. When I'd first visited this deep shadow realm, the only way to reach it had been via the Hollow. That path had since broken. This meant that for the Council mages to reach me, they'd have to go from our world, to Hyperborea, to here. And likewise, to get back home, I'd have to go through Hyperborea first.

The second thing about deep shadow realms is that their laws of reality can be very different from ours. Some have variable gravity, or mutable terrain. This particular deep shadow realm had an altered flow of time: an hour spent here was the equivalent of days or weeks in our world. The exact ratio waxed and waned, depending on how metaphysically "close" the deep shadow realm was. At the moment, based on my tests, the ratio was around 70:1, meaning that for each minute I spent in here, an hour and ten minutes would elapse at home.

Hence why I'd been in such a hurry to get away from the entry chamber. The Council doesn't have any great expertise with deep shadow realms, and Talisid and the rest of the Council team would certainly take precautions before entering. But the time dilation meant that from my perspective, even the most exhaustive checks would be finished very fast. It was hard to use my divination here, but my best guess was that I had a minute at most.

Gate spells briefly equalised the passage of time between the two realms, but not for long. Once Talisid and his group stepped through, the ratio would snap back, and time would continue passing seventy times faster than in our world. Talisid and the others shouldn't notice anything, at least not until they got back. I hadn't.

The deep shadow realm felt strange, alien. My divination showed me flashes of futures, chaotic and bizarre. It would be dangerous to stay here for long, dangerous to draw the attention of whatever inhabited this place. I could feel the dreamstone stirring as I ran, pulsing to some inaudible frequency. It was here that I'd found the crystal, taking it from a larger outgrowth. There had been other things there too, ones that *weren't* crystals, who had worn faces and spoken to me. The experience had shaken me, and I'd walked away intending never to come back. It was only a year later that a chance remark of Arachne's had set me thinking about a way to use the time dilation to my advantage.

I'd come up with something that I was pretty sure would work, but it was dependent on two things. First, I was betting that this time, the Council wasn't going to underestimate me or Anne. And second, I was betting that they really, *really* wanted to get rid of us.

From behind me, I felt the pulse of gate magic. I slowed down and took out my communicator. "Talisid," I said once I'd caught my breath. "You took your time."

"We had to take precautions," Talisid replied.

"Yes," I said, "I noticed it took a whole minute for you to go through the gate into Hyperborea."

"As I said. Precautions."

"So I see."

I'd arrived in a small, curving corridor. From here I'd be able to use the dreamstone to gate back to Hyperborea, but if I did that now, there was too high a chance that I'd be detected. I needed a better head start. I waited, looking down at the communicator, feeling the futures flicker.

"So," Talisid said. "Are you ready?"

"For what?"

"To make the trade."

"Oh, right," I said. "Ready as you are." I paused. "Why did you agree to that last demand, Talisid?"

"I'm sorry?"

"For me to be put back on the Junior Council."

"I'm not sure what you mean."

"A truce was on the table," I said. "Maybe. But getting my seat back? After what happened with Sal Sarque? Levistus would never agree to that. Bahamus would never agree to that. Neither would Alma, neither would Druss."

"I am not fully privy to Senior Council discussions, but regardless of how they came to it, they have agreed on this exchange."

"Yes," I said. "An exchange that would put me and Anne and Levistus's synthetic intelligence all in the same place at the same time."

"Verus, I understand that you have reason to be cautious," Talisid said. "But we've abided by all the terms of our agreement. I even elected to bring two members of the Council security forces, rather than Keepers, in a show of good faith."

"I'd say you brought considerably more than two people."

Through the communicator, I heard Talisid sigh. "I brought two, Verus. Only two. I know you're using your divination magic to watch us. Go ahead and observe. If you like, have Mage Walker employ her lifesight. No matter what spells you employ, what sensory magic you use, they'll tell you the same thing. There are only three of us here."

"I already used my divination," I said. "Back when you entered Hyperborea. And you're right. As far as I could see, there were only three of you."

"So we're agreed?"

"Not quite," I said. "Why did you hold the gate open for one minute?"

"As I said, we were ensuring that it was safe."

"So, funny story," I said. "Remember back when I was a journeyman Keeper? None of the other Keepers were willing to work with me, so I had nothing to do but sit in my office all day. So one of the things I did to pass the time was read. I read the whole Order of the Star doctrine manual cover to cover."

"Good grief, really? Even most Keepers don't read that thing."

"It *was* pretty boring. But it was interesting seeing where a lot of Council habits come from. Like, you know how Keepers will send someone through a gate the instant it opens? If it's dangerous, they might send a security man first, but they always follow through right after. It turns out that the doctrine manual says that Council operatives should make a point of keeping gate exposure as low as possible. And it's a funny thing, but everyone in the Council follows it without thinking. From open to close, they usually keep a gate running no more than fifteen seconds."

"I . . . suppose they do."

"You hid all those people very well," I said conversationally. "You'll have to tell me how you did it sometime. I'm guessing a combination of illusion and divination. Divination to lay a false future, and illusion to conceal them every other way. Illusionists can do a lot, can't they? They can make a subject invisible, hide the sounds they make, even conceal them from exotic senses like thermographic imaging or lifesight. But no matter how good they are, they can't hide the amount of time it takes to send that many people through a gate."

"You're being paranoid, Verus," Talisid said. But his voice had changed.

"Am I?" I said, and made an educated guess. "Then what was that signal you made just now?"

There was a second's pause.

Then *dozens* of magical signatures lit up from the room I'd just left. Elemental magic, air and earth and fire with the signature of utility spells, space and time magic flashes, barriers and protections, wards spreading outwards. The Council had taken the bait in jaws of steel.

A dozen voices spoke at the same time through the communicator. "—spread out, spread—"

"Alpha team, perimeter!"

"Wards up NOW, I want wards—"

"Clear, cle—!"

The light on the focus winked out and the voices cut off.

I was already working on my gate, using the dreamstone to weave the fabric of Elsewhere to join the deep shadow realm back to Hyperborea. The Council's search ring was expanding fast, but I'd known what was coming and they hadn't. The gate opened, and I stepped through into Hyperborea.

The hiss of Hyperborea's desert wind was very loud after the silence of the deep shadow realm. I took out my phone and checked the time. Excluding sync time, I'd been in there with the Council team for . . . call it four and a half minutes. Out here, it had been about five and a half hours.

It wouldn't take Talisid's team long to figure out that I was gone. But *not long* was going to have a very different meaning for them than for me.

Movement in the futures caught my attention and I slipped my phone back into my pocket. Time to deal with the rearguard.

Shapes emerged out of the desert haze, two, five, a dozen. There was a large Council security force in full battle gear, wearing body armour and holding submachine guns. The guns rose up to point in my direction as I came into view and didn't come down. Two unarmoured figures walked at the centre of the squad: mages. There was a man, tall and middle-aged, and a stocky woman with a mouth full of chewing gum. They slowed as they saw me.

"Avenor," I said. "Saffron." I kept my tone courteous. If there's a good chance you're going to have to kill someone, you should at least be polite about it.

Avenor and Saffron halted, their eyes shifting from me to behind me. They looked on edge, and it wasn't hard to guess why. They would have heard Talisid's team go in, then settled down to wait, expecting to be here for no more than ten or twenty minutes. Instead they'd been left alone for over five hours.

"Mage Verus," Avenor said cautiously.

I looked at the security men. "Sergeant Little," I said. "It's been a while. Nowy, Peterson, good to see you as well."

The men watched me warily. They didn't lower their guns, but from looking at the futures, I could tell they weren't about to fire. I'd spent a long time leading combat missions as a Junior Councilman. Half of these men knew me personally, and the other half by reputation. From their body language and the shape of the futures, I knew they really didn't want to get into a fight.

"Where's Talisid?" Avenor said.

I raised my eyes. "Did you lose contact? Your communicator stopped working as soon as that gate closed behind him, maybe?"

Avenor watched me closely.

"Awkward," I said. "Well, it's been nice to catch up, but I'm afraid I have to go."

"We'd prefer you didn't."

"I wasn't asking."

Avenor's voice was hard. "Until your agreement with the Council is concluded, you are still a wanted fugitive under Council law. Attempt to leave and you will be placed under arrest."

I looked straight at Avenor and spoke softly and clearly. "Talisid's entire strike force just tried that and failed. You think you're going to stop me with what you've got here?"

Avenor went very still. I felt a couple of soldiers take a step back. Avenor's eyes flicked past my shoulder, and I knew what he was thinking. He was hoping that Talisid's reinforcements would appear, and was starting to realise that they wouldn't.

Saffron was less hesitant. "You're under arrest."

I looked back at her.

Saffron turned to glare at the security men. "Sergeant! Have your troops arrest that man."

There was a dead silence, broken only by the whine of the wind. Several of the Council security men looked at each other.

"Sergeant!" Saffron shouted. "Little, or whatever your name was!"

Little nodded to her cautiously. "Keeper."

"I gave you a direct order! *Arrest that man!*"

"Keeper Saffron," Little said respectfully. "I feel that in this particular case this would be an inadvisable way to commit my men."

"I don't give a shit what you feel!" Saffron turned, addressing the men. "Arrest him now! Shoot him if you have to!"

The security men looked at her, at me, at each other. Then one of them lowered his gun. Two more glanced at him and followed suit. One by one the barrels descended to point down at the sand, until none were aiming at me.

Saffron stared, apparently lost for words.

"What'll it be, Avenor?" I asked. "By the way, very shortly you're going to be getting an urgent message from the Council. I'd suggest that you and your security team would be much better served by responding to that message than by getting yourselves killed in an attack on me. But it's your call."

Avenor looked from side to side. None of the men met his eyes, and the last futures in which he tried an attack faded away. He looked back at me, face hard. "This isn't over."

I let Avenor have the last word. With a nod to him and Saffron, I walked past. Both mages and the security men watched as I walked through the crowd, out through the other side, and disappeared into the desert haze. No one tried to stop me.

        ||||||||

Once I was clear of the shadow realm, I made a short call to Morden. Then I went to the Hollow to gear up.

For the meeting with Talisid, I'd deliberately gone in underequipped. It was all but certain that they'd had a diviner or some other mage with a way of getting a look at me, and I'd been doing my best to lull their suspicions. That wasn't a concern anymore, and I loaded for bear. I took my armour, my dreamstone, and my old MP7, as well as my usual dispel focus. A combat knife and handgun rounded out my weapons, and for defence I added a mind shield, an aquamarine in the shape of a teardrop that hung around my neck. It was the best mental defence focus I'd been able to get my hands on, and for some years now I'd had it stored away, just waiting for the right opportunity. Now I'd see if it was worth what I'd paid for it. I added my usual collection of miscellaneous tools and one-shots, then gated to the Heath, at the old entrance to Arachne's lair.

I arrived as the sun was setting behind the western hills. Gleams of sunlight penetrated the trees, casting long black shadows that stretched away without end. The air was warm, but the atmosphere was curiously hushed; a few voices were carried on the wind, but not many. The summer evening was quiet and still.

The ravine that had once led to Arachne's lair was deserted. The tunnel leading down into the earth had been sealed, and the spells that had opened and closed it were gone. If you didn't know better, it looked like just a mound of earth. There were no guards or alarms: the place had been looted when the Council had raided it, and apparently they'd decided they were done with the place. With no one living there and nothing valuable to find, it would probably be abandoned. Over the years, fewer and fewer would have any reason to visit, until someday, in fifty or a hundred years, no one would remember it at all. Men and women would walk their dogs, and children would play, not knowing that a cavern complex lay beneath their feet.

Maybe Arachne would return sometime around then. It was a nice thought. I wouldn't be around to see it.

I sat on a fallen tree and waited. Birdsong carried on the evening air. From far above, I heard the distant roar of an airliner, heading westwards.

Soft footsteps sounded, shoes on earth. "This," Anne said, "had better be good."

I turned to see Anne half-lit beside one of the trees. Spatters of sunlight fell across her bare arms and legs, swallowed up by the black of her dress. Her expression was shadowed, but didn't look welcoming. "Sorry about the wait," I told her.

"I *hate* waiting." Anne took a step forward into brighter light. "You made me wait *five hours*."

"I told you my best estimate was four to eight, and I explained why."

"No, you didn't. You ran off some random crap about deep shadow realms and I stopped listening. Now how about you go back to explaining why I've been hanging around these woods all day?"

"If you'd bothered to listen the *last* time I explained," I said, "you would have had to wait an hour or two at the most. And if you'd stopped being so paranoid and just given me a phone number, you wouldn't have had to wait even that long. The reason it's taken this long is that I had to wait for the Council to—"

"Bored."

"Okay, let's try this another way. It took five hours because the time flow—"

"Bored."

"Do you want me to explain this, or not?"

"Too many words." Anne made a spinning motion with one finger. "TLDR."

"Okay," I said. "I'll explain this in terms that are simple enough for your attention span. What do you think we're here to do?"

"You want me to kill Levistus."

"And as soon as we go after Levistus, the Council is going to send a response team to kill *us*. A response team that's going to have their best combat mages and their best weapons. Right now, that response team is stuck in a deep shadow realm for the next few hours. We're going to kill Levistus before they get out. Clear?"

"See, you should have explained it like that the first time." Anne folded her arms. "What's stopping them sending more?"

"The Council's first priority is to protect itself," I said. "Right now, they think there's an attack being launched against the War Rooms." Morden was seeing to that. It wouldn't be a very thorough feint, but it wouldn't have to

be—the Council would be in a state of maximum paranoia after losing contact with Talisid. "They have enough
reserves left to defend the War Rooms against a full attack from Richard's cabal, and they have enough reserves
left to send a strike force to crush us. They don't have
enough to do both."

"And what if they pick Option B?"

I shrugged. "What's life without a little risk?" I held
out a hand. "Coming?"

Anne looked back at me, then a smile flashed across
her face. "You know, I've been waiting for you to do that
for a *really* long time." She jumped lightly across the ravine, then strode up to me, the sunbeams casting her in
alternating dark and light. "Let's do this."

I gave Anne a nod. Together, we walked away.

chapter 11

You can tell a lot about a mage by where they live. Some live in little terraced houses in the suburbs. Some live in mansions out in the country. Others live in places that are so well hidden you'll never see them at all. Levistus's house and base of operations was a house on a street in London called Kensington Palace Gardens.

Calling Kensington Palace Gardens rich is like saying that Heathrow Airport is big. It's true, but doesn't explain the scale. Let's say you live in the U.S. or the U.K. or some other Western country, and let's say you work full-time earning an average sort of salary. If you managed to save fifty percent of that pretax salary, then the amount of time it would take you to save enough money to buy a house on Kensington Palace Gardens is longer than the amount of time between today and the birth of Christ. If you decided to get the money by playing the lottery, you'd have to win the U.K. national jackpot five times running to get even halfway there. The people who live on that street are the sort who buy Ferraris without noticing the difference in their bank balance.

So I have to admit, I got a particular satisfaction out of watching Anne blow Levistus's front door into a thousand pieces.

Wooden splinters went skittering across the floor. The doors had been warded against scrying, three or four different types of sensory magic, and against any attempt to pick or bypass the lock. They hadn't been warded against overwhelming force. Anne and I came through side by side and scanned the front hall, seeing a room floored in white marble, with black veined pillars flanking open doorways, all decorated in an elegant, minimalistic style. A curving staircase disappeared upwards. Running footsteps sounded from several directions, and Anne and I halted.

Men appeared from both sides. They were wearing polished shoes and well-tailored suits, but they were clearly security guards. More interesting to me was the way the lines of their futures moved: they were human, but unnaturally rigid and constrained. I suppose it shouldn't have surprised me that Levistus had mind-controlled guards, but I hadn't expected quite so many. All six of the guards were holding handguns, which they levelled. "Freeze!" one shouted.

Anne stared at the men, eyebrows raised. "Seriously?"

"Stay where you are," one of the men called. "Hands up and get down on your knees."

Anne looked at me. "These guys aren't even worth my time."

I shrugged.

"Second warning," the man announced. "Hands up, now!"

Anne sighed. She raised a hand and clicked her fingers.

Black death streamed in out of the night, flowing around us and into the mansion. There was the flash and bang of gunfire. It wasn't aimed at us. Claws flickered; screams rang out in stereo; blood painted the walls. A bullet hit the chandelier, sending a tinkle of broken glass falling to the marble.

As quickly as it had started, it was over. Six corpses lay on the floor. Spindly figures stood over them, man-sized but thin and inhuman, moving in fits and jerks. These were jann, lesser jinn that Anne could summon. Or that the jinn could. I'd fought against the things, but it was a new experience to have them on my side.

"*This* is what he sends to stop us?" Anne said. "I'm honestly kind of insulted."

"These were just the sentries," I told her. Glass crunched under my feet as I advanced. A jann looked up from where it was crouched over a body, hissed, then flitted away. I heard a scream from deeper in the mansion: the jann had fanned out ahead. I felt a flicker of conscience and ignored it. Gunfire sounded from the first floor, and I sensed the signature of spells; I headed for the stairs.

The stairs led into a big drawing room which had been converted into an office. Desks near the bay windows provided work spaces for the men and women who worked here. Or *had* worked here. Two bodies were shapeless heaps on the carpet: near to them, one jann was dissolving and another was kicking weakly as it died.

A woman was standing behind one of the desks, her face pale and spotted with blood, holding up a focus item like a holy symbol. It was a force magic focus, and it was generating a transparent cylindrical barrier a few feet in radius. Three jann tore at the barrier with their claws. Pressed up behind the woman, a young man was shouting into a communication focus. "—need help now! This is an emergency! We need Keepers here *now*!"

A female voice spoke from the communicator, calm and unemotional. "No Keepers are available to respond at this time. We recommend you withdraw from your present location and await instructions."

"There isn't any time! We need—!" The man heard a gasp from the woman behind him and whirled. He saw me with Anne at my back and brought up something in his other hand.

Anne reacted instantly. Green-black death tore through the barrier as though it were tissue paper, stripped the life and flesh from the bodies of the man and woman, and smashed their remains through the bay window and sent them falling into darkness towards the lawn below.

I wanted to tell Anne that killing them hadn't been necessary, but stopped. She wouldn't care and we didn't have time. "Lifesight readings?" I asked instead.

"Few more on the second and third floors," Anne said, looking upwards at the ceiling and frowning. "No sign of Levistus or Barrayar."

"Hmm." I strode over to the nearest desk and glanced quickly through the papers, searching in both the present and future. "This isn't well guarded enough." A thought struck me. "What can you see down below?"

"You mean the basement? I don't think there's . . ." Anne's eyes widened. "Oh. It's shrouded. How'd you know?"

"It's how the Council builds. Let's go back down. And please stop your jann from going up through the house killing Levistus's maids and cooks."

Anne shrugged.

｜｜｜｜｜｜｜｜｜

I t took us a couple of minutes to find the hidden entrance down to the basement, and another minute to disarm the traps and descend the stairs. Long enough for the defenders to get organised.

The wood-panelled staircase went down a long way before opening up into a wide chamber. It was an entrance hall, but while the one on the ground floor had been sized for a house, this one was sized for a palace. A white-and-black stone floor stretched out to the size of a tennis court, engraved with geometric patterns, and wrought iron staircases wound up to a gallery running around the walls at half the height of the ceiling. Doors at the far end led into what must be the heart of Levistus's operations.

The hallway was crowded with people, and all of them were waiting for us. More security guards were stationed up on the gallery and down on the ground floor, crouched behind bulletproof barriers. Unlike the men above, they were carrying submachine guns. Behind and between the barriers were icecats, graceful and low to the ground, panther-like constructs with wisps of cold rising from their claws.

The next group were the adepts and staff members, and it was clear they weren't here by choice. They were wearing outfits more suited to an office than to a battle, and wielding a highly uneven collection of weapons. They were shooting uneasy glances around them, and seemed unsure whether to huddle together for protection or to scatter.

And finally there were the mages. There were three, standing at the very back of the formation, evenly spaced across the hall. One was a man I'd never seen before, tall and slim with a refined cast to his features: he watched us both with an expression of boredom. The second was Barrayar. He was wearing his expensive business suit and looked as if he'd just been interrupted from work and was very irritated about it.

But it was the third mage who caught my attention. She was round-faced and heavyset, her arms and legs thick with fat and muscle. Unlike the first two, her face was blank as she watched me. To my magesight, the pale brown of earth magic glowed around her.

I hadn't expected Caldera. I'd expected her to have gone with Talisid's hit team; how she'd ended up here instead I didn't know. The last two times I fought Caldera, I'd been able to disengage and avoid her. There'd be no avoiding her this time.

"Okay," I said to Anne. "*This* is what I'd call well guarded."

Anne and I had come to a stop only a couple of feet from the doorway. A half cylinder of force magic barred us from going any farther, running from floor to ceiling. It didn't block sound—I could hear the breathing and the shuffle of feet of the crowd facing us—but it would take significant power for any intruders to break through. Assuming they had the chance. There was an antipersonnel mine buried in the floor right beneath our feet, and I knew from glancing at the futures that Barrayar was holding the detonator in one hand.

But Barrayar obviously didn't know everything that I could do, or he would have pressed the button already. As soon as I'd detected the explosive, I'd started to work on it with the fateweaver, picking out the futures in which it failed. Behind us, the jann started to sidle into the room, staring at the security guards with hungry eyes.

"Verus," Barrayar said coldly. "You've gone too far this time."

"Hello, Barrayar," I said. "So, that exchange that was supposed to happen today? I didn't like the delegation you sent very much. Thought about sending a strongly worded letter, but figured I might as well tell you in person."

"You know, Talisid had one job," Barrayar said. "I should have known he'd fuck it up. Did he tip you off, or was he just that incompetent?"

"Do you care?"

"I suppose I don't."

"Hey," Anne interrupted. "You two going to kiss, or shall we kick this off?"

Beneath our feet, the mine's electronics failed. It was easier than the ones in Sal Sarque's fortress had been: Levistus hadn't kept this one well maintained. Probably he'd never seriously expected to need it. "You know, I really thought your boss would be here," I told Barrayar. "What's he doing, watching on camera?"

"Whatever you're hoping to achieve, it won't work," Barrayar said. "I'll give you and Miss Walker one chance. Turn around and leave."

"Hey, Barrayar," Anne called. "Just curious. Was it you who signed off on that order for Lightbringer and Zilean to torture me?"

Barrayar looked back at Anne with raised eyebrows. "Is that why you're here?"

"No, I'm going to kill you anyway. It'll just make it a bit more satisfying."

Without changing expression, Barrayar pushed the button on the detonator. The faint *click* was loud in the silence. There was a moment's expectant pause.

I spoke into the vacuum. "*Now* you can kick off."

Black energy stabbed from Anne, meeting the force barrier with a *crack* of black lightning. The barrier flickered and died. The jann charged, flowing past and around Anne in a black wave as Levistus's forces opened fire.

Light and sound hammered the entrance hall, a dozen battles and duels breaking out across the room. Fleeting images caught in my memory, fractions of a greater whole. An icecat and a jann hit each other in midair and tumbled to the floor in a whirl of claws and teeth. Fire stabbed down from the gallery on the left, grim men almost invisible behind their weapons, jann falling as they tried to close the distance. Cutting blades of air and force flew the length of the room to shatter against Anne's shield. More jann poured down the stairs, throwing themselves into the meat grinder, drones dying for their queen.

I had only a second to take in the larger battle before I

had to focus on myself. Two icecats charged me as fire tracked in, and I snatched futures from the rushing tide. One icecat was struck mid-leap by a jann; bullets whistled by on my left and right. The second icecat leapt for me, missed, and was pounced on before it could turn.

There were so many enemies that they were blocking each other. I broke into a swerving run, aiming for a doorway on the right side of the hall, firing a burst from my MP7 as I did. A burning red line streaked past my head, carrying the smell of ozone. More security men and one of the icecat handlers tried to bar my way; I wove through the attacks, death waiting in the futures and in the present, snapping off short bursts, only vaguely aware of the men falling away as their futures wisped out. It was a surprise, somehow, to reach the door and realise there were only bodies left to guard it.

A storm of air and force magic drove me to cover. I crouched inside the doorway, my back against the wall as bolts of electricity crackled off the stone. My MP7 was empty and I reloaded, taking a second as I did to scan. The icecats were all crippled or destroyed, along with a good number of the jann. Many of the security men were dead, but on the left side of the hall a tight group had held their ground and were killing any jann that tried to approach.

Anne was duelling the mages. Shadowy black wings seemed to stretch out from her shoulders; things that might have been limbs overlaid her arms. Her eyes were alight, and she fought with a fierce joy. Barrayar and the third mage were engaging her with force and air, but the translucent black threads of the jinn's magic formed a shield that deflected all their attacks. It was the first time I'd had the chance to watch the new Anne going all out, and it was frightening to watch. She had all of her old speed and lethality, with the jinn's power behind it. The jinn's magic didn't seem to follow the rules of most combat spells. What it reminded me of most was death magic, pure destruction and nothing else.

Pounding footsteps sounded from around the corner, and I stepped back as Caldera appeared in the doorway. She aimed a punch at me that would have broken my neck, and I backed into the room. Caldera stalked after me, heavy footfalls ringing on the stone.

The room I was in was a swimming pool. God knows why Levistus had one. The water, tinted blue-green from the pool tiles, stretched out down one side of the room, sculptures and houseplants standing around the other. I backed away into the side of the room where there was space to move, Caldera following.

A young man appeared in the doorway behind Caldera; one of the adepts. He was carrying a wand with a glow of red energy hovering at its tip; he levelled it at me but I'd already moved to place Caldera between us. "Keeper!" he called over the screams and gunfire behind. "Move!"

Caldera didn't take her eyes off me. "Back off."

"Give me a clear shot!"

I raised my MP7 and fired. Caldera moved instantly, trying to block the shots; the adept in the door activated a shield ring. I'd seen both events and compensated accordingly. The first and second shots of the three-round burst deflected off Caldera's hand and the adept's shield; the third blew his brains out.

Caldera whirled, saw the body, then turned on me with her face twisted in rage. She charged and I dropped left, leaving my leg extended. Caldera tripped, sliding on the polished tiles to crash into a display of plants. I turned and waited for her to rise.

Caldera came up, earth and leaves in her hair, breathing heavily. "You murderous piece of *shit*."

"Pot and kettle, Caldera."

Caldera thrust out her hand at the entrance hall behind, where shouts and gunfire mixed with the flash of battle-magic. "You did this! You set it all up!"

"How many times have you come after me?" I said harshly. "Did you expect me to just sit there and take it?"

Caldera lunged. Her arms and limbs were wreathed in earth magic, giving her the toughness of stone and the strength of a bear. I stepped away from her punches, blows like hammers whistling past my head. "I'm here for Levistus," I told her. "Not you."

"I. Don't. Give. A. Shit." Caldera sent a punch with each word.

I stepped back from the blows, putting my back to the swimming pool. "I'm not here for you," I repeated. "But I'll kill you if I have to. First warning."

"Fuck your warnings!"

Caldera tried to slam me into the pool. I ducked, caught her shoulder, twisted in a hip throw. Caldera went over my thigh and into the water with a *boom* of displaced water, sending a wave splashing up over the sides.

I was already moving, crouching by the adept's body. As Caldera broke the surface, floundering and gasping, I scanned the adept's items. The shield ring I discarded at a glance. The wand was more interesting. It was a combat focus that produced some kind of directed energy attack; I didn't recognise the effect but it looked powerful. I clipped it to my belt and strode back into the main hall.

The tempo of the fight had changed while I was gone. All of Anne's jann were dead, but they'd done heavy damage: all the icecats were gone, the adepts were down to a couple of survivors, and the only remaining security men were in a cluster up on the gallery on the far side. Barrayar and the other mage had closed ranks; their shields were overlapping and they were engaged in a furious long-range duel with Anne.

But the biggest change was that Levistus had sent in

reinforcements. There were two giant four-armed gold-and-silver constructs at the far end of the hall, radiating magic and power in equal measure. Mantis golems. One had its feet planted and was spitting golden death at Anne from an energy projector. The second had been advancing towards my door with a heavy tread; as it saw me its energy projector came up and it fired.

No time to think. I acted on instinct, darting forward to the nearest staircase, then up the stairs to the gallery. The golem's energy projector tore fragments from the wall, melted the iron steps just behind my feet. I reached the gallery and sprinted clockwise. The security guards on the opposite side added their fire to the golem's, shots glancing off pillars and striking sparks from the railing. I caught a glimpse of Anne below; Barrayar and the other mage and the golem were battering her shield with attack spells. The roar of gunfire and battle-magic hammered at me from all around.

As I reached the corner of the room I went into a roll, coming up in a kneeling stance with my gun levelled, aiming down the gallery. The knot of security guards had been waiting, but a pillar had blocked their view of me for just long enough and their aim was high. I fired down the length of the gallery, sending three-round bursts as fast as I could pull the trigger. Caught out of cover, the guards were slaughtered. Bullets drilled through flesh until the MP7 clicked empty.

Only one guard was left, half-shielded by a dying man in front of him. His gun sighted on me as I pushed hard at the future I needed; the guard pulled left as he fired and the bullets plucked my sleeve. I closed the distance in five running strides, ducked his panicked blow, hit him in the throat and face. On the floor below, the mantis golem aimed its energy projector: I shoved the guard back against the railing and the energy blast caught him in the back, exploding his body and spattering me with blood.

Down on the lower level, Anne and the two enemy mages were still engaged. Anne was more powerful, but the overlapping air and force shield from the other two mages was deflecting her attacks, and I could see frustration on her face as her death spells were turned away. I scanned the battlefield below, analysed it in a split-second, then grabbed one of the dropped SMGs, clicked it to full-auto, and threw it with an overhand swing.

The gun went flying over the heads of Barrayar and the other mage, and as it did I sorted through the futures, pushing away hundreds, choosing one. The weapon hit the floor and went off, chattering flame. Bullets tore into the shield's weaker side, some breaking through. The other mage staggered, his shield flickering.

Anne struck instantly. Green-and-black death flashed down the hallway, and the other mage died.

My precognition shouted a warning. I looked across to see Caldera in the doorway to the swimming pool, dripping wet and furious. Ignoring Anne, she raised a hand towards me. The gallery cracked and broke under my feet, the metal railing twisting as the stone came rumbling down.

I jumped clear of the avalanche, hitting the floor and rolling as the gallery fell in a cloud of dust and a roar. The mantis golem was lining up another shot, and I sprinted through another doorway and out of sight.

I'd come through into a canteen. White tables dotted the room, with orange-upholstered benches along the walls. Trays and half-eaten food were still laid out. A cloud of dust hung in the air around the doorway, obscuring sight.

I could still hear shouts from the entrance hall, combined with flashes of magic and the sounds of running feet. Caldera had broken off her pursuit—even she wasn't going to run right past Anne in battle mode—but the mantis golem hadn't. It would be on me in another ten seconds. I unclipped the wand from my belt and waited.

Heavy footfalls sent a tremble through the floor, and the mantis golem loomed out of the dust, striding forward before planting its feet and coming to a halt. I studied the construct, watching the solid line of its future shift in response to my actions. The golem was seven feet tall and looked like an enormous insect sculpted in silver and gold, with faceted eyes and triple-jointed legs. The upper two arms held a sword and some sort of stunning weapon; the lower two held the metal energy projector. Mantis golems are enormously strong, and invulnerable to all but the most powerful attack spells. But this wasn't the first time I'd fought one, and I knew their weaknesses. They're slow moving, they're stupid, and those energy projectors they carry are deadly but unstable.

The mantis golem aimed its projector at my chest.

I'd been waiting with the wand aimed. I sent a surge of energy into the focus; its tip glowed red and a beam of scorching red light went down the energy projector's barrel, piercing its inner workings just as it tried to fire.

The projector exploded in a burst of golden light, shards of white-hot metal flying in all directions. I'd closed my eyes against the flash; as I opened them I saw that the middle section of the golem was melted and shredded. Both lower hands had been destroyed; the armour on the abdomen had been burned away to reveal glowing silver veins with deep gouges from the shrapnel.

The golem ignored the horrific damage. It stood still for a moment, momentarily blocked in fulfilling its command, then the futures shifted and it began striding forward, its footsteps sending tremors through the floor, the sword and stun weapon lifted. I studied the golem as it closed in. I could make out the spell powering the golem, chains binding the spirit at the construct's heart. It was enormously complex, energies working in weave and counterbalance. The sword whistled out and I stepped back, still calculating. There were holes in the construct's armour, and a shot would hurt it, but if I wanted a kill . . .

There. A tiny node where several lines of energy met. I didn't understand how it worked or why that spot was the one that mattered, but that's how it is when you're a diviner. I used the fateweaver, sifting through the lines of the construct's future.

The construct attacked again and I dodged, my movements neat and precise. A table came between me and the construct and was crushed to splinters. The sword made a whistling noise as it passed my head; that blade was heavier than any normal sword and one hit would explode my skull like a water balloon. The future I needed drew closer and I set my foot back, getting into position. Duck the sword, step aside from the stun . . . and for an instant, the golem's movements caused the rents in its armour to line up, exposing its core.

I fired the wand, and the scent of ozone filled the air. The golem didn't react, reversing the sword for another strike. I ducked the backswing and fired again, the beam spearing the construct, burning into its heart.

The energy node snapped. Strands of magic lashed as the spell went wild, restraints breaking. The golem shuddered and came to a halt, the light going out of its eyes. *Something* huge and formless seemed to flow out of the construct's legs and down into the earth: I had a fleeting sense of some ancient presence, cold and massive, then it was gone. The golem was a lifeless statue, arms extended and still.

Weakness rippled through me, the wand suddenly feeling like it weighed twenty pounds. There's a reason I don't like these kinds of combat focuses: those three shots had used up too much of my own energy. I clipped it to my belt and strode out of the canteen.

The entrance hall was empty. Bodies of humans and constructs littered the floor, and a haze of dust hung in the air, but there were no traces of the survivors or the other golem. Skirmish battles are fast: my fight with the golem had taken only a minute or two, but that had been more than enough time for the battle to move on. I could hear running footsteps in the distance, but there was no sign of Barrayar or Anne.

At the end of the hall was a pair of closed double doors that looked like they led somewhere important. I started walking, and as I did reached out through the dreamstone. *November.*

Oh! Oh good, you're still—I mean, I'm glad you're well.

What's the status at the War Rooms?

They're restricting official communications to synchronous focuses, November answered, *but I've managed to gather some data. Apparently they're quite agitated. Orders are still to stay on high alert in preparation for an anticipated attack on the War Rooms.*

Levistus getting any reinforcements?

No. Actually, one call I intercepted gave the impression that he's been calling personally. No one seems very keen to help.

I was nearly at the double doors: I looked to see what would happen if I opened them and walked through. *Send the money and notices we discussed to that adept team now.*

. . . Done. I have receipt of transfer.

Good.

The double doors were thick wood, heavy and unlocked. I pushed them open and stepped to one side.

A violet disc of force blurred past, cutting through the

space I'd been occupying a second ago. "Hi, guys," I called from around the wall.

The room beyond the doors was a gate room, designed for entry and exit. The floor was dull metal with a polished sheen. Columns of rough, unworked stone ran from floor to ceiling, illuminated with an eerie green light, and flanking the columns were plain metal walls spaced to allow for gating. At the back, a raised observation gallery ran from wall to wall; the gallery was fronted with one-way glass that made it impossible to see in. At the centre of the room, three mobile barricades had been set up, heavy steel shields reinforced with magic and standing five feet tall.

There were four people in the room: Caldera, and the three adept mercenaries I'd run into at Heron Tower. Caldera and Crash were behind the left and right barricades, while Stickleback and Jumper were behind the back one. I could sense defensive spells designed to deflect ranged attacks coming in from outside. On top of that, the wards that prevented gate and teleportation magic over the mansion were limited within this specific area, meaning that Jumper would be able to use his teleportation abilities just fine.

I stayed behind the wall and waited to see if the four people inside would make a move. They didn't. I knew that Stickleback would attack the instant I poked my head out into the doorway, but until then, it seemed they were willing to wait.

"Not coming out?" I called.

"Why don't you and your pet monster come in?" Caldera called back.

"Anne's not here," I told her. "Far as I can tell, she's chasing Barrayar."

"That's nice."

I smiled to myself. "Let me guess. Planning to camp out till reinforcements arrive?"

"You tell me."

It wasn't a bad plan. The wards made ranged attacks almost impossible. Anyone wanting to force entry would have to advance through the choke point under fire from Stickleback, then fight Crash and Caldera at close range. Anne would still kill them all, but she'd have to work for it.

"Crash," I called. "As I understand it, you're the spokesman for your group."

There was a pause. "What if I am?" Crash said at last. It was the first time I'd heard him speak. For a tough guy, he had quite an educated voice.

I nodded. "I am hereby notifying you that your employment with Councillor Levistus has been terminated, effective immediately, as per section seven of your contract. Authorisation codes have been sent to your contact details as specified. Your outstanding fees have been paid to the account specified in appendix one, including a cancellation fee as per section twelve."

There was a moment's silence. "What?"

"Go ahead and check," I said.

Another pause, then through the futures, I saw Crash pull out a phone. He tapped at the touchscreen, keeping a wary eye on the door.

"What are you doing?" Caldera demanded.

"Any problems?" I asked.

"Our contract's not with you," Crash said.

"Your contract's with the Council, as represented by Levistus. I'm still a member of the Council and authorised to make negotiations in their stead. In any case, the contract doesn't specify who has to deliver notice of termination. Only that they need the proper authorisation codes, which I've supplied."

"You don't seriously expect anyone to buy this," Crash said.

"Put it this way," I said. "You have two options. Option

one is you and your team take the money and leave. The Council won't be happy, but you can point to the fact that you fulfilled the letter of your contract, even if it wasn't in the way they wanted. Option two is you and your team stay and fight against me and Anne, who have, in case you haven't noticed, killed pretty much everyone else in the building. You will lose at least one member of your team and probably more. I don't personally think you're being paid enough to make that worth it, but it's up to you. So. Which is it going to be?"

Silence. I could sense Crash, Stickleback, and Jumper looking at one another. Caldera stared between them. "What are you doing?" she said again, more sharply. "You're not listening to this shit?"

Jumper said something to Crash, and Crash answered, both of them speaking rapid-fire Japanese. Stickleback interjected something, and a quick three-way exchange took place.

"Hey!" Caldera said. "Talk to me!"

Crash looked back at her. "We need to confer." He made a signal. Jumper and Stickleback moved up, closing on his position in a few quick strides. Crash watched my position warily right up until Jumper put his hands on Crash's and Stickleback's shoulders, and the three of them teleported out.

And all of a sudden, Caldera and I were alone.

"Well," I said. I took the sling of the MP7 off my shoulder and walked out into the open. "Looks like it's just the two of us."

Caldera glared at me. "If they come back—"

"You really think they're going to?"

Caldera didn't answer. There was a kind of baffled fury in her eyes. Once again, the ground had been cut out from underneath her, and she didn't know how.

I nodded past Caldera to the glass observation gallery and the door set into the wall underneath. "Levistus is through there. I'd appreciate it if you could let me pass."

"Well, you're shit out of luck then, aren't you?"

"I suggest a compromise," I told her. "You withdraw and call for reinforcements. Once they show up, you can come after me again and we'll carry on where we left off."

"A compromise?"

I shrugged. "Nobody's happy, but nobody's dead."

Caldera stared at me in disbelief. "*Screw you.*"

"Fine," I said. "A contest, then. Just like our old sparring matches. I get one good hit through your defences, you withdraw. If you get one good hit on me, then I will."

"A *contest*? You think that's what this is?"

"I'm trying to—"

"No," Caldera said. "Shut up. You do not get to talk. You and your psycho girlfriend just walked in here and killed everyone in this room. And before that, the two of you helped kill an entire base's worth of Council people, including a member of the Senior Council. And before *that*, the two of you killed *another* base's worth of security at San Vittore. And now you walk up and tell me you want me to withdraw so you can add *another* Senior Council member to your body count, and you *actually have the fucking arrogance to think I'll let you*?"

I looked at Caldera in silence.

"I can't believe I ever sponsored you to the Keepers," Caldera said. "Slate and the rest gave me so much shit for that, but I stuck up for you. I put my neck on the line for you! And you pay me back with *this*?" Caldera snorted in a half laugh. "You are going to go down in history as the worst traitor the Light Council's ever had! And when mages look up the records to find out how you ever made it into the Keepers, they'll find my name as the reason why!"

"I think you should be less worried about the history books and more about the next five minutes."

"Shut up!" Caldera shouted. "I'm sick of how you think this is a joke! Being a Keeper is supposed to matter! The law is supposed to matter! But all you give a shit about is yourself!"

"The law is whatever the Council says it is," I said. "They signed a piece of paper, and I became a criminal. They signed another, and I wasn't. Their whims write the laws; the Keepers enforce it. And at the end of the chain, some unlucky mage or adept gets sentenced to death because a Senior Councillor was able to get four votes instead of three by blackmailing the others with a bunch of sex tapes."

"You sound like every other Dark mage," Caldera said. "You think I don't know about the Council's dirty secrets? I was dealing with this shit back when you were fleecing teenagers for crystal balls. But at least I work for something bigger than myself. For you, all that matters is Alex Verus."

"Working for something bigger than yourself? All the times we hauled off some adept to the cells, or played the heavy, you think that makes it okay?"

"Yeah, I've arrested a lot of adepts," Caldera said. "Mages too. You know what I didn't do?" Her arm shot out towards the corpse-filled hallway. "I didn't go fucking judge-jury-executioner on everyone who got in my way!"

"No," I said contemptuously. "You just threw them in a cell and washed your hands of what happened afterwards. Just following orders, right, Caldera? That way, nothing is ever your fault."

"You know, I'm done talking with you," Caldera said. She stepped back into a combat stance and beckoned. "Bring it."

"I gave you one warning," I said softly. "This is your

second. That's more than I'm in the habit of giving these days."

Caldera spat.

I closed in. Caldera held her ground, watching me narrowly. I made a few attacks, probing. Caldera batted them away but didn't try to counter. She was fighting defensively, not giving any openings.

I'd sparred against Caldera many times, back when we were both Keepers. Once we'd had a chance to get a feel for each other, the matches had usually ended in stalemate. Caldera wasn't quick enough to catch me, and I wasn't strong enough to hurt her. In the end I'd have to back off, or be worn down.

I slipped past Caldera's guard to hit her with a palm strike to the head. The impact stung and jarred my arm; Caldera barely noticed. I withdrew slowly, leaving a clear opening, but again Caldera didn't take it. She just watched, eyes hard and suspicious.

No good. I wasn't going to lure her into a trap. Well, in that case . . .

I focused my magesight on the spells reinforcing Caldera's body. The earth magic flowed through her limbs, sluggish and heavy. In one pocket I carried a slim metal dispel focus. It could break Caldera's protective spells, leave her vulnerable. Trouble was, I'd used that trick before, and Caldera would be expecting it. She'd pull back instantly, giving ground while she rebuilt her spells, and she could do it fast.

Well, I'd give her what she expected, then.

I slid the dispel focus into my left hand, my dagger into my right. I kept them concealed, but Caldera shifted her stance in reaction. I began circling, feinting and sliding, looking for an opening. As I did I began to weave together a future, twining several strands to converge on a single target.

The future grew, strengthened, drew closer. I feinted again and struck.

The dispel focus discharged into Caldera's side. A pulse of countermagic surged through her body and instantly she jumped back, weaving a new set of spells to replace her defences.

I pushed with the fateweaver, the future snapping into place. The spells I'd disrupted went wild, maintaining their pattern but discharging their energies in the wrong way. Surges of strength went through Caldera's muscles, uneven and erratic; her stoneskin magic poured all its energy into hardening parts of her body while leaving others unprotected.

Caldera staggered, almost falling. Her new spells fizzled out; the malfunctioning spells were blocking them. To fix the whole mess she'd have to rebuild it from scratch. I wasn't going to give her that long.

I attacked again and this time Caldera struck hard, trying to drive me away. I ducked the punch and sliced her arm, the blade cutting across an unprotected piece of flesh. Caldera flinched and pulled away. She gave ground, trying to gain herself the chance to rebuild her defences, and I pressed her harder.

My knife stabbed, opening up wounds in Caldera's shoulder and thigh. Her movements had lost their smoothness: they were jerky, almost fearful. It was probably the first time Caldera had ever been cut with a blade; all of a sudden she was discovering that when you aren't invulnerable, knives are scary. I drove her back against one of the rough stone walls, getting in close. Caldera swung a hook; I ducked and the punch smashed chips out of the rock face, and as it did my knife sank into her gut.

Caldera lost her breath in a gasp. I pulled back slightly, watching Caldera put a hand to her lower stomach. It came away red, and she looked up at me in shock.

"Last warning," I said quietly. "Walk away."

Emotions flashed across Caldera's face; shame, fear, rage, others too fleeting to read. The futures jumped wildly. A dozen Calderas stood and fought, walked away, went berserk and attacked, broke down and screamed. Flicker-flicker-flicker . . .

The futures settled. Caldera stared at me in pure hatred. "*Screw you.*"

My face hardened and I moved in.

Though Caldera still had her magic, and though her wounds weren't crippling, what followed was more like an execution than a battle. The stone wall heaved, trying to pull me in, and Caldera swung wildly, her punches still carrying enough force to kill. I evaded, stabbed, stabbed again. Red bloomed on Caldera's shirt and jacket. Caldera tried to tangle my feet and I put my blade through her thigh. The only sound was the panting of breath, and the scuff and thump of footsteps on the tile. Light flashed on my knife, blood dripping to the floor.

Caldera broke away, bleeding from a dozen wounds. I watched her steadily as she pulled herself upright, trying to rally. I'd taken a couple of bruises, no more. Our eyes met and I saw a kind of dawning realisation, then her expression went blank.

I don't know why Caldera went in for that last attack. I think at some level she had to know what was going to happen, the battle experience that had served her for so many years turning on her at the end. Maybe she just didn't know how to do things any other way. Or maybe she was like so many battle-mages, and when it came right down to it, she could never really believe that someone as tough as her could ever lose to someone like me.

I met Caldera's rush with my own. Her strike missed. Mine didn't.

Caldera staggered, turning to me with an odd sort of surprise. Then, slowly, she crumpled to the floor.

I looked down at Caldera. She was still breathing. My

knife was red with her blood, and I looked from her to the blade and back to her again. Seconds stretched out as I hesitated.

Then, from the direction of the entrance hall, I heard the sound of clapping.

I turned to see Anne, strolling towards me unhurriedly. "Nice," she said with a smile. "Very nice."

"What were you doing?" I snapped. I forced my muscles to stay still to stop my hands from shaking. "Sightseeing?"

"Oh, I've been watching for a while," Anne said. "Was tempted to step in, but I figured it wasn't fair if I got to have all the fun." She nodded down at Caldera. "Do you mind?"

I paused, then stepped aside.

"Thanks." Anne crossed the room and knelt at Caldera's side, careless of the spreading blood. "Huh, you really did a number on her. Did you drag it out on purpose?"

"No."

"I would have." Green light glowed around Anne's hand, her life magic weaving through Caldera's body.

"What are you doing?"

Anne rose to her feet, brushing off her hands. "Just first aid."

I looked down and saw that the blood had stopped spreading. "Why? You've never liked her."

"Hey, don't make it sound like it was my fault," Anne said. "She hated me from the first time we met. Tried to hide it with that I'm-an-impartial-Keeper act, but I could tell. And that was *before* she suffocated me."

"Why the act of mercy then?" I asked. "Also, where's Barrayar?"

For answer, Anne clicked her fingers. Four of the summoned jann stalked in from the entrance hall. One of them was carrying Barrayar in its claws, the mage's head and arms hanging limp. I scanned ahead and saw that Barrayar was alive but unconscious.

I looked at Anne, eyes narrowed.

"What?" Anne asked innocently.

"What are you up to?"

"Me?"

Two of the jann stalked past, their eyes resting on me coldly as they passed. They bent down and picked Caldera up, shifting under her weight. "You're taking prisoners now?" I said. "Why?"

"Don't worry about it."

"You telling me that is a *very good reason* to worry about it."

"Oh, relax," Anne said. "People are more useful alive than dead, right? Seems like the sort of thing you'd say." The jann turned and began moving in the direction of the entrance hall, leaving us behind. "Anyway, this is where I get off."

"What?"

"I'm done here. You have fun with Levistus."

"The whole reason I brought you here was *because* of Levistus!"

"And that's my problem how?" Anne gestured to the entrance hall. "Look, I took out most of his private army, plus a mantis golem, plus Barrayar. Oh, and that other mage. What was his name again? Ilmarin? No, that was some other guy." Anne frowned, thinking, then shrugged. "Well, not like it matters. Anyway, I'm sure you can finish up on your own."

"While you do what, take a tea break?"

"Hey, I'm not your bodyguard anymore." Anne turned and walked away after the jann. "You'll be fine. Good luck!"

I stared after Anne's retreating back. She didn't turn to

look at me, and I very briefly considered going after her. But that wasn't what I'd come here to do.

Anne disappeared, leaving me alone. From the look of the futures, I didn't think she was coming back. I picked up my gun and walked forward.

chapter 12

The control centre under Levistus's mansion was a wide, one-storey room, filled with desks and chairs. Computer equipment and magical focuses split the desktop space between them. The floor was polished and squeaked under my shoes, a grid of lights shone from above, and the hum of machinery was a steady noise in the background.

The room was empty, but it didn't feel deserted. Someone had been here only minutes ago. I had the feeling I knew who.

The MP7 was back in my hands, the dispel focus back in my pocket. I channelled a steady thread of power into the focus, letting it recharge as I strode down between the desks. Banks of security monitors displayed CCTV images of the mansion, the swimming pool, the gate room. A projection focus sat dark and inactive, but I could sense a fading charge. A moment's study told me that it had been set to view the entrance hall in the basement. Someone had stood here watching the battle. I could almost smell Levistus's scent, trace his footprints.

A space magic signature at the back of the room caught my attention. I moved closer.

There was a freestanding gate against the back wall, a dark wood arch seven feet tall carved in intricate patterns. Like the projection focus, it held a fading magical residue. It had been deactivated, but it was locked, not burned out. A quick search revealed a password and a small override focus hidden in the wall. I said the password, touched the focus, and felt the gate stir to life. I'd only need to channel a little energy and I could step through. It would lead me into . . .

I frowned. *A ruin?* Why would Levistus have a permanent gate to an empty ruin?

I focused with my magesight, checking futures. As I studied the lines of the gate spell, I noticed inconsistencies. This wasn't the destination that the gate had been originally set to. It had been altered recently, and the changes concealed. A misdirection.

There was no way to tell where the gate had originally led, but the gate focus had been used for a very long time to go to the same place over and over again, and the focus "remembered" that destination, just as a book will fall open to a frequently read page. I reached out with the fateweaver to see if there was any chance that the gate would slip back to its original target. There was, but it was a very, very small chance.

A moment's work with the fateweaver and it was a one hundred percent chance. I touched the gate and channelled. Energy flowed; the lines of the spell shifted, and the archway darkened into a masked portal.

I knew as soon as I stepped through that I'd found Levistus's shadow realm.

Columns of crystal and frosted glass spiralled to a pale blue ceiling, circular walls framing a large rounded room.

Pedestals and standing shelves held magic items of all kinds, radiating dozens of overlapping magical auras. The shadow realm felt small, probably reaching barely further than the walls of the room.

Levistus was bent over a desk, concentrating on something. As I stepped through he whirled, with an expression as close to shock as I'd ever seen on his face.

It had been six years since I first met Levistus, and he'd changed very little. Thinning white hair, odd colourless eyes set in a face smoothed to stillness. "You!" he said. "How did . . . ?"

"Your gate protections aren't as good as you think," I told him.

Levistus's expression calmed, returning to the mask-like, impassive look that I remembered from all those Council meetings. "So I see," he said. "I take it Caldera is dead?"

"Do you care?"

"I had imagined you might."

I began walking, circling Levistus. He turned to face me as I moved. "You know, I was expecting you to be there for the big fight," I told him. "Not that I'm complaining. If I'd had to deal with you throwing mental attacks at the same time as I fought that mantis golem, I might actually have been in trouble."

"A leader's role is to direct, not fight in the trenches," Levistus said. "A lesson your time on the Council apparently failed to teach you."

"Well, when it comes to staying off the front lines, you're certainly the expert. And you're right. Maybe if I'd spent less time leading raids and more time building up political power, the way you did, I wouldn't be here now. But then again, leading from the front teaches you things. Like how to win a battle."

"Win?" Levistus said. "You believe you've won?"

I'd circled half the room, passing focuses and weapons

and scrying items. I'd drifted closer as I moved: I'd started maybe fifty feet away from Levistus, and now the distance was down to more like forty. "Not yet."

Levistus didn't answer.

"I assume you know why I'm here."

"Yes, Verus, I know precisely why you are here," Levistus said. "Once a Dark mage, always a Dark mage. Crude, destructive, and ultimately predictable."

"Yeah, that was what you thought back when you picked me to be your disposable diviner to get the fateweaver for you," I said. "Has it ever occurred to you that the whole reason I was drawn into Council politics was because of you? If you hadn't spent so long trying to destroy me, I wouldn't have become the person I am right now. It's funny, but in a way, you kind of created me."

"I had no part in creating you," Levistus said sharply. "Your path was set by your master a long time ago."

I gave a slight smile. "Touched a nerve? I hope so, Levistus, because I really want to make sure you understand just how much of this is your own fault. Don't get me wrong: the fact that I'm going to kill you in a few minutes is one hundred percent my decision, but you had so many chances to stop this. Back when we first met in Canary Wharf, do you have any idea just how little I cared about Light politics? Yes, I didn't like the Council, but I really didn't give two shits about who was *on* the Council. You were the one who changed that. First you tried to use me to steal the fateweaver, then you tried to have me assassinated when I got involved with Belthas, then you pointed the Nightstalkers in my direction the year after . . . I don't think a year's gone by when you haven't tried to murder me or someone I care about. You know the worst thing? How *pointless* it all was. At any time, all you had to do was walk away. You could have stopped it after that failed death sentence; you could have stopped it after I was raised to the Council. Even right up until this week, I was still willing to call a truce. But you just couldn't let it go."

Levistus's eyes flashed. I'd sat at the same table as him for scores of Council meetings, maybe hundreds, but I think this was the first time I'd ever seen him openly angry. "You think this is some sort of grudge?" Even furious, Levistus's voice was tight and controlled. "Your arrogance is beyond belief. I sought your removal because I recognised from the very beginning that your influence upon the Council would be a purely destructive one. Bahamus and Druss were both foolish enough to believe that you could be manipulated. I was not. You care nothing for order, nothing for stability. Your only concern is for yourself. Your presence on the Council was an insult to everything it stands for."

"And what *does* it stand for?" I asked. "See, that's the thing about Light mages like you and Caldera and Talisid. You love to talk about these high-minded ideals that the Council supposedly stands for, and you think that makes you so much better than Dark mages. But you never seem to feel any particular need to *act* better than Dark mages. You love to talk about how evil your enemies are, but when *you're* the ones doing the destroying or lying or killing, you never seem to have a problem with it."

Levistus looked at me in contempt. "Like most Dark mages, you have the intellectual development of a child."

"Yeah, well, children can still see the obvious," I said. "You want to lecture me about only caring about myself? How many lives have you destroyed to get to where you are now, Levistus? Oh, I'm sure you don't kill them personally. You just sit in your comfortable chair and sign orders with your fountain pen. Have you ever bothered to count? I don't think you have. They're just numbers on a page."

"Your feelings are irrelevant," Levistus said. "As are your infantile ethics."

"You know the other thing about people like you?" I said. "You get cocky. You order people's deaths, and because you're not the one who has to get your hands dirty, you avoid the consequences. After a while, you stop thinking about consequences at all. You figure you're untouchable, and for the most part, you're right. And so when you finally go too far, it takes you a long time to notice. You know what it was in your case, that knocked down the whole house of cards? It was when you and Sal Sarque ordered for Anne to be captured and tortured two years ago. Back then, I doubt either of you gave it a second thought. But it gave Anne the push to pick up the jinn, and if you follow that chain of events all the way through, it ends up with Anne killing Sal Sarque in his island fortress a month back."

I'd closed the distance to thirty feet. A few more steps and I'd be in range to rush him. "You really do not see it, do you?" Levistus said. "Sal Sarque's death at your hands demonstrates precisely *why* you and Mage Walker needed to be removed."

"Anne killed Sarque because of what you did."

"She killed Sarque because she valued her self-preservation over the good of the country," Levistus said. "As do you. Consider, Verus. Let us say that you succeed, that you and Mage Walker manage to overthrow the Council, kill enough of them to cause their resistance to collapse. Will it be worth it? When historians look back, what do you think their judgement will be? Are your lives worth more than this country?"

I was silent.

"You never even considered it," Levistus said. "And that is why you are unfit to wield power."

"Did you expect us to lie down and die?"

"Of course not. If you valued the good of the country over yourself, you would have. But you do not, and you did not, and instead you chose the vicious and destructive path you follow now."

I stared into Levistus's colourless eyes for a moment. "You know, people like you are always talking about sacrifices and the greater good," I said. "But there's a funny thing I've noticed. No matter how many people get sacrificed, you're never one of them."

Levistus looked back at me indifferently. "And?"

"I think maybe it's your turn."

I started my lunge on the last word, but Levistus was ready. Ice flashed across the room, running from wall to wall and from floor to ceiling.

I came to a stop. The wall of ice split the room in half, with me on one side and Levistus on the other. It was transparent, and nearly a foot thick. I know what ice mages are capable of, and even the strongest of them can't throw up walls that big that fast. Levistus must have had some item or trick.

"I'd heard rumours that you were an elementalist as well as a mind mage," I said. "Should have guessed ice would be your style."

"The key words," Levistus said, "are *as well*."

Mental force struck me like a hammer. It wasn't anything like the domination attempts I'd faced from Crystal and Abithriax: this was a brute-force attack designed to stun the target, crush their mind and leave them unconscious. But just as Levistus had anticipated my move, I'd anticipated his. I'd been channelling my power through the mind shield I carried, and Levistus's attack ran into my mental defences.

Levistus struck again and again. The ice was no barrier to him, and he hammered my defences with blows of psychic force. It felt like a boxer pounding against my guard, fists slamming into my brain. But I'd had years of practice at defending myself against psychic combat, and the focus was the best I'd been able to find. Waves of hostile energy crashed against my mind, breaking against the fortress of my will.

I forced myself to ignore the mental blows and focused on the ice wall. It was thick and strong, but it was real ice, with the weaknesses that came with it. I focused on vulnerable points, using the fateweaver to amplify them, then I lifted my MP7, clicked it to single-shot, and began firing, slowly and deliberately, one bullet per second. The flat report of the gun echoed in the chamber, my divination guiding each bullet as it slammed into the ice.

"If you expect to shoot through—" Levistus began.

My fifth bullet hit, and there was a rumbling *crunch*. Cracks spiderwebbed through the wall and Levistus stopped talking.

I fired a sixth bullet, and a seventh.

Levistus made a gesture and the air next to him shimmered. A humanoid figure took form, visible only to my magesight, floating just above and beside him, sculpted out of lines of vapour. It was an air elemental like Starbreeze, but where Starbreeze's face was expressive and ever-changing, this one's face was blank.

"It took me some time to replace Thirteen," Levistus said. "The changes proved more complex than predicted. Still, I suppose this is as good a time as any for a field test. I think you'll find it quite effective at its purpose."

I kept firing. Eight shots, nine. There was another rumble and a section of wall five feet up cracked and fell.

Levistus twitched his hand.

The elemental soared up, quick as lightning, darting through the hole I'd made, then curving down. Those eerie blank eyes were locked on my face as it dove towards me. Air elementals don't need to strike or buffet their targets; they can turn a living being to air and scatter them across a thousand miles. This one wasn't intending to do that—some limitation of whatever Levistus had done to enslave it, maybe. It was going to try to flow straight down my throat and asphyxiate me. Just as fatal.

I'd pulled the wand from my belt the instant the elemental began moving. As it went into its dive, I fired.

Red light flashed out, carrying the scent of ozone. The elemental tried to dodge aside, but somehow, despite its speed, the beam caught it in the head. In my magesight I saw the beam tear through the core of animating magic within the creature and burn through the other end. The elemental wisped into vapour, destroyed in an instant.

Weakness rippled through me, and I lowered the wand, meeting Levistus's eyes. "Not effective enough," I told him.

Levistus's face twisted in anger, but I was already firing. The final bullet sent a shock wave along the ice wall's major fracture and split it open. With a keening crash, a whole section of the ice wall from floor to ceiling collapsed.

Levistus tried to throw up a smaller wall of ice to block the hole. I broke into a run, firing from the hip, twisting the futures as I did. The bullets intercepted the ice as it formed, shattered it before the structure could take shape, and then I was through, with nothing between me and Levistus but empty floor.

Levistus snapped a command word. From one of the pedestals, something metal unfurled and leapt towards me. I dived and rolled, catching a glimpse of the thing as it flew overhead: a black metal chain, hooked and barbed and glowing with red light. Instead of falling, the thing arrested its forward motion, then reversed course, accelerating back towards me.

In the moment's breathing space I dropped the MP7 and drew my dispel focus. As the chain enveloped me, I stepped in and struck. The chain was some sort of enormously powerful focus item, animated with a simple governing intelligence, and it was shielded against dispel magic. The fateweaver found a chink in the protections, and the dispel attack caused the focus spells to go wild and fail. Metal barbs lashed my back, but they were already lifeless and falling away. The chain clattered to the floor.

The seconds it had taken me to deal with the chain had given Levistus the chance to open the range. His shield was up, a translucent barrier of crystalline light, and a nimbus of blue energy glowed around him. Ice shards materialised behind and above his shoulders, hovering in the air and pointing towards my heart.

The ice shards flew at me as though fired from a gun. I leapt to one side and they shattered on the floor and against the pedestal behind. Before I'd even landed, more were materialising and Levistus was firing again, with still more after that. It wasn't a single attack but a barrage, like a machine gun that never ran out of bullets.

I dodged, ducking and twisting under the rain of ice. The shards were thin slivers of blue energy, needle-sharp, and in the futures I saw them spear through my flesh as though it were paper. Levistus's control was tight, directed by his iron will, but there were too many of the shards for him to focus on them all, and in that gap the fateweaver did its work, opening up safe paths through the deadly rain.

The room flashed blue, the light illuminating Levistus's face. I didn't watch his eyes; all my attention was on the lines of the futures, thread-thin paths of safety forking through a sea of death. An ice sliver took a few hairs off my head; another brushed my sleeve. Cold seeped into me but my armour seemed to pulse with life, holding back the chill.

Levistus was getting closer. I'd started thirty feet away; now the distance was closer to twenty. Every now and again there'd be a gap in the barrage, and I'd use the opportunity to take a step forward. Step by step, Levistus drew nearer.

Out of the corner of my eye, I could see strain on Levistus's face, mixed with concentration. He backed away, giving ground. The barrage of ice didn't slow: shard after shard materialised and flashed out towards me, but as each attack came out, I marked it and plotted a new course so that it would miss. My path formed a zigzag, cutting back and forth but always turning towards Levistus.

Levistus came up against the wall. He tried to escape to the right and I moved to block him. Barely ten feet separated us now. The barrage intensified, growing wilder, faster, but all that did was open up more chinks for the fateweaver. The sound was a constant roar, the keening crash of ice shards striking the floor and walls, the scuff of footsteps.

A final step and I was within arm's reach. Levistus was right in front of me, close enough to touch. His shield shimmered, a glowing barrier. I was so close now that the shield was an obstacle against the rain of shards, and I moved to use it as cover, placing it between me and Levistus each time a new icicle materialised. The paths of safety were wider now, and I was able to turn my attention away from keeping myself alive, and towards Levistus.

Levistus's shield shone, reflecting the image of the knife in my hand. The blade glanced off the steel-hard planes, but with each strike I was probing for a weakness. Levistus was spending most of his energy on defence now; only the occasional ice shard made it around the shield to slash down. I dodged them all, searching, seeking.

Levistus tried to reinforce his shield, change his attack pattern to drive me back. The futures shifted and for an instant there was a crack in his defences.

The fateweaver drove into that crack like a wedge. The future I needed opened up, one tiny possibility amid thousands, and my divination found it.

Levistus's shield shattered as I drove my knife through it point-first, the edge gleaming. Shards of frozen magic spun in the air as I rammed the blade into Levistus's gut. My impact slammed him up against the wall. I saw the shock in Levistus's eyes, felt his clothes as I gripped them with my free hand, then I twisted the knife, pulled it out, and drove it between his ribs and into his heart.

Levistus and I stared into each other's eyes from inches away. The shock in his eyes became pain, then that familiar look of surprise that you only see on dying men. I felt Levistus shudder, warm blood oozing over my fingers, slick on the knife handle. Then those odd colourless eyes seemed to fade and the life went out of them. Levistus slid down the wall. I let him down slowly, then let him crumple to the floor.

I looked down at Levistus's body. His face was expressionless again, blank in death as it had been in life. There was blood on his clothes, the wall, my hands.

Mechanically I wiped the knife on Levistus's robes and sheathed it, then straightened and looked around. The shadow realm seemed suddenly very empty, half-real without its owner. Some of the pedestals and shelves had been destroyed in the battle; others were intact, their contents radiating magic.

There were enough treasures here to make any normal man rich for a hundred lifetimes, but I could sense active spells in the background, and I didn't know what I might have triggered or what might be coming. My body was still hyped from the adrenaline but I could feel exhaustion creeping up on me. I needed to finish and get out.

I took a few things. A crystal vial, seemingly fragile, with something glowing inside. A headband of beaten copper, dull and tarnished, worked into the shape of a crown of feathers. Finally, there was a long, spear-like weapon, suspended in some kind of containment field. The haft was black, and though it had been a long time, I thought I recognised it as a Russian design called a *sovnya*. Both it and the copper headband were imbued items, and possibly the vial too. I held them cautiously at arm's length, keeping a neutral mental posture, carefully not attempting to claim them, but even so I could feel them stir and uncoil as they reacted to my presence.

I gated out and through a series of staging points, jumping from continent to continent.

Night had long since fallen by the time I got back to the Hollow, and as the gate closed behind me, it was all I could do not to collapse. The aftershock of the combat was starting to hit, and I wanted to run away and fall asleep and throw up. I dumped the imbued items and my weapons, then stripped off my armour and fell into bed. I was asleep in seconds. Dimly, I was afraid of what dreams would come, but if I had any, I was too far gone to remember.

·········

There's a very specific feeling when you wake up in the morning with something hanging over you. It makes your stomach and heart sink, a mixture of anxiety over what you did and worry over what's going to happen next. When you're young, you get it for things like an overdue library book, or a fight with another child. As you get older, you outgrow worries like that, but you don't outgrow the feeling at all—you just get it for different reasons. For some people, it'll be fear of a bad grade, or an angry manager. For others, it's money, or the police.

But I'm fairly sure no one else woke up that particular morning wondering what was going to happen now that they'd just assassinated one of the leading politicians in the country. It was so extreme that I had trouble grasping it. There are lots of people who'll tell you how to handle a bad breakup, or losing your job. There isn't much advice out there on how to deal with killing a government minister and their entire personal staff.

I dressed, cleaned my teeth, and shaved. The imbued items I'd stolen last night sat around the room, their presence oppressive. I didn't want to eat with them watching me, so I took some fruit and a protein bar out of the cottage and ate my breakfast sitting on a fallen tree in the Hollow's morning sun. After the chaos and ugliness of last night, it was a relief to look at the sunlight and feel the wind.

Karyos arrived just as I was finishing up. The hamadryad seemed to glide through the undergrowth without brushing it, almost as if the plants bent aside to let her pass. "We have a visitor."

I paused, holding the remains of my apple. "Outside?"

Karyos nodded. "He has disturbed the sensors but has not attempted entry. I believe he is waiting for a response."

"Anyone you know?"

"No."

I looked quickly through the futures to see who I'd find if I stepped out of the Hollow and to its mirrored location in the Chilterns. My eyebrows rose. "Huh."

"Do you recognise him?"

"Yes," I said. "He's a Light mage, and very powerful. I don't think he's an enemy though." Or at least he hadn't been before last night.

"Will you receive him?"

I thought about it for a second and then nodded.

⁣ ⁣ ⁣ ⁣ ⁣ ⁣ ⁣ ⁣ ⁣

The gateway at the Hollow's entry point opened and Landis stepped through.

Landis is tall and rangy, with sandy-coloured hair and an abrupt way of moving. He spends half his time acting oblivious and the other half acting like a lunatic, but I've learned over the years that he's more observant than he looks.

Landis is one of the most dangerous battle-mages I know. He's not well-known outside of the Order of the Shield, but he's as experienced and powerful as any elemental mage I've ever met, and even with the fateweaver, I wouldn't like to take him on. Which was a problem, because as a member of the Order of the Shield, he had a duty to at least arrest me, and more likely kill me on sight. Inviting him in was a risk, but right now both my instincts and my divination were telling me that he was here to talk.

"Ah, Verus!" Landis said. "So good of you to see me on such short notice. I imagine you must have a busy schedule these days."

"That's one way to put it," I said. "Why are you here?"

Landis looked from left to right at the forests of the Hollow, smiling. "This really is a wonderful shadow realm. 'A thing of beauty is a joy for ever,' as they say. I must remember to visit more often once this is all over."

"It's very pretty, yes," I said wearily. "Landis, I don't mean to be rude, but I just killed around a dozen people last night. I'm not really in the mood for discussing aesthetics."

"Yes, I know. I find it's important to centre oneself at such times."

I looked at Landis. He looked back at me pleasantly.

"Would you like to take a walk?" I asked.

"Of course."

We began to stroll through the woods of the Hollow, the path winding gently between trees and through clearings. "I imagine you're wondering whose side I'm on," Landis said.

"You're a Keeper of the Order of the Shield," I told Landis. "You answer to the Council, which means at any time they could order you to go kill me, and you'd be forced to do exactly that. Don't get me wrong; I appreciate all you've done for us. But it seems to me it's going to be very hard for us to stay friends."

Landis nodded. "Quite understandable. Have you noticed that virtually no Keepers from the Order of the Shield have been sent after you?"

That caught me off guard. I thought for a second, going through names. "There have been a couple."

"Ares and McCole. Both have extensive ties to Council Intelligence."

"Okay," I said. "I'll bite. Why haven't the Order of the Shield been sent after me?"

"Because senior members of the Order of the Shield—notably myself—have politely but firmly communicated to the Council that we view pursuing you as counterproductive."

I looked at Landis with a frown. He looked back at me with eyebrows raised. We continued to walk through the woods of the Hollow.

"You've been protecting me," I said.

"Effectively."

"Why?"

"For years now, some among us have recognised that Levistus was more dangerous to the Council than Richard Drakh could ever be. Drakh struck at the Council from outside; Levistus was rotting it from within. Worst of all, Levistus had displayed a disturbing ability to suborn or blackmail others to his will. In another ten years, he would have been a dictator."

"Probably less," I said. "But back up. You're telling me you and your friends in the Order of the Shield knew about all this all along?"

"Yes."

"And what were you planning to do about it?"

"Our hope had been that your conflict with Levistus

would present some opportunity to weaken his political position."

"Wonderful," I said. "So you, some of the most competent and dangerous battle-mages on the entire Council, have been sitting around all this time doing . . . nothing. You couldn't have gotten rid of him yourself?"

"Being a Light mage has a price, Verus," Landis said. "Yes, we could have removed Levistus directly. But doing so would in all probability have started a civil war. The Keeper Orders have many privileges, but in exchange for those privileges, we must accept certain limitations on our freedom of action."

"Limitations," I said bitterly. "Yeah, that's a nice way to put it. You know how many people died last night because you didn't feel like you had enough 'freedom of action'?"

"Forty-eight confirmed dead and four missing, the last I checked," Landis said. "Twenty-eight security personnel, eleven Council employees and functionaries, nine members of Levistus's personal staff, and four mages. I knew six of them personally. Lorenz was the one I was best acquainted with, after Caldera, of course. An ex-member of the Order of the Shield, liked to play the flute. Affected boredom much of the time, though it was something of a pose. Quite a talented air mage, but he did have some rather careless personal habits and fell in with Levistus as a result. Married, though he and his wife had been separated for years. I hope the news doesn't hit her too badly. From the autopsy, I assume he was killed by Anne, though the bullet wound was presumably your work. Then there was Casper. An adept, only in his mid-twenties, if I recall. I used to talk to him during court appointments at the War Rooms. He always struck me as quite idealistic. Genuinely believed in the Council, though some of the things he saw as liaison to Levistus were beginning to make him uncomfortable. He might have found a different position quite soon if those jann hadn't torn out his throat. Then there was Christina, whose body they found on the front lawn. She didn't work for Levistus at all, she simply was unlucky enough to be there on an errand at the time of your attack. I believe she was engaged to be married this coming spring . . . did you want me to go on?"

"Please don't," I said. What Landis had just said was probably going to stick in my memory for years. It's bad enough when the people you kill are faceless strangers. Knowing their names makes it so much worse.

"And then of course there's Caldera, who you know very well. We actually roomed together for a little while; I don't know if she ever told you. I'd been a journeyman for a good few years but they passed that law requiring members of the Order of the Shield to meet the same qualifications as the Order of the Star, so she and I ended up in the same class. She was always rather disappointed that I didn't have what she considered a proper apprecia- tion for high-quality beverages, but she did her best to educate me all the same, and I was introduced to quite a few fascinating drinking establishments as a result." Lan- dis paused. "I advised her to accompany Talisid's force. She refused. She was quite certain you'd find some way to evade them, and she wanted to be ready when you did. She always did have excellent instincts for fieldwork, but they didn't bring her much happiness."

I was silent.

"You aren't the only person who's had to make hard choices, Verus," Landis said. "I've been a Keeper for quite some time, and I've made a great many decisions that have led directly or indirectly to people's deaths. Be- lieve me, I am fully aware of their consequences."

We walked for another minute or so without speaking. "All right," I said. "Assuming I accept everything you're telling me, I don't think you came here just to thank me for taking care of your business. What is it you want?"

Landis nodded. "I want you to stop assassinating Council members."

"You're not the only one."

"By burning away the dead wood, the forest fire allows new growth," Landis said. "However, at a certain point, that fire must stop. I have now specified the point at which it must stop."

I looked sidelong at Landis. His manner was pleasant and there was no threat in his words, but I knew that if I replied with *or what?* I wouldn't like the answer.

"It's all very well to say 'stop,'" I said. "But as you may or may not be aware, the entire reason I'm fighting this private war is that the Council refuses to call it quits."

"I may be able to exercise some small influence in that regard. At the very least, I suspect when you next call, they'll be more inclined to take you seriously."

"Yes, because I just killed one of them. Backing down now is the absolute *worst* thing I can do. What I've done is bad enough, that would make it be all for nothing!"

"All you have to do is make the same request as before. Who knows? Maybe this time they'll listen."

I thought for a second. My instincts were telling me to say no. I finally had the Council on the ropes and I didn't want to back off.

But making an enemy of Landis was a bad idea. He was Variam's master, and his word carried a lot of weight in the Order of the Shield. If he was telling the truth, then he was the only reason I didn't have a whole extra Keeper Order to deal with.

And then there was the personal side. Landis had done me some very big favours over the years. He had taken a chance on Variam when nobody else would, and he'd backed me up in some scary fights. I owed him a lot.

"All right," I said. "Because it's you, I'll try it. But I can't promise it'll work."

"Good show!" Landis said cheerfully. He clapped me on my shoulder hard enough to rock me sideways. "I won't keep you any longer, then. Do feel free to contact the Council at your earliest convenience."

ıııııııı

I escorted Landis out of the Hollow. The portal closed behind him and I was left alone.

With Landis gone, I felt at a loss. I thought about getting in touch with November or Variam and catching up on the news, but it felt like the wrong thing to do. Council communications would be in chaos right now, and I really couldn't see any point in eavesdropping. I probably knew more about what was going to happen next than they did.

In the end, I couldn't come up with anything better than my original plan. I left formal meeting requests with the Council via two different sources. Usually I'd have just called Talisid, but either he was still stuck in that deep shadow realm or he wasn't answering his phone.

I heard back from the Council within the hour. Apparently I finally had their attention. As afternoon came, I prepared for what I hoped would be the last time I'd ever have to speak to them.

chapter 13

I stepped out of my cottage to find Karyos and Luna waiting in the clearing. "Heard from Vari?" I asked Luna.

"Yeah, he's on standby. Again." Luna shook her head. "I can't believe Levistus is finally dead."

I shut the door behind me. "Wanted to settle the score yourself?"

"No, I got over that way of thinking a long time ago. You really think you can pull this off?"

"One way or another. You good to stay here for a few hours?"

Luna frowned. "Be nice if you'd tell me why."

I sighed. "I wish I knew."

"You could always try, I don't know, divining the future."

"Don't be snarky," I told her. "I've tried. No matter how I conduct this audience with the Council, I can't see any direct threat."

"So what are you afraid of?"

"I don't know," I said. "That's the problem. The futures look . . . volatile. I can't see any threat right now, but that could change. And the sort of interview I'm about to have, with lots of unpredictability and decision points, is *exactly* the kind of thing that's virtually impossible to see past."

"But why do you want me here and not in my shop?" Luna asked. "If the Keepers are watching, it's going to look suspicious as hell."

"I know, but if anything happens, the Hollow's a lot better protected. Please, Luna, just do this as a favour. It'll put my mind at rest."

Luna shrugged. "Well, I suppose I didn't have anything really important to do. I'll stay here till you get back."

"Thanks."

"Why did you also warn me?" Karyos asked. "You believe the Council will connect us?"

"Honestly, no," I said. "It's much simpler than that. I've lost too many people I care about by now, and you're two of the only ones left. I'd have asked Vari to stay here as well if I thought he'd do it."

"Yeah, fat chance," Luna said. "Shouldn't you be going?"

"Yes," I said. But I still hesitated. "Hermes is here, right?"

Luna rolled her eyes. "Will you stop fussing? Look, we put up the gate wards on this place together. If the Council or someone else decides to break in, we are going to have more than enough time to do something about it. Now how about you start worrying about the problem you actually have?"

I wanted to say that Levistus's shadow realm had had gate wards, too, and that hadn't stopped me. But I knew that Luna's response would be to ask whether there was anyone else running around with a fateweaver, and I'd have to answer no. There was still Richard to worry about, but if Richard had wanted to go after Luna, he'd had more than enough chances already and he hadn't seemed to—

"*Alex*," Luna said. "You're going to be late."

"All right. I'll come back as soon as I have news."

⎪⎪⎪⎪⎪⎪⎪⎪

gated to the spot I'd picked out for my audience with the Council. It was a clearing in a forestry area in Wales, in a dip between two hills. I'd picked out a selection of spots like this before my first time contacting the Council, and this was number three of ten. The others had been mostly in North and South America, but Wales felt appropriate. A lot of things had started here; this was a good place for them to end.

I made my preparations with more care than usual. Perimeter alarm focuses to warn me if anyone got close— my divination could do the same thing, but I wanted the extra layer of protection. Tripwires hidden in shadows between trees, where I could jump them but any pursuers wouldn't see. Antipersonnel mines set up at key locations, where attackers would be funnelled into kill zones. Once I was done, I stepped back and studied my work.

It looked good. If anyone launched an attack, I should have more than enough time to decide whether to escape or to turn and fight. And to attack me, they'd have to find me, which would be quite a trick. I hadn't used this site before, and in fact I hadn't even decided to use this one at all until the very last minute. Once I started transmitting, they could track me down, but they'd have to get through my shroud, and it would be enormously difficult not to leave some warning that I'd sense well in advance. I checked back in with Luna and Karyos—they were fine. I checked in with November—he was safe in his new flat and reported nothing to be concerned about. I used the dreamstone to call Variam—he told me that he was on standby and no, he wasn't being mobilised to go after me, and why was I sounding so worried if I wouldn't tell him what about?

No matter what I did, I couldn't sense any danger. Still, the uneasy feeling didn't go away.

It was half an hour to the deadline when the first thing went wrong. The futures shifted and I could see that someone had the potential to find me. They weren't here yet, but by the time the meeting was due to start, they'd have narrowed down my location and would be able to gate to me with little notice.

I could get away easily. But I'd spent hours preparing this site, and there was no way I'd be able to do all this setup again for a new location. Besides, if I did, what was to stop them following?

I could find some different and better-fortified location, but that would mean missing my window with the Council. That would send exactly the wrong message. I'd worked towards this for so long, I couldn't screw it up now!

Shit. I checked the time. Twenty-seven minutes. What to do?

I paced, watching the futures grow more and more defined. I couldn't see any evidence of actual aggression. Maybe they weren't here for a fight.

With eighteen minutes to go, I made the decision to hold my ground. I'd wait him out, pretend he wasn't there, and dare him to do something about it.

Fifteen minutes. Ten. I checked the futures obsessively. At this point it was pretty much useless and I knew it, but old habits die hard. Five minutes. One.

My com focus flashed exactly on time. I took a deep breath, then channelled through it. "Good afternoon, Alma," I said. "It's been a while."

"Verus," Alma said, her voice cold. "I believe you had something to discuss."

Futures unfolded before me, different approaches, different words. Enough to tell me who was listening. "And Druss, and Bahamus, and Spire," I said. "Oh, and can't forget you, Undaaris."

"We don't have time for games," Alma said. "Say your piece and get out."

All of a sudden, I was calm. The focus was audio-only, but in my mind's eye I could see the people I was talking to, sitting around the Star Chamber's long table. Alma, straight-backed and unsmiling, grey-streaked hair framing a pair of cold eyes. Bahamus, silver-haired and aristocratic, courteous but missing nothing. Druss, a bear of a man with a thick beard. Undaaris, his eyes flicking from one person to another. And last of all, Spire, tall and silent and aloof.

But there were two more chairs around the head of that table, and right now, it was those two empty seats that the remaining members of the Senior Council would be thinking about. I'd sat at that table in the Star Chamber so many times, but always as an observer. This time I was the one in the driver's seat.

"Oh, I'd say you quite clearly have time for games, Alma, given that for the past week you've done nothing else. First you stonewall me while your hunters follow my trail, then you pretend to agree to a negotiation and send a small army. You've tried to kill me, you've tried to betray me, and most importantly, you've wasted my time. On the positive side, this time you're at least picking up the call yourself, which suggests you might be starting to learn from experience."

"You have your audience, Verus," Alma said. "Don't push your luck."

"Luck has nothing to do with it." If Alma's voice was cold, mine was ice. "You will listen to me because you are fully aware of what the consequences will be if you don't."

"Verus," Bahamus cut in before Alma could reply. "Let us try to stay on point, please. I believe you have a proposal."

"I have exactly the same proposal that I gave you a week ago. An end to hostilities. It would have saved a great many deaths if you'd taken me seriously the first time."

"There were reasons for our decision."

"Yes. The biggest reason was sitting in the chair to your right and he was called Levistus. That reason has now been removed."

There was an uncomfortable pause. "This really all you want, Verus?" Druss said. "Everyone walks away?"

"It's all I wanted from the beginning. You're the ones who've been making it complicated."

"Because you still refuse to recognise what you are asking," Alma said sharply. "You broke the Concord."

"Deal with it."

"You cannot break the most important laws of this country and tell the Light Council to 'deal with it.'"

"Yes, I can."

"Verus, be reasonable," Bahamus said. "This is not only about you. Even if we were to overlook your . . . activities . . . the current state of your compatriot Miss Walker cannot be ignored."

"You are *directly responsible* for the current state of Anne Walker," I said. "And when I say you, I mean the Council as a whole. For years you turned a blind eye while mages like Sagash abused her. You voted to sentence her to death. After that was rescinded, Keepers reporting to Sal Sarque and Levistus attempted to kidnap and torture her, not once but multiple times. Maybe not all of you were responsible as individuals, but the Council is very much responsible as a whole, and the five of you lead the Council. And the Council treated her so badly that when she was trapped between that jinn and a Council task force, she turned to the jinn. Do you realise what it says about your behaviour that a jinn seemed like the *better option*?"

"Regardless of any sympathy I have for her current state—and I do have some, though you may not believe it—the fact remains that in her present condition, she is simply too dangerous. If you really want to help her, you should be trying to bring her in."

"And if you wanted *my* help, you shouldn't have sentenced us to death. *Again*."

"The order was for your arrest," Druss said.

"And how long do you think I'd have lasted in a Keeper cell?" I asked. "Whatever. I didn't call to argue. I called to deliver a message. Do not go near me, do not go near Anne, and do not go near anyone I place under my protection. Clear?"

"We cannot simply ignore Anne," Bahamus said.

"I will take care of Anne if it becomes necessary. Until and unless things reach that point, you will not move against her."

"Your intentions regarding Anne Walker are irrelevant," Alma said sharply. "You do not have the authority to make demands."

"My authority is the two empty seats at your table."

Alma's voice was cold and menacing. "Are you attempting to threaten us?"

"That was not me threatening you," I said. "*This* is me threatening you." I leant forward and put every bit of my intensity into my voice. "There were seven of you at that table when you voted to sentence me to arrest and interrogation and death, and when you sent those Keepers to hunt me to the corners of the earth. There were six of you at that table when you refused my offer of a ceasefire and ordered Talisid's team to ambush me. There are five of you at that table now. If you refuse my offer again, I will continue this war with every resource and ally at my disposal. I will use the information from Levistus's files to sow discord in your ranks and destroy your base of support. I will ally with your enemies and use the information I've gathered over the years to strike where you are most vulnerable. And if that still doesn't work, then I will come after you personally. I will arrange your destruction at the hands of others, as I did Sal Sarque, and I will kill you with my own hands, as I did Levistus. I will hunt you down one by one, so that there are four of you around that table, then three, then two, and if you still won't listen then I will keep going until every last member of the Senior Council is dead and the Star Chamber is empty except for a records clerk sitting in an empty room!"

There was dead silence. I could almost hear the shock. *No one* spoke to the Council like that.

"You overreach yourself." Alma tried to rally. "You were fortunate against Levistus. You will not be so lucky again."

"Do you have *any idea* how many mages before you have told me that? Last night it was Levistus, and Lorenz and Caldera, and Levistus's adepts, and Levistus's security. Before that it was Talisid and his team. Before that it was Symmaris. Before that it was Jagadev. Before that it was Sal Sarque. Before that it was Onyx and Pyre. Every last one of them at some point looked at me, weighed up what they thought they knew, and decided that they liked their chances. Every last one of them is now defeated, dead, or both. So when you decide you can take me, Alma, I want you to understand very clearly that you are just the latest in a line of *hundreds* of people who thought the exact same thing!"

"Is that really all you're bringing to the table, Verus?" Bahamus asked. "Threats?"

"Yes. Because for all your talk of law and stability, the only thing that you and the rest of the Council have ever really respected is power and the threat of force. There's no real difference between you and the Dark mages. You're both playing the same game; you're just on different teams. So let me make this very clear. You will accept this ceasefire and you will stop coming after me or *I will destroy you.*"

There was no sound at all from the focus. Seconds ticked by.

"We will consider your proposal," Bahamus said at last in an expressionless voice.

"Consider, then choose," I said. "I'll be waiting."

The focus went dead. I stood in the clearing. Far overhead, clouds drifted in a clear sky. I watched the futures shift.

It was fifteen minutes later that the focus reactivated. "Verus?" Bahamus said.

"I'm listening."

"We have . . . after some consideration . . . decided to accept your proposal," Bahamus said. "We will cease any offensive operations against you and your immediate associates. Your legal status will become that of an unaffiliated mage. In exchange, you will undertake to take no aggressive action against us or provide any assistance to our enemies in the current war. Further details will be negotiated at a later date. Is this acceptable?"

"Yes."

"Thank you." Bahamus paused. "I hope we can develop a better relationship in the future."

"I really don't care," I said. "Good-bye."

I cut the focus. The light on the item went out and the connection went dead. I let out a long, slow breath.

And then, from the trees, I heard the sound of clapping.

I turned to see Morden step out into the clearing. The Dark mage was smiling. "Very well done," he told me.

"On the one hand, thanks," I said. "On the other, could you be a little less patronising?"

"My apologies," Morden said. "But I meant it sincerely. You conducted your negotiation skilfully and with force."

"I suppose I should take the compliment. What are you doing here, Morden?"

"Nothing very important. This is more of a social visit."

"Tracking me down after the amount of work I put in to stay undetected today is not my definition of a social visit."

"I suppose I could have left a phone call, but I felt this would be a better way of getting your attention."

"Okay, you've got it," I said. My guard was still very much up. I couldn't sense any danger, but I wasn't going to relax until I was back in the Hollow. "What do you want?"

"It's a courtesy notice, really," Morden said. "I thought I should inform you of my retirement."

I blinked. "Your what?"

"I feel as though the time has come for me to exit the political sphere," Morden said. "The British one, at least."

"And do what? Teach adepts?"

"Possibly. I took up the practice through necessity but I've discovered I quite enjoy it."

"Right," I said. "I don't want to come across as discouraging here, but I don't think the Council is going to take 'I'm retiring to become a teacher' as a valid reason to leave you alone."

"Not if presented that way, no," Morden said. "Which brings me to the other reason I was observing your negotiations. I had something of a personal interest in your success."

I frowned.

"The Council and I have been in contact," Morden said. "They are currently under the impression that you and I are acting as associates."

"I'm not working for you anymore."

"I didn't say you were. Still, given the assistance I've provided . . . and that you requested . . . it's not an unreasonable conclusion."

I started to answer, then paused. I'd approached Morden in his shadow realm, and it had been on his guidance that I'd attacked Heron Tower. Then he'd helped with that diversion last night as well . . . "I suppose not," I said. "Though I don't see—"

I stopped as I remembered what Bahamus had said. *We will cease any offensive operations against you and your immediate associates.* I'd assumed he meant Anne, but if he had, why hadn't he used her name? "Associates" implied more than one . . .

I looked at Morden. Morden looked back at me with his eyebrows raised.

"You used me for this," I said.

"Just as you used me."

"I *wondered* why you were being so helpful," I said. "Let me guess. You also gave them the impression that we both had access to Levistus's blackmail files, and it'd be in their best interest to leave you alone."

Morden inclined his head slightly.

I studied Morden. "I could tell them you were lying."

"You could," Morden said. "Though it would result in a rather awkward conversation where they attempted to decide which of us to believe. I also suspect it would encourage them to reconsider your deal. You forced them to the negotiating table by projecting an image of strength, but if they sense they could play the two of us off against one another . . ."

Shit. Yeah, that was *exactly* how the Council would see it. I might be able to make it work, but it'd be a risk . . .

. . . a risk that would gain me nothing. It wouldn't help me, it wouldn't help Anne, and it wouldn't help my friends. On the other hand, if I kept quiet, it'd give me leverage over Morden in the future. He wouldn't be able to threaten me the way he had in the past.

And besides . . . did I actually *care* whether Morden got one over on the Council?

Not really.

I looked at Morden. He was watching me calmly, and I wondered how much of my thoughts he'd been able to guess. "Why are you really doing this?" I said. "And don't tell me it's for health reasons, or that you want to spend time with your family. You and Richard worked towards this for years. Why step away now?"

Morden nodded. "I am willing to gratify your curiosity, on condition that you keep the remainder of our conversation private."

I thought for a second. "All right."

"My arrangement with Richard worked most effectively while the two of us operated in separate spheres," Morden said. "I was on the Council and dealt with Light mages; he stayed in the shadows and dealt with Dark ones. Unfortunately, once I made my final break with the Council, that was no longer sustainable. For a while I took the role of teacher, training adepts in Arcadia, but the distance between us was greatly reduced. As time passed, Richard and I were forced to take decisions that encroached upon each other's freedom of action."

"You wanted different things," I translated. "The differences weren't a problem to begin with because you weren't in a position to act freely. Once you started winning, though . . ."

"A common problem with revolutions," Morden said. "Fortunately, I had been aware of the risk, and decided that my stewardship of Arcadia would be my final act in this conflict. Once it was destroyed, I began making preparations to take my leave."

I studied Morden, thinking. "Seems to me that if you

saw it coming that far in advance, you should have prepared your departure a bit more carefully."

"Perhaps."

"I think you *did* prepare it more carefully," I said. "Then all of a sudden you had to improvise. Something happened to move up your schedule, didn't it?"

Morden nodded. "While my issues with Richard were a source of tension, they were not immediately urgent."

"Let me guess," I said. "Anne."

"Richard intended to employ Anne and her jinn as his trump card in a series of key conflicts with the Council. Your actions not only prevented this, but introduced a new and highly unpredictable variable. Richard has been forced to modify his plans."

"Which plans?"

"Why don't you ask him?"

I snorted.

"In any case, I feel that this is an appropriate moment for me to make my exit," Morden said. "You, Anne, the jinn, Richard, and the Council are all quite busy with one another, and I see no particular reason to continue to involve myself."

"In other words, you don't want to end up like Jagadev or Levistus."

"Essentially."

"I wouldn't really have pegged you as the type to run."

"Verus, when you reach my age, you'll learn that sometimes the best course of action is simply to walk away. Both Jagadev and Levistus ultimately failed to do that."

"Walking away wouldn't do very much good in my case."

"Perhaps in your case I should have said 'if' instead of 'when.'"

I gave Morden a narrow look. "Are you trying to tell me something?"

"I think, thus far, you have played your cards in this conflict quite well," Morden said. "However, your successes have come from joining forces against mutual enemies. As the number of players on the field continues to fall, that will become steadily more difficult."

"You're making it sound as though there's something in the future you're trying to avoid," I said slowly. "Exactly how far away is this something?"

"A good question," Morden said. "However, I suspect it's one you'll quickly be able to answer yourself." He nodded to me. "Good-bye, Verus. Though we've had our differences, I've found our association to be quite educational. I will be happy to renew our relationship at some point in the future. But not just now."

Morden walked away. I watched him disappear into the trees, until I felt the signature of a gate spell and knew he was gone. I had the feeling I wouldn't be seeing him anytime soon.

Morden's last words had left me uneasy. I scanned the futures, first quickly, then in detail. Still no danger. The clearing was empty of anything that could be a possible threat. I looked to see what would happen if I tried contacting other people . . .

And froze.

Oh shit.

There was no time to gather up my traps and gear, no time to use staging points. I pulled out my focus for the Hollow and made the quickest gate I'd ever done in my life.

। । । । । । । ।

I felt the difference the instant I set foot in the Hollow. The woods were hushed and the birds weren't singing. There was a brooding, waiting feeling to the air, like approaching thunder.

I broke into a run and as I did, I reached out to Luna. *Where are you?*

Karyos's clearing. Luna's voice was terse. *Hurry.*

The journey from our front door to Karyos's clearing was maybe a minute at a full sprint. I made it in less than that. As I broke through the treeline, I skidded to a halt.

The image of Karyos's clearing made me think of a painting, one of those classical scenes with the figures captured on the brink of action. Karyos was under her tree, standing protectively in front of the trunk. To her right was Luna, close enough to Karyos to support her but not so close that an attack against one of them could threaten both. Luna's stance looked casual, but she held her whip in one hand and a shortsword in the other, and I knew she was ready to burst into movement.

Hermes was on the far side of the clearing. The blink fox was almost hidden in the foliage, and only the amber gleam of his eyes marked him out in the shadows. He was crouched low to the ground, tail and paws flat on the grass, ready to run or teleport. Hermes, Luna, and Karyos formed a narrow arc, their gazes all fixed on the clearing's other side.

Occupying the point where their gazes met was Anne. Alone out of all the people in the clearing, she looked relaxed, standing in a lazy hipshot stance. The black dress seemed to soak up the light, emphasising the pale skin of her arms and legs.

"Oh, look," Anne said. "Daddy's home." From her tone of voice, it was clear she was not happy to see me.

"If you wanted to stop by for dinner," I told her, "you could have asked."

"What I *wanted* was to talk to Luna without you breathing down my neck." There was an edge to Anne's voice. "And we should have been done by now, except she keeps stalling."

How bad is it? I thought at Luna.

Luna's answer was instant. *Bad.*

I gave Anne a shrug. "If all you want to do is chat, I'm not going to stop you."

"Good." Anne's tone was threatening, but she turned back to Luna. "Okay, you've got Alex to hold your hand. *Now* are you going to give me a straight answer?"

"It's not that simple." Luna sounded like she was choosing her words very carefully. "You talk about straight answers, but you won't give me one."

I'd already reached out with the dreamstone and found the person I needed. Without waiting for questions, I poured thoughts and images through the link far quicker than could be conveyed in words.

There was no pause before the reply. *On my way.*

"There is nothing complicated about this." Anne was obviously running out of patience. "You pick up the monkey's paw, you win. Which part are you not following?"

"The part where that thing *eats* anyone who tries to use it," Luna said. "Every time I say that, you just brush me off."

"I told you, I'll handle it."

"Handle it how? It's done the same thing to the last thousand people who picked it up, why would I want to be number one thousand and one?"

"The monkey's paw isn't the only thing around here with a jinn."

"And what if the other one doesn't cooperate?" Luna asked. "You keep talking as if you own it."

"Okay, I'm getting *really* tired of this," Anne said. She swivelled. "Karyos."

Karyos inclined her head. "Lifeweaver."

"Sorry I wasn't there when you hatched," Anne said. "You know how it is. How about I make it up to you?"

"In what way?"

"Jinn don't have to partner with humans," Anne said.

"They prefer them, but nonhumans work too. What do you say? You've been at the mercy of mages long enough. How about turning the tables?"

"I thank you for your offer," Karyos said. Her manner was grave and formal, at odds with her young face. "But I regret that I must decline."

"Why?" Anne demanded. "Mages have been after you for centuries, haven't they? They invaded the Hollow, burnt your old tree. Are you just going to sit there and take it?"

"The path you offer would lead to the burning of every tree in my grove until the Hollow was nothing but ash." Karyos's voice was clear. "You look at me through the eyes of a human girl, but I know you for what you are, ancient one. I will not be a soldier in your war."

"Don't call me that," Anne said sharply.

Karyos looked back at her in silence.

"Hermes," Anne called. "How about you come with me at least?"

Hermes stayed crouched. His tail curled between his legs.

"Seriously?" Anger flashed across Anne's face. "I was there when we pulled you out of Sagash's shadow realm, you ungrateful little—!" With an effort Anne cut herself off.

Hermes sank a little lower to the ground, eyes glinting.

"Well." Anne turned to me. "So that's how it is." She gave me a too-bright smile. "I'm losing all the kids in the divorce, huh?"

"They're not buying what you're selling, Anne," I said. "Though I'm not sure I should be calling you 'Anne' anymore."

"That's who I *am*."

"I'm not talking about your other self," I said. "I don't think either of you is in the driver's seat right now." Anne was about to speak, but I kept talking. "What are you trying to recruit all these people *for*? You're putting together an army, right? What are you going to do once you've got it?"

"Whatever I have to."

"And what's the endgame?" I said. "Rule the world? Kill anyone who gets in your way? Or just keep fighting until someone stops you?"

Anne looked back at me angrily.

"Think, Anne," I said softly. "Think about all the time we spent together. Living with us in the shop in Camden. Living alone in your flat above that little nature reserve in Honor Oak. You never wanted this. Not even when I was talking with you in Elsewhere. You wanted to be powerful, wanted to get your own back . . . all of that, yes. But you weren't a megalomaniac."

"It's not . . ." Anne hesitated. "Okay, look, I might have had to make some . . . compromises. You don't get anything for free, right?"

"This is beyond compromises," I said. "The jinn's taking you over. This isn't you."

"I don't . . ." Anne trailed off. She shook her head, and all of a sudden she looked vulnerable, afraid. "Look, I need this. Can't you guys help? Don't you owe me that much?"

It was Luna who answered. "I owe you *more* than this much," Luna said. "I'll do whatever I can for you and I always will. But it has to be for *you*. Not some creature wearing your body."

"We can sort that out later." Anne held a hand out towards Luna. "Just come with me. Please?"

Luna looked back at her, and very slowly, shook her head.

The futures danced, but not towards a choice. One by one, the possibilities heading in a certain direction winked out. Multiple branches were left, but now they were all pointing the same way.

Anne's face darkened. "So it's going to be like this?"

Uh-oh. I reached out through the dreamstone. *Luna— I know! Stop distracting me.*

"I've been there for all of you over and *over* again," Anne said. "The whole reason you're *alive* is because of me. Now that I really need it, you can't do this one thing?"

"It's not about—" Luna began.

"No," Anne said. "I'm sick of hearing you say the same things. I've really been trying to be nice, but you are just not listening."

"She is listening." I kept my voice calm, but I could feel things slipping away. "But you're not doing much to reassure us here."

"I'm not here to reassure you. I'm here to call in some favours, which *you* don't seem very keen on doing."

"Look," I said. "We don't have to—"

"No, I think I'm done talking," Anne said. "This is what you always do, isn't it? You spin stories and you make it sound oh so reasonable. And all the time you're setting them up for a fall. You've done it with everyone else, now you're trying it with me, right?"

"I'm not trying anything with you," I said. But it was hopeless and I knew it. Already I was planning out which way to move.

"Sure you're not." Anne raised a hand and snapped her fingers.

Movement stirred from around us. Slender shadows appeared from all around the clearing, slipping between the trees. Cold eyes stared at Luna and at Karyos and at me. They were jann, and this time there were more of them. A lot more.

"Okay," Anne said again. She made no signal that I could see, but one of the jann to her left stepped forward into the clearing. It held out something in its claws, a lacquered tube of blue and white. The monkey's paw.

"Maybe you might have forgotten," Anne said, "but I

helped build this place. I know how to get through the gate wards. And I know where you keep your stuff." She looked at Luna. "Now I'm done asking nicely. You *are* coming with me and then you're going to see I'm right. Only question is, are we doing this the easy way or the hard way?"

Luna stood very straight. "I don't belong to you."

The jann moved. Claws flexed; slender bodies slipped forward. They were all around me and closing in from every direction; already I could barely see anyone else through the ring of shadowy figures and cold, flat eyes. Yet only half of the jann were surrounding me; the rest were around Luna.

I'd kept up the mental link, and through it I could hear Luna's thoughts, tense but calm. *Alex, if you've got any ideas, now would be a really good time.*

I felt a weird tug of déjà vu. I'd been in this position before, in Sagash's castle, an army of magical creatures around with no way out. Except back then Anne had been the one at my side. We'd come full circle.

Try to make it to my cottage, I told Luna. *It's you she's after.*

And the fifty jann in the way?

I'll do what I can.

"I haven't told them to hurt you," Anne said. I could only see glimpses of her through the closing ring of jann. "If you just—"

Luna moved. I couldn't see through the crowd of jann, but I saw the aura of her curse flash, and a jann gave a weird whining scream. Then my weapons were out and I was charging.

The nearest jann reached for me, claws extending. I evaded easily, shot it through the head, rammed my knife through its body and ripped it out sideways. It staggered, still moving, until two more strikes finished it off. But in the time it had taken me to kill one, five more were on me.

The future narrowed into a whirl of strikes and grasping claws. I slid between the futures in which I was hurt or pinned, finding paths of safety through the danger. I'd lost sight of everyone else. I could sense magic from where I'd last seen Karyos and Luna, and knew that they were fighting, but the press of jann all around me was too close to do more. I ducked under an arm, slashed it in the same motion, kicked another aside, fired into a shadowy face. They were trying to wound and catch me, but not actually kill me, and that gave me an edge. And their sheer numbers were working against them. I knew Anne was near, but she couldn't see me through the crowd, and any attack spell she tried to use would hit the jann instead of me.

But it wasn't enough. I'd gone out today equipped to deal with the Council, not a horde of summoned monsters. My knife and gun were poor weapons against the shadowy bodies of the jann—they had no veins to open or vital organs to pierce. Enough damage could destroy their physical form and banish them, but my weapons couldn't deal that much damage that quickly.

Alex! Luna called.

I tried to dodge past a jann towards where I'd last seen Luna; two more blocked my way and forced me back. *I can't get through—*

I sensed something over the miasma of background magic: a gate flicker. Hope leapt within me. *Cancel that. Just hold on.*

There was panic in Luna's thoughts. *Help!*

Hold on!

Three jann attacked me from all directions. I managed to dodge two, contorting; the third hit me, its claws scraping my back. My armour became rigid, deflecting the blow. I spun into the jann, twisted to trip it, but already another was reaching for me.

Alex! There was pain in Luna's thoughts now, the sense of flowing blood. *Too many!*

I didn't have time to answer. Everything was a rush of violence and flashing claws. The light seemed to be fading. I wove through the melee, losing all sense of direction, focused on the future coming closer. *Come on, come on . . .* The whirl of claws drove me to a halt, and it was all I could do to dodge them, counting down in my head. *Four, three, two, one . . .*

The sky lit up with fire.

Looking up, I saw a figure descending on wings of flame. Variam. His spell was slowing his fall, and as he sank he raised a hand, fingers extended.

Bursts of heat scorched the clearing, tearing holes in the crowd. Jann screamed, their bodies flaring like paper in a bonfire. All of a sudden I could see again, and I could make out Luna just a little distance away.

Darkness seemed to bloom, and Anne stepped out of the crowd. Her eyes flashed with anger, and behind her I could half see, half feel the jinn, unfolding like a shadow. A green-black wave of death flashed upwards at Variam: he threw up a shield of fire and the spells met with a clap of thunder.

I was already running, aiming for Luna. A jann tried to get in my way and I slashed it and kept going. Luna had two jann trying to pull her to the ground; she'd lost her wand and was struggling to stay on her feet. Hermes blinked into existence behind one jann, sank his teeth into the back of its ankle, blinked away again as it lashed out. The distraction let Luna pull an arm free, stab the second jann, then break away.

I heard a shout from Anne, and turned to see her point at us. "Stop them!" She took a step towards us, but a wall of fire from Variam cut her off and she jumped back with a curse.

Variam had burnt at least ten jann to ash. There were still dozens more. Every one of them charged us.

Luna and I turned and ran. The jann were converging

on us, and we sprinted into the trees, running side by side. I couldn't see Variam or Karyos or Hermes, and I couldn't spare the time to check; that many jann hitting us at a full charge would bring us down in seconds. We wove through the trees, hearing the crash and snap of foliage behind us as the jann tried to force their way through.

Vari— Luna said.

He's doing his job; we need to do ours. Get to my cottage—weapons.

We broke out of the woods twenty yards from my little house. The sky was still lighting up from the battle behind, but we'd gained a few seconds on our pursuers. I ran to my front door and yanked it open with Luna right behind.

I took two steps inside and paused. In one corner was my black weapons bag. My MP7 was still lying on top: I hadn't touched it since last night. It would be better than my handgun, but not by much. The shortsword in the bag underneath might be better still.

But propped in the corner where I'd left it was the spear I'd taken from Levistus's shadow realm. The long, slightly curved blade glinted in the light from outside, and I could sense something from the weapon, something awake and hungry.

Sometimes you have the time to divine the future and figure out a plan. Sometimes you have to trust your instincts. I tossed my empty gun onto the desk, grabbed the spear, and walked back out of the cottage just as the first jann burst from the tree line.

Time seemed to slow as I strode across the clearing. Three, seven, a dozen jann streamed from the trees, converging on me. Behind them, the sky flashed dark green and fire red in the light of Variam and Anne's battle. The first jann was a couple of steps ahead of the others, and it charged, claws extended. I brought the spear across—

The spear cut the jann in half. The blade lit up with red

light as it carved through the centre of the jann's body, leaving a dull red glow on the top and bottom halves of the jann's torso. There was so little resistance that I nearly fell.

I managed to recover my balance just in time to catch the second jann with a backswing, then set the spear against the charge of the third. The second one was cut in half just like the first; the third impaled itself in its rush. It flung back its head, and a high, whining scream filled the air, then red light flared from within its chest and it burned from the inside out. The spear seemed alive in my hands, radiating a fierce joy. It wanted more.

More were coming. Jann were pouring from the tree line and they threw themselves at me, ignoring the threat of the spear. I struck and dodged, using every bit of my skill and magic. No human would have fought so suicidally, but the jann seemed to care about nothing except Anne's command, and their total lack of self-preservation pushed me to my limits. Claws scraped at my armour. I'd never used a spear in combat, but I'm good with a staff, and the weapons aren't so different. The spear itself seemed to help, twisting in my hands to slash and impale, revelling in the slaughter. Dimly I was aware of Luna guarding my back, but I had no attention to spare. Strike with the haft, reverse and thrust, tear the blade out with the next slash. A blow caught my head; another jann grappled my leg, and I brought the spear around high to low, cutting through its arms. Parry and dodge, find the thread through the futures, kill, kill, kill—

Panting, I rammed the spear through the chest of a jann, watching it jerk and spasm as red energy burnt through it, and realised that it was the last one. All around me, black bodies littered the clearing, the first of them already starting to dissolve into smoke. My breath was ragged and the blood was pounding in my head. I had no idea how long the fight had lasted; it could have been ten minutes or ten seconds.

"Come on." Luna was panting as well; she looked exhausted, and now that I had the chance to notice, I could see that there was blood down her right arm. Still, her eyes were fixed on the lights in the sky. "Help Vari."

My muscles felt like water and all I wanted to do was rest. I managed to nod, and broke into a jog, back towards Karyos's clearing.

We came out of the trees to see Anne and Variam facing off against one another, fifty feet apart. A shield of flame surrounded Variam, making him hard to look at; only his eyes and his dark face showed above the flickering fire. Karyos stood a little way behind. The hamadryad looked hurt, but she was staying near her tree. And opposite them both was Anne, green-black light wreathing her. The shadow of the jinn extended behind and above her, a looming presence, but Anne still looked very human, and very pissed off.

"What is your *problem*!" Anne shouted at Variam. "Can't you take a hint?"

"I saw this coming a long time ago." Variam watched Anne, his dark eyes unreadable. "Alex is dumb enough to trust you. I'm not."

"I wouldn't *have* to do this if you'd all stop fighting!" Anne turned to glare at me and Luna. "Oh, and you're here as well. Did those jann round you up? No, of course they didn't, there's no way they could possibly do anything useful."

Fires were burning in half a dozen places around the clearing. Karyos's tree seemed intact, but others had been charred, and more had been knocked over, branches and tree trunks snapped off as if by some invisible force. The spear seemed to quiver in my hands, pulling towards Anne. It wanted her . . . or the thing inside.

"How the hell are you still up?" Anne demanded of Variam. "Did you take up Harvesting in your spare time or what?"

"Like I said," Variam said. "I saw this coming. You, though—I bet you didn't make any plans at all. Just figured you could win without even trying."

Anne narrowed her eyes at Variam. "It's that cloak. Isn't it?"

I couldn't see through Variam's flame shield, but now that I looked, I could sense another magical aura wrapped around him. Maybe it was the item he'd taken from Jagadev . . .

"Anne!" Luna said. "Stop! You have to see this isn't working."

"Oh, for God's sake, shut up," Anne said. "Maybe you haven't noticed, but there is a *really good reason* I'm doing this. As soon as the Council are done with their war with Richard, they're going to be after us again, and who's going to stop them? You've just been hiding in your shop hoping they'll take someone else first. Vari's working for them. The only one of you who's done anything useful is Alex, and he still needed me to do the heavy lifting. If you don't have a jinn of your own, then it's just a matter of time before you end up the same way I did!"

"The Council aren't going after her," I told Anne.

Anne snorted. "Seen that in the future too?"

"Did you really think you were the only one who'd noticed we had a problem?" I said. "While you've been running around settling old scores, I've been calling in favours and putting together a plan. A plan which just came off. As of an hour ago, the Council have agreed to a truce. They won't come after me or my associates. I even got them to specifically include you."

Anne paused. "Well, they're lying."

"No, they're not. Because this time I made sure I had

enough leverage to back it up. Our war with the Council's over."

"Bullshit."

"You did all this for nothing, Anne," I said calmly. "You've been telling yourself that there's no other way, right? Attacking me and Luna, having to fight Vari, all the compromises you made and whatever you've had to promise that jinn . . . in your head, it was all okay because you were the hero. But you haven't saved anyone. Right now, you're the one that Luna and Vari are trying to save each other *from*."

Anne opened her mouth for a retort and nothing came out. She stared between me and Luna and Vari and for once had nothing to say. Emotions battled in her face, shame against anger.

"It's not too late," Luna said quickly. "You've hurt me, you've hurt Karyos, but it's nothing you can't fix. Nobody's dead, not yet."

"And if someone *is* ending up dead," Variam cut in, "you should think about whether it might be you."

Anne hesitated, and in one of those strange moments of insight I was suddenly sure that what Luna and Variam had done was enough. Dark Anne was ruthless and she was violent and she was terrible at thinking long-term, but she wasn't a total psychopath. She did care about some people, the three of us most of all. We'd shown her that, to beat us, she'd have to risk killing us, and that wasn't a price she was willing to pay.

Unfortunately, that was only a price that *Anne* wasn't willing to pay. And though Anne didn't know it, she wasn't calling the shots anymore.

"Okay," Anne said. Her face hardened. "Okay."

"You started this fight with one of you and fifty jann," Variam told her. "Now there's one of you and zero jann. Let me break down the maths on that for you. *You're losing*."

"One of me?" Anne said softly. "Is that what you think?"

The green light around Anne seemed to die, but the darkness grew. The presence behind her loomed larger, shadows spreading across the clearing like giant, batlike wings, a sense of something watching, cold and hungry. Anne spoke again and there was an echo to her voice, dissonant and frightening. "I've been holding back from the moment I stepped in here. I think it's time I showed you what you're really dealing with."

Vari, Luna! I snapped out through the dreamstone. *Shield!*

A sphere of green-black light flared outwards from Anne. It was a basic attack spell, one I'd seen before from death mages, but never on this scale. Normally my best defence against battle-magic is evasion, but evasion only works if there's somewhere to evade *to*. This was a full sphere, hitting everything around her. The amount of power it must have taken was enormous. No battle-mage I'd ever met could cover half that volume.

I forced the best future I could with the fateweaver, and twisted to let my back armour take the blast, trying to lessen the impact. It did a little, but not enough. Pain and nausea swept over me, draining my energy. I stumbled and fell, black spots swimming in my vision.

Through blurry eyes I could see that Luna was on her knees. Anne was already casting another spell, this one something I'd never seen. It looked like the teleportation spells space mages used, but its weave was alien, utterly different from human magic. In one hand she was holding the gate focus that she'd used to enter our shadow realm; the other was extended towards Luna, and a net of black lines wove outward, growing through the air towards Luna like shoots of a plant.

But she'd forgotten Variam. Alone out of the four of us, Variam had a real shield, and with the instant's warning he'd managed to weather Anne's spell. Flame darted from his hand, blocking off the black tendrils from reaching Luna.

The grey mist of Luna's curse darted out.

It all happened too fast to see. Luna's curse intersected Anne and Variam's spells, and as the three magics met, energy burst outward in a clap of thunder. Every hair in my body stood on end and the world went white.

Somehow I made it to my feet. I couldn't see or hear, but I still had my divination and I looked ahead, searching for danger to me or to anyone else. But there was nothing. The futures were clear. Gradually my vision returned, revealing an empty clearing, the grass pressed flat and leaves blown from the trees. Fires were still burning, but the sense of menace was gone.

I looked around as the spots receded and the ringing faded from my ears. Karyos was still there, rising a little shakily from beside the tree. Luna was struggling to her feet. The silver mist of her curse was barely visible; it was returning, seeping back along her limbs, but it seemed to be recovering, as if it had been depleted.

There was no sign of Anne. And there was no sign of Variam.

"Vari," Luna called, looking around. "Vari!" She turned to me. "Where is he?"

I closed my eyes, reaching out through the dreamstone. *Vari.*

A moment, then I made contact. Variam's thoughts were frantic, intense; he was fighting. *I'm here! Anne gated us out and she's pissed.*

Where are you?

No time. Get Landis. Tell him—

Shock and pain flared in Variam's mind, making me stagger. An instant later the link snapped.

Vari! I cast about for Variam's mind, trying to establish the connection. *Vari!*

Nothing.

I opened my eyes and looked at Luna, troubled. "What's happening?" Luna demanded. "Where is he?"

"I don't know," I said quietly.

Karyos crossed the open grass to join us. The three of us stood alone.

chapter 14

"You have to find him," Luna told me for the third or fourth time.

"I'm trying."

I was sitting with my back against a tree. Karyos was kneeling next to Luna, frowning slightly as she bound herbs to the wound in Luna's arm. It seemed to hurt, judging by the way Luna was flinching, but her attention was on me. "Can you figure out where he is?"

Across the clearing, animals were working to clean up the damage from the battle. Birds plucked up burned leaves; squirrels and mice nibbled off splintered twigs and carried them away. Not all were working; some were searching. A squirrel came bounding out of the woods to hop up to Karyos. Karyos met its eyes for a second, then the squirrel bounded away. Karyos glanced at me and shook her head.

"Alex," Luna pressed.

I sighed and broke off the path-walk. What I was trying to do wasn't easy, and Luna was making it harder. "I can't reach Vari through the dreamstone in the present or in any future I can see."

"Then what about—" Karyos pulled the bandage tight and Luna winced. "Elsewhere," she said once she'd recovered.

"If I enter Elsewhere," I said, "I'll be able to touch Variam's dreams."

Luna brightened. "Then he's—"

"I'm also going to be intercepted," I said. "A jinn, or more than one. They're powerful in that realm. Much more than me."

"But he's alive?"

"He's alive. But adding that up, he's either Anne's prisoner or under her control."

"There," Karyos said, rising to her feet and taking a few steps back from Luna. "Your wounds are not severe."

"Thanks," Luna said. As she relaxed, the silver mist of her curse spread down over her arm; she'd been holding it under tight control. A faint tinge had still reached Karyos, but at Luna's gesture, it flowed from the hamadryad down into the ground.

"Nothing?" I asked Karyos.

Karyos shook her head again. "I do not believe it is here."

"What isn't?" Luna asked, flexing her arm.

"When we were facing the jann in this clearing, one of them was holding the monkey's paw," I said. "When we fought them outside my cottage, I didn't see it. Karyos's animals have been searching the Hollow."

"And finding nothing," Karyos said. "I believe she took it away."

Hermes came trotting out of the trees. He sniffed the air, then walked a few steps towards me before stopping, his eyes narrowed.

"Hermes?" Luna asked. "What's wrong?" She followed Hermes's eyes.

"I think I can guess," I said, getting to my feet. The spear was lying on the grass by my side. I reached down and picked it up.

Immediately I felt the spear's presence in my mind, alive and hungry. Killing all those jann hadn't sated it at all. It wanted to drink Hermes's blood, but nowhere near as much as it wanted to kill Karyos. I could see her flesh opening up beneath the blade, red blood bright on the—

With a shudder I let go of the spear and the image winked out. The spear bounced on the grass and lay still. "I think I'm figuring out why Levistus left this thing hanging on his wall."

"I do not like that weapon," Karyos said.

"When you picked it up," Luna said slowly, "I thought I felt . . ." She drew back slightly. "Does it want to kill *everyone*?"

I shook my head. "Not you or me. But Hermes, and Karyos, and all of those jann—that's another story. I think it's an imbued item meant to kill magical creatures. Or maybe anything nonhuman."

"Remove it from this shadow realm," Karyos said clearly.

I nodded.

"This isn't getting us anywhere," Luna said. "What do we do about Vari?"

"I don't know."

"Then find him!" Luna said. "The longer we wait, the harder it's going to be."

There was a frantic note to Luna's voice, and I looked at her sideways. I knew Luna cared about Variam, but this . . .

Luna read my expression. "You don't get it," she said. "Anne wasn't going for Vari."

"At the beginning—"

"*Not* at the beginning. At the end. That gate spell was meant for me. I was out of it, but my curse wasn't. It couldn't stop Anne's spell, but it could redirect it. The curse made her take Vari instead of me." Luna stepped closer, eyes alight with urgency. "We have to save him. Please."

I looked back at Luna and hesitated. But before I could form an answer, something flickered on my precognition. I looked up, my eyes narrowing.

"Alex," Luna said.

"We've got trouble," I said.

A chime sounded, echoing through the Hollow. The note was harsh, warning. It sounded twice more before falling silent.

Luna frowned, looking around. "Wait, is that . . . ?"

"Breach alarm," I said. Since we'd set up the wards, we'd never had an enemy successfully force entrance to the Hollow. Now we were getting two in one day.

"Breach alarm?" Karyos asked.

"We set it up when we moved in," I said. "Gives us warning when someone tries to force their way through the gate wards."

"Can they do it?" Luna asked.

I'd already seen the answer to that. "Yes."

It was the worst possible time for us to be facing an attack. Variam was gone, Anne had switched teams, and both Karyos and Luna were hurt. And I was already tired.

But who would be attacking? Anne wouldn't trip the alarm. The Council would, but I couldn't for the life of me think why they'd choose now of all times. Morden was gone, Rachel was gone, Onyx was gone. The only one that really left was—

Reason and divination gave me the answer at the same time. "Oh, shit," I said, my heart sinking.

"What?" Luna said. "What's wrong?"

"Both of you, take Hermes and get out," I said. "Right now."

"And leave my tree?" Karyos asked. "Humans may flee their homes. I cannot."

I looked at Luna.

"No," Luna said. "We need to go after Vari. We are *not* splitting up."

I let out a breath. I wasn't sure if running would do any good anyway. "Fine."

⁍⁍⁍⁍⁍⁍⁍⁍⁍⁍

The wards on the Hollow failed thirteen minutes later. Luna, Karyos, and I were standing ready. I'd identified the spot where the breach would occur, and we'd taken up positions around it, myself on point with Luna and Karyos flanking me a good distance back. I was wearing my armour and holding the spear, and could feel the presence of both imbued items, one defensive, one aggressive. It was the best display of strength we could manage. I wasn't sure it was going to be enough.

A patch of air a little way ahead began to darken. With my magesight, I could see the strands of a gate beginning to form.

Let me do the talking, I said through the dreamstone.

The air darkened, becoming opaque, and the darkness took the form of a ragged oval. The strands of the gate completed as the spell activated. A foot broke the surface of the black portal, and a mage stepped through. His feet came down on the grass of the Hollow, and the portal faded away behind him as he stopped, his eyes glancing over Karyos and Luna before coming to rest on me.

"You are not welcome," I told Richard.

"You can lower your weapon, Alex," Richard said. As always, his voice seemed to dominate the area, resonant and clear. "I haven't come to fight."

"That's funny," I said. "Normally, forcing your way through gate wards means exactly that."

"You've been making rather a habit of entering shadow realms uninvited, as I understand," Richard said, but held up a hand before I could answer. "I offer a truce. I have come to speak to you, and nothing more. You have my word."

I looked back at Richard.

I don't trust him, Luna said. I'd kept the mental link open, and her thoughts were sharp and wary. *Is he working with Anne? Why is he here?*

I know, I thought back at her. I lowered the spear slightly. "Very well."

Richard made an inviting gesture. *Hold*, I told Luna and Karyos, and advanced. I came to a stop maybe ten feet away from Richard, studying my old master. At this range, I could reach him with the spear in less than a second. I couldn't sense danger, but I knew better than to rely on that.

"I have come to extend you an invitation to a meeting between myself and the Council," Richard told me.

I looked back at him for a second before replying. "A meeting about what?"

"I will be proposing a temporary alliance."

"And you expect them to agree?"

"The decision is of course theirs," Richard said. "But ultimately, yes."

I looked back at him.

"Shall I assume you will be attending?" Richard asked.

"Sorry, I was distracted," I said. "I'm trying to figure out whether you're lying or just delusional."

"Neither is the case."

"As of this moment, you are possibly the only person in this country that the Council has more reason to hate than me. So please do explain to me why they would have the *slightest* interest in an alliance."

"They have an interest in an alliance," Richard said, "because otherwise, they have perhaps a week before your lover effectively destroys this country."

I stared.

"I am inviting you to this meeting for two reasons," Richard said. "Firstly, because I believe you can contribute in ways that neither my cabal or the Council can fully match. And secondly, because this whole mess is entirely your fault. By freeing Anne's jinn, you have triggered a threat that has the potential to cause more destruction than any war in recorded history."

It took me a long time to come up with an answer. "I don't believe you," I said at last.

"Then listen and I will explain," Richard said. "But make no mistake. You caused this. And I fully expect you to clean it up."

⁙⁙⁙⁙⁙

Richard kept talking. For the most part, I listened. Once he was done, he left. I watched the gate close behind him, then once the last wisps of darkness had disappeared, I turned and walked slowly back to Karyos and Luna.

"So that is your old master," Karyos said thoughtfully, looking over my shoulder.

"What happened?" Luna demanded.

"He invited me to a meeting," I said absently. My thoughts were far away. The spear was still pushing me to strike at Karyos, but all of a sudden that seemed a very small concern.

"Yeah, screw that," Luna said. "How are we going to find Vari?"

I hesitated for a long moment. "I think . . . we might have a bigger problem."

Luna opened her mouth angrily, but before she could

speak, I cut in. As I kept speaking the anger faded from her face, her eyes widening. Karyos watched me, her expression unreadable. Above us, the sun of the Hollow sank through the multicoloured sky, evening fading slowly into dusk.

Ready to find
your next great read?

Let us help.

Visit prh.com/nextread

Penguin
Random
House